RIDING SHOTGUN
A RED RYAN WESTERN

William W. Johnstone
and J. A. Johnstone

PINNACLE BOOKS
Kensington Publishing Corp.
www.kensingtonbooks.com

PINNACLE BOOKS are published by

Kensington Publishing Corp.
119 West 40th Street
New York, NY 10018

PUBLISHER'S NOTE
Following the death of William W. Johnstone, the Johnstone family is working with a carefully selected writer to organize and complete Mr. Johnstone's outlines and many unfinished manuscripts to create additional novels in all of his series like The Last Gunfighter, Mountain Man, and Eagles, among others. This novel was inspired by Mr. Johnstone's superb storytelling.

All Kensington titles, imprints, and distributed lines are available at special quantity discounts for bulk purchases for sales promotions, premiums, fund-raising, educational, or institutional use. Special book excerpts or customized printings can also be created to fit specific needs. For details, write or phone the office of the Kensington sales manager: Kensington Publishing Corp., 119 West 40th Street, New York, NY 10018, attn: Sales Department; phone 1-800-221-2647.

PINNACLE BOOKS, the Pinnacle logo, and the WWJ steer head logo are Reg. U.S. Pat. & TM Off.

ISBN-13: 978-0-7860-4432-0
ISBN-10: 0-7860-4432-2

First printing: June 2019

10 9 8 7 6 5 4 3 2 1

Printed in the United States of America

Electronic edition:

ISBN-13: 978-0-7860-4433-7 (e-book)
ISBN-10: 0-7860-4433-0 (e-book)

CHAPTER ONE

"Ryan! Red Ryan, I'm calling you out! Damn your eyes, fill your hand, and get down here!"

"Red, do you hear that?"

"Yeah, I hear that. Ignore him, Dolly, and he'll go away," Ryan said. "Now, where were we?"

The naked woman in the bed smiled. "I was asking if you love me, Red."

"Love you? I sure do, and that's a natural fact."

"Do you tell the other girls that you love them?"

"Nah, Dolly, I just tell it to you."

"Patsy Prentice says that every time you're in town you talk all kinds of pretties to her. You never talk pretties to me."

"Yeah, I do, all the time. Hell, Dolly, you're as pretty as a speckled pup under a wagon. When I first rode into Cassidy Crossing and saw you standing on the balcony with the other ladies that time, I thought, 'Well, Red, she's the only gal for you an' no mistake.'"

"That time? Red, it was only yesterday."

"Times flies when you're having fun, don't it? Now,

come closer and give me some more of that good ol' Texas lovin' . . ."

"Ryan! Are you coming down or do I have to come up there after you?" The man's voice from the street, strident and angry. "I aim to shoot you down like a dog, Ryan, and be damned to ye."

"Go away!" Red called. "At the moment, I'm real busy!"

"Come down here, Ryan!"

"Later!"

"Now!"

"Give me ten minutes, you damned nuisance, whoever you are. You should be hung for disturbing a man."

"Get down here now, damn you!" The bullet that crashed through the bedroom window added the exclamation point to the end of that sentence.

"That's it, I'm out of here!" Dolly said. "Everybody told me you were a crazy man, Red Ryan, and you are."

The girl rolled off the bed, gathered up her frillies, and then stood at the door, staring expectantly at Red. Even when she frowned as she was doing now, he had to admit that she was a real purty little gal. "In my wallet," he said.

Dolly grabbed the wallet from the dresser and took out some bills. "There's only three dollars here."

"And you're most welcome to it, l'il darlin'," Ryan said.

"That's all?" Dolly said. "That's all the money you have?"

"It's all I got, and when three dollars is all a man has, he's giving you his entire fortune."

"You damned cheapskate, Red Ryan," Dolly said. "Who's going to pay for the window?"

"I'll talk to Dark Alley Jim, tell him I'll pay him for

the window next time I'm in town." Ryan ducked as a bullet shattered another pane. "Uh-oh, make that two windows."

Now there was a deal of shouting and screaming in the upstairs rooms of the Golden Garter Saloon & Sporting House, and the proprietor, Dark Alley Jim Mortimer, loudly demanded to know who was trying to murder his whores.

Dolly Barnes opened the bedroom door and yelled, "Jim, it's Red Ryan. He's been called out."

"Ryan, you damned troublemaker, git away from here and deal with this afore my place is all shot to pieces," Mortimer hollered. Then the man himself burst through the door, saw Ryan struggling into his long johns, and said, motioning with a Greener 10-gauge for emphasis, "Git out there on the street and don't come back here ever again."

"I thought you were my good friend, Jim," Ryan said.

"I've shot good friends afore," Mortimer said. "And you're not my friend, good or any other kind."

Ryan pulled on his boots, slammed a derby hat on his unruly mane of red hair, and slid his Colt from the holster, leaving his own Greener shotgun in a corner. Scatterguns always meant a killing, and he was hopeful that this situation could be resolved by prudent words rather than buckshot.

Red stepped to the window, flung it open, and yelled, "I'm coming down!" He caught a brief glance of an angry but respectable-looking gent in the street who held a revolver in each hand.

Dressed only in hat, boots, and fire-engine red underwear, Ryan brushed past Mortimer and thumped down the stairs and onto the porch that ran the length of the building.

The respectable-looking gent was obviously not in the mood for words, prudent or otherwise, and he didn't waste any time in palaver. He cut loose with both six-guns, and Ryan ducked as bullets crashed into the door and the woodwork around it, and one round, better aimed than the others, drilled a neat hole through the crown of his derby.

"Well, the hell with this," Red said.

He thumbed off a shot, and the respectable-looking man clutched his right shoulder, dropped his guns, and howled, "Damn! He's shot me!"

Ryan stepped off the porch into the street, his Colt hanging by his side, and said, "What the hell did you expect me to do? Mister, with all that shooting you did, you could've plugged Dolly Barnes, the best value-for-money whore this side of the Concho River."

"I was trying to kill you, not a lady," the respectable-looking man said. His face was ashen, and he was in obvious pain, grimacing under his mustache.

"Why? I never seen you before in my life," Red said.

"You're Red Ryan, ain't you?" the man said.

A crowd had gathered and looked on Ryan with hostile eyes, seeing a known rowdy who'd just drilled a respectable-looking gent in a frock coat and morning top hat.

"Yup, that's my name," Ryan said.

"You ride shotgun for the Patterson and Son stage?"

"I have that honor, at least some of the time."

"Then you're the one that killed my young brother."

Amid cries of "Shame!" and "Disgraceful" and "String him up," from one half-drunk, banty rooster who'd just stumbled out of the saloon and had no idea what the hell was going on. Ryan said, "When was this, and who was your brother?" And then, voicing his growing irritation, "As of right now, I'm starting to regret not putting another bullet into you, mister."

"There speaks a born killer," a man wearing a store-keeper apron said.

"String him up," the banty rooster said.

"Here comes the doctor," a woman said.

Dr. Miles Davis, short and stocky with gray hair and a melancholy face, helped the wounded man out of his coat and then stared hard at the bloodstained shoulder.

"My brother's name was Lou Richards, and you gunned him five miles east of El Paso, not three weeks ago," the respectable man said. He winced as the doctor worked his arm up and down, testing his shoulder.

"I remember that. Your brother Lou Richards was a road agent," Ryan said. "He tried to hold up my stage, him and Banjo Bob Kidd. I knew Kidd from a couple of years back when he was a younker. He was still carrying the buckshot in his ass he got from my Greener when he tried to rob a Butterfield I was guarding. He was lucky that day. I wasn't aiming for his ass."

"It's only a scratch," Dr. Davis said, "Mister . . ."

"Richards, Hugh Richards."

"Well, Mr. Richards, you're burned up some, but no bones broken." He looked at Ryan, not liking what he saw, and then back to the wounded man. "Here, take your coat. Come to my office later, and I'll give you a salve for the bullet burn . . . if you're still aboveground."

"Listen to me, Richards, you damned fool. Yeah,

I killed Banjo Bob on that El Paso run three weeks ago," Ryan said. "But I didn't kill Lou."

"For shame," a woman in the crowd said.

"Then who did?" Archie Richards said, grimacing as his wound pained him.

"Dallas Stoudenmire did. That's who," Red said. "Only a halfwit like Lou would try to steal a gold watch from an almighty dangerous gunfighter like Dallas."

"How did it happen?" Richards said. If he was skeptical he didn't let it show.

"How did it happen? I'll tell you how it happened," Ryan said. "As it came down, Stoudenmire was one of my passengers, and after the holdup, Lou said to him, 'Gimme your wallet, watch, and chain.' Dallas said, 'Try and take them and damn you fer a common thief.' Then Lou said, 'Your funeral, Mary Ann' and he brought up his Colt. But quick as greased lightning Dallas drew two revolvers and put four bullets into Lou. Now, Lou was hit hard, but he managed to put one round into our near-side wheeler horse. Buttons Muldoon, my driver, was sure cut up about losing that two-hundred-dollar hoss, and he would have shot Lou all over again if he hadn't already been dead."

"You swear all that on the Bible," Richards said.

"I don't have a Bible, but I give you my word for it," Red said.

"Then considering how it happened, it seems like I owe you an apology, mister," Richards said. He seemed crestfallen and out of sorts from the pain in his shoulder and from shooting at the wrong man.

"You owe me more than an apology," Red Ryan said. "Call it five dollars for the three panes of glass you broke and three for the services of Dolly Barnes that I paid for but didn't get. That's eight dollars, and

I'll forget about the ten cents for the bullet you forced me to shoot at you."

Richards's face stiffened. "You're a hard man, Red Ryan."

"No, pardner, not hard, just broke, and I don't much feel like telling Dark Alley Jim Mortimer that I can't pay for his broken windows. He has a quick temper and a quicker draw to go with it."

Richards reached into his coat pocket and produced his wallet. "There's a ten, Ryan. We'll call it quits."

"Much obliged," Red said. "Now go see Doc Davis and get that shoulder fixed. And pick up your pistol, and don't ever think of throwing down on a man again. Gunfighting sure ain't one of your hidden talents."

"There's no change back, Red," Dark Alley Jim Mortimer said. "You scared the hell out of my whores and ruined this morning's business. Besides that, one of them bullets went through your wall into the next room and burned across Deacon Elijah Dogmersfield's bare ass. Now he says it's a sign from God that he should quit consorting with fallen women and tread the path of righteousness alongside his three-hundred-pound wife."

"Sorry to hear that," Ryan said. "Seems that everybody is getting burned with bullets this morning."

"You're sorry? Think how sorry I'll be if Deacon Dogmersfield spreads the word that a sporting man can get shot at the Golden Garter and I lose the gospel-grinder trade. This is a serious concern to me, Red."

"Sorry about that too, Jim," Red said, trying his best to look penitent.

Mortimer sighed and said, "All right, here's the way I see it, Red. Loss of the services of four scared whores . . . twenty-five dollars. Loss of revenue obtained from champagne sales to the clients of those four whores . . . twenty-five dollars. Add that up and it comes to fifty dollars."

"And I'll pay you the very next time I'm in town," Ryan said, blinking.

"Figured you'd say that, Red." Jim Mortimer's smile was not pleasant. "That's why I'm holding your shotgun, cartridge belt and holster, your fancy buckskin shirt, and your pants hostage until the debt is paid in full."

Red Ryan was shocked. "Now just hold on there, Jim, you can't do that."

"Yes, I can."

"I can't face the world in my underwear."

"Get used to it," Mortimer said.

Sick at heart, Red Ryan sat on the porch step outside the Golden Garter, his head in his hands, wondering how a morning that had begun so full of promise, so full of the fair Dolly Barnes, could have turned to such complete . . . horse dung.

A shadow fell over Ryan, dark as his mood, and he looked up and saw the large form of his driver, Patrick "Buttons" Muldoon.

"Taking in some sun, Red?" Buttons said.

Ryan shook his head. "Ran into some trouble this morning."

"What was it this time? Fist or gun?"

"Gun. Feller by the name of Richards called me

out, the brother of the road agent Dallas Stoudenmire gunned that time on the El Paso run."

"Hell, Red, why blame you? You didn't do it. The only feller you shot all day long was Banjo Bob Kidd. Seen that my ownself."

"Well, we got it sorted out in the end," Ryan said.

"You plug the Richards feller?"

"Scratched his shoulder. He's over at Doc Davis's place getting a plaster."

"Where are your duds?"

"Jim Mortimer is holding them hostage, says I owe him fifty dollars because Richards shot up the place, scared his whores, and shot Deacon Dogmersfield up the ass."

"And you don't have fifty dollars."

"What you see, is what I got."

"You're a sorry sight, Red, and no mistake. I'll talk to Dark Alley Jim," Buttons said.

The stage driver stood only five-foot-six, but he was as wide as he was tall, and a lifetime of rasslin' half-broke horse teams had given him tremendously strong arms. And he had a volcanic temper that showed itself now and then. And now was one of those times.

Muldoon stomped into the Golden Garter, and a few moments later Red Ryan heard bottles smash and furniture splinter . . . and a few moments after that, Dark Alley Jim crashed through the front window of the saloon, landed in a heap, groaned, and lay still. Red stood . . . in time to see an almost naked Dolly Barnes sail through the now destroyed window, but her landing was softer because she fell on top of her unconscious boss.

Muldoon, dressed in a blue sailor coat decorated with two rows of silver buttons that gave him his name, reappeared, Ryan's Greener under his arm, gun leather and duds thrown over his shoulder.

"Jim says you don't owe him a damned thing and I got your three dollars back from the whore he said you was with this morning since services were not rendered," he said. "Now get dressed and saddle your hoss. Did you remember we got a stage to pick up in Fort Concho?"

Red Ryan and Buttons Muldoon rode out of town, dodging rocks thrown by four highly irritated whores led by Dolly Barnes who yelled at Red that he was dirty, no-good, low down . . .

Ryan agreed with what the women called him, but the dirty part hurt.

He and Buttons reached Fort Concho three days later.

CHAPTER TWO

Throughout its twenty-two-year history, construction never ended at Fort Concho, and the day Red Ryan and Buttons Muldoon rode in under a black, growling sky, the post consisted of forty buildings on forty acres surrounded by a vast wilderness of flat, treeless prairie. The buffalo soldiers of the 10th Cavalry occupied the fort, commanded by Colonel Benjamin H. Grierson, a stern man who'd never recovered from his grief over the death of his twelve-year-old daughter, who'd died in an upstairs bedroom of one of the houses at the post.

Red and Buttons rode past the sutler's store, the bakery, and the blacksmith's shop to the sandstone headquarters building. A Patterson & Son stage was parked a distance away, brought there by a relief driver a few days before.

Muldoon stopped to inspect the coach and Ryan swung from the saddle and looped his horse to the hitch rail. He looked around at the scouts coming and going across the parade ground, recognizing big Tam McLeod, who'd scouted for Grierson during the colonel's successful 1880 campaign against Victorio that had ended the Apache threat to West Texas.

"Tam!" Red yelled, waving.

The big man stopped, turned, and looked at Ryan and shook his head. "Hell, I heard you was dead!" he hollered. "And buried."

"Not yet," Ryan called back. "I'm still aboveground."

"I see you got a bullet hole in that fancy hat of your'n," McLeod said.

"Long story," Red said.

The scout, looking more Indian than white man in greasy buckskins and feathered hat, walked up to Red and said, "All right, I got two versions of the happy story of your demise. One is that a jealous husband caught you in bed with his wife and shot you through and through with a pepperbox pistol. The second was that you was hung for a hoss thief in El Paso a year ago by Dallas Stoudenmire. Now which one o' them is true?"

"Neither, Tam, since I'm still alive and kicking."

"Well, that's surely a sore disappointment. Ain't it?"

Ryan watched an eight-man patrol commanded by a boy second lieutenant ride out, their accoutrements jingling, a Pima wearing the blue headband of an army scout ahead of them.

"What's going on, Tam?" Red said. He and the scout went back a ways, and his smile showed that he held no ill will in regard to the big man's chagrin that he was still breathing.

"The Apaches are out. The colonel is bringing in the settlers, them that will come anyway."

"I thought Victorio's death had ended all that warpath stuff."

"And you're not alone, so did a lot of people. For the past two months, there's been a heap of coming and going around the Mescalero wickiups and then a couple of weeks ago about twenty young Chiricahua loiterers left the San Carlos and were welcomed by the Mescalero with open arms."

"How many hostiles are we talking about, Tam?"

"Counting both Mescalero and Chiricahua, about fifty, all of them young bucks, and they're already playing hob. So far, they've murdered twenty-seven Americans, settlers, miners, army supply train escorts and the like, and that number is likely to grow before the army catches up with them."

"Who is leading the broncos? Old Nana? Or is Loco still alive?"

"Yeah, Loco is still alive, but him and Nana are in Mexico where the pickings are easy, and they ain't likely to raid north of the Rio Grande again. This present bunch is led by a young war chief who calls himself Ilesh. In Apache that means Lord of the Earth. From what the Pima scouts tell me, Victorio's spirit came to Ilesh in a great dream and promised him that if he led the united Apache tribes in battle they'd drive out the white man and become lords of the earth." McLeod shook his head and then spat a stream of tobacco juice onto the sand. "It's a bad business, Red."

Ryan watched Buttons Muldoon closely inspect a bright yellow stage wheel and then said, "I reckon the Patterson stage isn't going anywhere until this is over."

"Kinda depends on the attitude of the passengers, don't it?" McLeod said.

"I have two patrols out and in addition the B Company under Captain Taylor scouting the old Butterfield stage route as far as Ketchum Mountain," Colonel Benjamin H. Grierson, tired and looking older than his years, said. "It's a show of force but a token one. The company is understrength, and if the hostiles are in the area I doubt they'll be impressed. Thank God settlers are few and far between in this part of the country, a good reason for the Apaches to avoid Fort Concho. We just aren't important enough."

Red Ryan didn't like what he heard. "Colonel, I've been hired to guard the Patterson stage to Fort Bliss," he said.

"I know, Mr. Ryan. The passengers have already made that clear." Grierson glanced out his office window and said, "Ah, I see Buttons Muldoon heading this way, and he looks none too happy."

"Somebody must have told him about the Apaches," Red said.

A rare smile from Grierson and then, "That would be my guess."

And the colonel was right. Muldoon's round, whiskered face was wrinkled in concern. He took off his leather glove and extended his hand. "Good to see you again, Colonel. It's been a spell."

"Since the Victorio campaign, Buttons," Grierson said. "You're looking well."

"Wish I could say the same about how I feel," Muldoon said. "I've just been told that the Mescaleros are out."

"And about twenty Chiricahua bucks with them. They left the San Carlos two weeks ago," Grierson said.

"Me and Red have been hired to take the Patterson stage to Fort Bliss," Muldoon said.

"Yes, Mr. Ryan has already informed me of that fact," the colonel said. "I can guarantee your safety as far as Ketchum Mountain and perhaps a distance beyond, at Captain Taylor's discretion. I'll give you a note giving him my permission to use his best judgment."

"Colonel, it's four hundred miles of rough country between here and Fort Bliss," Red Ryan said. "That's four or five days on the trail and maybe longer. I doubt the passengers will want to make the trip."

"On the contrary, Mr. Ryan, they seem eager to leave. At least two of them do. I advised them to wait until the hostiles are corralled, but they insist on making the journey, Indian uprising or not."

Ryan shook his head. "Colonel, who are those people? Are they rubes from back east that don't know any better?"

"Two of them are the wives of enlisted men, and they're traveling to Fort Bliss to join their husbands," Grierson said.

"My God, a couple of washerwomen," Muldoon said.

"No doubt, Buttons, no doubt," the colonel said.

"Are those women the two that want to make the trip?" Ryan said.

"No, the stalwarts are Mrs. Stella Morgan, the wife of soon-to-retire Major John Morgan, currently stationed at Fort Bliss, and Mr. Lucian Carter, a San Antonio bank clerk heading farther west in hope of finding a better career situation. To the best of my knowledge the two are traveling companions but are not related in any way."

"I'll talk to them," Ryan said. "Tell them—"

But a commotion outside the door to the colonel's office stopped Red in mid-sentence. The door burst open and a tall young man barged inside, followed by a harried-looking desk sergeant. "Sorry, sir," the soldier said. "I couldn't stop him."

"It's all right, Sergeant," Grierson said. Then, "What can I do for you, Mr. Carter?"

Carter was blond, blue-eyed, and handsome, but he had a sulky, petulant mouth, almost effeminate in its fullness, and a pale skin that would flush easily and burn in the sun. There were bulges under the armpits of his expensive gray sack coat and Ryan pegged him as a two-gun man, rare in the West and probably unique among bank clerks.

"I'll tell you what you can do for me, Grierson," Carter said, his face bright scarlet. "You can guarantee Mrs. Morgan and me a cavalry escort between here and Fort Bliss."

"On the frontier there are no guarantees, Mr. Carter," the colonel said. "My command is already spread thin, and I cannot spare men for escort duty. I suggest you remain here at the fort until the Apaches are rounded up and returned to the reservation."

"No, that won't do," Carter said. "Mrs. Morgan is an army officer's wife and she's anxious to be reunited with her husband because she has some tragic news to impart. She will brook no delay and neither will I. As a gentleman, it is incumbent on me to see her safely to her destination."

"There are two other army wives involved, and they are willing to remain at the fort until the Apache threat is over," Grierson said.

Carter's peevish mouth twisted into a contemptuous grin. "A couple of fat women married, or so they claim, to corporals," Carter said. "Who cares about such people?"

"I do," Red Ryan said. "If the two ladies in question

are passengers of the Patterson and Son Stage and Express Company and they paid the same fare to Fort Bliss as you did. Until they reach the fort they are my responsibility."

"And who the hell are you?" said Carter, a truculent, arrogant man Ryan had disliked on sight.

"Name's Ryan. I ride shotgun for Abe Patterson."

Again, Carter's insolent grin, then, "Yeah, then that makes me feel a whole lot safer."

"You should," Buttons Muldoon said. "Red's the best scattergun guard there is, and I've ridden with a few."

Carter turned to Grierson. "You still insist that I can't have an escort?"

"I'm afraid it's out of the question," the colonel said.

"Then you will take us there, Ryan?" Carter said. "We've paid our fares."

"Listen to the colonel, Carter," Ryan said. "Wait until the Apaches are penned."

"I'll pay you double what Patterson is paying," Carter said.

"No deal," Ryan said.

"Triple."

"I'll be on my way, Colonel," Ryan said. He stepped past Carter, but the man shot out his arm and with considerable strength grabbed Ryan's right bicep and squeezed . . . hard. "Don't you ever walk away from me when I'm talking to you," Carter said.

There were a couple of warning signals Carter should have noticed about Red Ryan, but didn't.

Most obvious was the fact that Red stood six feet and a half-inch tall, and under his buckskin shirt his shoulders and arms bulged with a pugilist's muscle, a holdover from his days as a bare-knuckle booth fighter with Dr. Edwin Drake's Medicine & Curiosities Show. Red had taken on all comers in the ring, had never once failed to come up to scratch, and his quick fists earned him a record of sixty-three wins with only one defeat, and that at the hands of an up-and-coming youngster by the name of Joseph Choynski, the California Terror, who would later in his career fight the likes of James J. Jeffries, James Corbett, and Jack Johnson.

The second fact Carter should already have known . . . that it's never a good idea to muscle a quick-tempered, redheaded man with an arm as hard and big around as an iron stovepipe.

Lucian Carter paid dearly for his oversight.

Ryan twisted a little to his left as he wrenched his arm free and at the same time unleashed a powerful left cross that connected with Carter's chin. The man's legs turned to rubber and he staggered back a few steps before crashing into the office door, splintering the lock. But as Carter slid to the floor, his right hand moved under his coat and emerged with a short-barreled Colt in his fist.

"I wouldn't," Buttons said, his own Remington hammer-back and ready. "Mister, you could be about to make the worst mistake of your life."

Carter thought it over, but he knew the portly stage driver wasn't bluffing, and now wasn't the time to take chances. He holstered his gun and rose to his feet, a trickle of blood running down his chin from the corner of his mouth.

Carter pointed at Red and said, "Damn you, you'll live to regret this."

The man turned on his heel, threw the door wide, and lurched outside.

Buttons looked at Grierson and said, "Colonel, whenever this show hits the road, I've got the feeling it's gonna be a fun trip."

Both Red Ryan and the colonel laughed their agreement.

CHAPTER THREE

Red Ryan and Buttons Muldoon shared a spare room that in the past had been reserved for a couple of infantry sergeants. Apart for a threadbare rug on the stone floor and a couple of chairs, two iron cots, a dresser, and a full-length mirror were its only furnishings. Buttons was cleaning his revolver, and Ryan sat in one of the chairs reading a book he'd found, *Middlemarch* by George Eliot, a morbid, depressing novel that was then unaccountably popular among Western men.

The moon was on the rise and coyotes yipped in the dreary darkness when a soft, hesitant tapping came to the door. Ryan marked his place in the book and rose to answer, allowing inside a young woman who instantly banished the bleak lamplight with her luminous beauty.

Buttons, ever a gentleman when he was around the ladies, especially pretty ones in their early twenties, rose to his feet and joined Ryan as the girl smiled and said, "Ah, which one of you gentlemen is Mr. Ryan?"

"I am," Red said. "And this here is Buttons Muldoon, the best whip in Texas."

"I'm so glad to meet you both. My name is Stella Morgan, originally of the Philadelphia Morgans. I'm booked on the Patterson and Son stage."

"Yes, you are indeed, pleased to meet you, Mrs. Morgan." Red waved to his recently vacated chair. "Would you care to sit?"

Buttons would later accuse Red of "grinning like a possum eating persimmons" when he first beheld the fair Stella, and Red readily agreed that he was smitten by the woman's dazzling loveliness.

"Ma'am, we have whiskey but no glass, if you'd care to make a trial of it," Buttons said.

"No thank you," Stella said. "I've already taken tea with Colonel Grierson."

Red smiled. "What can we do for you, Mrs. Morgan?"

"Please call me Stella. Mrs. Morgan sounds so formal, especially out here in the wilderness." The woman returned Ryan's smile and said, "Red . . . may I call you Red?"

"Please do."

"Red, the colonel told me of the unfortunate unpleasantness between you and Lucian Carter, and it distressed me terribly. I can tell you that Lucian is very upset about it."

"I imagine he is," Red said. He wanted to say that a left cross to the chin with a lot of shoulder behind it would upset just about anybody, but he didn't. Instead he did his best to look sympathetic. "We all let our tempers get the better of us at times."

"Well, please let bygones be bygones," Stella said. "Lucian told me he's most willing to forget the whole unhappy incident. But . . . Red . . . it is imperative that I reach Fort Bliss within the next few days."

"Why the hurry?" Red said.

"I've been living in San Antonio with my husband's mother—"

"Major Morgan's ma?" Buttons said.

"Yes, a dear, sweet lady, but unfortunately she passed away over a week ago. It was all very sudden, I'm afraid. But thank God, she didn't suffer too much."

"Sorry to hear about the lady's death, Stella," Ryan said.

"Well, she was old and very sick and it was her time," the woman said. "But John was very attached to his mama, and I want to be the one to break the sad news to him before someone less caring than myself does. I think you will understand that time is of the essence."

"Ma'am, you know the Apaches are out?" Buttons said.

"Yes, I do. But to spare John further heartbreak I'm willing to take my chances. I must be at my husband's side at this trying time."

Buttons said, "Mrs. Morgan—"

"Stella."

"Stella, do you know what Apaches do to women?"

"Buttons, I'm sure Stella has a pretty good idea," Red said, angling him a look.

"I am not well versed in the ways of the world," Stella said. "But I imagine being a prisoner of the savages would not be pleasant."

"You're so right about that, little lady," Buttons said, but when the woman took out a little handkerchief and dabbed her eyes it banished his smile.

"I must be with John . . . I just . . . must be on hand to succor my husband," she said. "I know he'll be heartbroken."

A woman's tears are corrosive enough to melt a man's heart, and Red Ryan was not immune.

"I must say that I admire your courage, Stella," he said. "Such fortitude is rare, even among Western women."

"Red, say you'll take me to Fort Bliss," Stella said, sobbing slightly. "Please, please say you will."

"I'll study on it," Ryan said. "You have my promise on that."

"I need more than a promise, Red," Stella said. "If I'm not with John when he learns of his mama's death, I'll never forgive myself. Red, he doted on her, loved her with all his heart and soul. I'm an army wife, and I can't fail my husband now because of some savages. John himself has faced so many dangers on the frontier, can I do any less?"

Red saw more tears budding in the woman's eyes, and he said hastily, "Well, it's a big country and the Apaches are few, it's just possible we can make the trip without encountering any hostiles."

Stella managed a smile. "Red, you are my gallant knight in shining armor. Mr. Muldoon . . . Buttons . . . we can't do it without you."

"No, you can't. That is, unless you can handle a six-horse team over four hundred miles of the worst country this side of perdition," Muldoon said.

"I beg you, Buttons, take me to Fort Bliss," Stella said.

"If Red is willing to make the trip, then I'll go along,"

Buttons said. "But I think you two are making a big mistake."

"No, everything will be just fine," Stella said. "I just know it will."

The girl leapt up from her chair and kissed Buttons on his whiskery cheek and then Red. "I'm so happy now," she said. "Thank you both, my wonderful . . . frontier heroes."

After Stella left, Red said, grinning, "I've got tears on my mustache. Imagine that."

He sat on his chair again, the room once more in dusky lamplight, and picked up *Middlemarch,* trying to regain his interest in young Dorothea Brooke, who married a husband so old, his head was almost a skull. But after a few minutes he closed the book with a thump and stared at Muldoon and said, "What the hell did we just do?"

Buttons shook his head. "You tell me, Mr. Knight in Shining Armor."

CHAPTER FOUR

Stella Morgan was quartered with the wives of the Fort Bliss corporals, plump, contented matrons who talked all the time as they knitted winter mufflers for their husbands and munched constantly on sugar cookies, of which they seemed to have an inexhaustible supply.

Making the excuse of a headache, Stella said she was going for a walk before she turned in. "Some fresh air may help," she said.

"You be careful, dearie," one of the women said. "It's cold outside. Take your shawl and don't get a chill in the bladder."

"And remember . . . there are bloodthirsty savages about," the other said.

"I'm not going far," Stella said, throwing her shawl around her shoulders.

She stepped into the starless murk and, keeping to the shadows, walked past the troopers' barracks and then angled across the parade ground toward the sutler's store. Colonel Grierson had pickets out, but they were invisible in the darkness, and the woman moved on soundless feet.

Stella passed between the side of the store and the blacksmith's shop and then walked more quickly toward the wood-frame cabin that lay some thirty yards away. She tapped on the cabin door, and it opened immediately. Lucian Carter, stripped to his pants and undershirt, stepped back to allow the woman inside. He stuck his head out of the doorway and looked around. Satisfied, he closed the door again and said, "You spoke to them?"

Stella smiled. "Yes, they'll do it."

"Thank God," Carter said. "The sooner we get away from this godforsaken post and put some distance between us and San Antonio the better."

"Take it easy, Lucian, and content your mind," Stella said. "Remember, the San Antonio police have nothing on us."

"They were suspicious, Stella. I knew that by the way they were sniffing around. One of the detectives said to me that it was surprising that a healthy, active old lady like Martha Morgan should die so unexpectedly of natural causes. He had a big copper's nose and sneaky eyes, the kind that told me he was saying one thing but meant another."

"Yes, perhaps it was all a little surprising," Stella said. "But the police said nothing about murder."

"I know, but that damned nosey little detective . . . was not the word murder on the tip of his tongue?"

"Hardly. Lucian, you left no mark on the miserable old biddy."

"No, I didn't mark her." Carter smiled. "It was a very soft feather pillow."

Stella put her arms around the man's neck, tilted

back her head, and spoke directly into his handsome face. "We've come far, Lucian, you and I, haven't we?"

"And we have farther to go, Stella. The money and jewelry we have is only a start."

"A small start, my darling. There is so much more ahead of us."

"What about that damned redheaded shotgun guard I had the trouble with?"

"What about him?"

"Did he swallow your story?"

Stella placed the back of her hand on her forehead and pretended to swoon. "Oh, I am undone. I must be with my husband when he hears about the death of his dear, dear mama." The woman's smile was hard, triumphant. "The fool fell for it hook, line, and sinker."

"What about the other one, the driver?"

"He's a harmless idiot."

"I plan to kill them both, Stella," Carter said. "I swear to God, I'll shoot those two barbarians in the belly and listen to them scream."

"Time enough for that when we reach Fort Bliss. Let them get us there first."

"Clever girl," Carter said. He ground his groin into the woman. "Stay a while."

Stella stepped back. "No, not here. What if someone saw us? It's too dangerous. We're just traveling companions, remember?"

"Then I'll wait until we get to Fort Bliss," Carter said.

"No, wait until we get to Washington, Lucian. You'll enjoy me all the more."

Carter grinned. "When we're members of the capital's high society, huh?"

"Exactly. Now, I must go. The fat washerwomen will miss me."

"Until tomorrow then," Carter said.

"Yes, until tomorrow, my one, my only love," Stella said.

Since her head was on his shoulder, Lucian Carter couldn't see the woman's eyes, hard as polished diamonds. Just as well . . . because they were amused . . . and calculating.

"How is your headache, dearie?" one of the army wives said.

"Better, much better now," Stella Morgan said, smiling.

Lucian Carter slid the carpetbag from under the cot. It was large, the kind that had a leather flap across the top fastened with a brass padlock. He took the key from his pocket, unlocked the bag, and peered inside. Dishonest himself, the threat of theft preyed on his mind. Yes, the contents were still intact, fifty thousand dollars in large-denomination bills . . . Martha Morgan didn't believe in banks . . . and jewelry, necklaces, rings, and bracelets mostly, worth at least an additional fifty thousand, and probably twice that. Even more precious was Martha's will, folded into a long manila envelope. Its contents were straightforward enough. In the event of her death—Carter smiled at that—she left all her property to her only child, her son John. The properties consisted of her San Antonio house, a Washington, D.C., town house, railroad shares, considerable holdings in a South African diamond mine, and shares in the White Star shipping line, in all, assets worth a few thousand dollars north of half-a-million. When Major Morgan died, and his impending demise was a guaranteed natural fact, his fortune would of course fall to his grieving widow.

Stella would be rich, and so would Lucian Carter, her next husband.

Carter stood with the bag open, lost in thought.

Did he love Stella? No, he didn't, not really. But he lusted after her lithe body. Would he be sad if she died? Well, a rich man could choose from plenty of willing women. Would he consider . . . making her die? Of course, murder was always an option, because then all the money would be his.

Carter raised his chin and slowly scratched his throat, his manicured fingernails scratching on bristles. He had a lot to think about, but not now. Later, after they were safely ensconced in a Washington town house and Stella wore his wedding ring on her finger. He'd make his decisions then.

CHAPTER FIVE

The Patterson & Son Stage and Express Company skimped on wages and passenger comfort but not on horses. The team Buttons Muldoon hitched to the stage was the best money could buy, six high-quality grade horses personally chosen by Abe Patterson himself. They'd go fast and far without tiring.

Red Ryan watched Buttons with Tam McLeod. The scout was in a sour mood, last night's whiskey punishing him. "Why did you change your mind, Red? That purty Morgan gal work her charms on you?"

"Uh-huh, you could say that," Red said. "She's anxious to join her husband in Fort Bliss."

"The two other army wives decided to make the trip," McLeod said. "I guess they're also anxious to join their husbands. More fool them."

"Who told you that?" Ryan said, surprised.

"Colonel Grierson . . . ah, and here he comes now."

The officer pulled on a leather glove as he walked across the parade ground under a morning sky ribboned with scarlet. He wore a faded blue fatigue blouse with no shoulder boards and a battered campaign hat.

He looked tired, like a man who hadn't slept in several days.

"Ready to go, Mr. Ryan?" Grierson said.

"Yes, Colonel. Tam tells me the other two women have decided to make the trip."

"Yes. They figure if a sweet young thing like Stella Morgan is going, then they'll tag along too. They probably think Mrs. Morgan wouldn't make the trip if she didn't think it was safe."

McLeod watched Lucian Carter help Stella into the stage. "Heard you had trouble with that ranny yesterday, Red," he said.

"Nothing serious," Ryan said.

"He's still aboveground, so I figured it had to be nothing serious," McLeod said. The scout rubbed his aching temples. "What do you count as nothing serious?"

"I won't be handled," Ryan said.

"I reckon you've plugged men for less."

"Not recently," Red said.

Colonel Grierson smiled. "Those ladies are having a time of it."

"So is Muldoon," McLeod said. He grinned. "Yeah, that's right, push on those bustles, Buttons. That's it . . . like loading a cow into a chute."

"Narrow door, plump lady. It's always a problem," Red said.

Buttons closed the stage door, wiped off his sweating face with a large blue bandana, and called out, "You ready, Red? Let's hit the road."

Six mounted troopers, one holding a red-and-white cavalry guidon, had formed up behind Grierson. "Red, I'll escort you part of the way to Ketchum Mountain myself," the colonel said. He seemed worried, his face lined and exhausted. "I'd expected to hear from Company B by this time." Then, visibly making an effort to appear confident, "Captain Taylor is a competent officer who was with me on the Victorio campaign. For all I know he may be in pursuit of the hostiles."

Red Ryan nodded and said what he didn't really believe. "I'm sure that's the case, Colonel."

When the Patterson stage rolled out of Fort Concho, Red Ryan was in the guard's seat, his shotgun across his knees. Colonel Grierson and his men had formed up behind, riding through dust. The scarlet sky had turned to pale lemon, and the new-aborning day was coming in clear, smelling of horses, leather, and buffalo grass.

Buttons Muldoon's hands were steady at the reins, his far-seeing eyes scanning the plain in front of him. Then he turned to Red and said, "The Carter feller is a two-gun man. Shoulder holsters. Odd that."

Red nodded. "I haven't seen many men carry guns that way."

"John Wesley Hardin did. Do you recollect we met him out Gonzales County way that time?"

"Lucian Carter isn't a patch on Wes Hardin," Red said. "On his best day, he ain't even close."

Buttons watched a jackrabbit bound in front of the horses and then veer away in panic, its feet kicking up little puffs of dust. "How do you know that?" he said.

"I just know."

"No, you don't. You have no way of knowing how he'd stack up to Wes."

Red smiled. "What are you trying to tell me, Buttons?"

"I'm telling you to be careful around Carter. All right, he may not be as fast as John Wesley, but he's sneakier, I guarantee it."

"I'll bear that in mind," Ryan said.

"And another thing . . ."

"I swear, Buttons, you must be the talkiest stage driver in Texas."

"Maybe so, but I see things."

"What did you see?"

"When that Carter ranny was helping Stella Morgan into the stage, I seen him run his hand down her back, from neck to bustle." Muldoon shook his head. "Odd that."

"Buttons, you think everything is odd," Red said.

"She's a married woman, but she didn't object. Seen that too."

"Stella is a pretty woman," Ryan said. "She's probably used to men touching her all over and no longer thinks anything of it."

"You reckon so? But I bet she'd object if I done it," Buttons said.

Red turned his head, stared at his whiskery companion, and said, "Come to think about it, I guess she would at that."

The stage rocked over some uneven ground, and after getting the team under control again, Buttons spat over the side and then said, "Well, we can't all be purty like you, Red."

After an hour, the vast, sun-scorched land empty around them, Colonel Grierson cantered his horse alongside the stage, and Muldoon brought the team to a jangling halt.

"Ketchum Mountain is in sight and this is as far as I go, Mr. Muldoon," the soldier said. "I don't want to get too far from the post. Give Captain Taylor my compliments and tell him that I'd like a report as soon as possible."

Red Ryan leaned across his driver and said, "Sorry to lose you, Colonel."

"I have only half a company back at the fort," Grierson said. "I can't be gone for long." He extended his hand. "Good luck, Mr. Muldoon." And then to Ryan, "Keep a close watch on the trail, Red." They shook hands. "And good luck."

"And you too, Colonel, good luck," Red said. "See you back at Fort Concho in a couple of weeks."

"I hope so," Colonel Grierson said, his face lined with concern. "I sure hope so."

CHAPTER SIX

Ketchum Mountain is a ridge about four miles long that rises nearly three thousand feet above the flat. Its slopes are surfaced by gravelly loam that supports a thick growth of bunchgrass and cactus. The bodies of Captain Andrew Taylor and thirty-eight troopers of Company B were scattered over its eastern slope, except for a tangled knot of men, a sergeant and six privates, who'd made a stand around their officer and died with him.

Red Ryan walked among the dead, so many ash-gray faces that he remembered from his previous visits to Fort Concho.

Juan Gomez, the Mexican corporal who'd once planned on becoming a priest but had joined the cavalry instead. Bill Moorehouse, the blue-eyed Englishman that nobody ever beat at dominoes. Private Patrick O'Neill, the big, drunken Irishman who laughed easily and had been a major in the army of the Confederacy. Tom Lake . . . Bob Anderson . . . Jed Franklin . . . all first-class fighting men . . . all dead.

Captain Taylor, his gray hair stained red from a

head wound, lay on his back among his men. They were huddled together, as though they'd sought solace in the nearness of each other when death came for them.

Already, fat black flies hovered over the corpses and made a low, soulful drone.

"Looks like they were taken by surprise, Red," Buttons Muldoon said. His face was like stone.

"Seems like," Red said. "How many Apaches?"

"Judging by the tracks I'd say at least fifty. They were mounted, and they came straight in."

"Then it was a dusk or a dawn attack, otherwise Captain Taylor would have seen them coming from a long ways off."

Muldoon said, "Dawn, I reckon. The Apaches will fight at night, but they don't like it much and try to avoid it when they can."

"How are the passengers?"

"Scared. Even that Carter feller looks scared, but he's still lugging that carpetbag that he never lets out of his sight."

Carter stood with Stella Morgan outside the stage, looking over at the carnage but reluctant to move closer. The two older women, their eyes averted from the scene, remained in the stage that shook with their sobbing. To look upon violent death puts a terrible burden on the soul, and Red Ryan, who'd seen more than his share, didn't blame them.

As Red did his best to console the army wives, Buttons wandered off a distance, and when he returned he took Red aside and said, "They didn't all die. Judging by the tracks, it looks like a patrol headed out before the attack, probably the previous day. I'd say ten, twelve men headed north."

"I guess that's why there's no dead scouts," Ryan said. "They went with the patrol."

"Could be," Muldoon said. "Company B would have had at least four of them."

"Pima?"

"Probably, but I didn't see Luke Spence or Pete Williams at the fort. They may have been with Captain Taylor and left with the patrol."

"Ryan!"

Lucian Carter stalked toward Ryan and then belligerently got into his face. "What the hell are you going to do about this?" he demanded.

"I can't resurrect the dead, Carter, so there's not much I can do," Red said.

"Yes, there is. You can climb aboard the stage right now and head for Fort Bliss."

"That's your advice, huh?"

"No, it's not advice, Ryan. As a paying passenger, I'm ordering you to do what I say."

Red Ryan's temper, always an uncertain thing, flared and his right fist clenched. Buttons Muldoon read the signs and said, "Man's got a point, Red. Unless his other patrols have come in, Colonel Grierson has half a troop of cavalry at Fort Concho and a few civilians. Right about now, staying with the stage is probably safer than heading back."

Ryan thought that through and decided Buttons was correct. Ilesh had scored a great victory, and by now the young war chief was a big man among the Mescalero lodges. The capture and burning of Fort Concho would be hailed as an even greater triumph than the slaughter of Taylor's command, and the aggressive young bucks might push him in that direction. By this time the Apaches must know just how weak Grierson's force was, how vulnerable, and how much power and fame they could garner by its anni-hilation. The capture of a U.S. army post by Apaches had happened only once before, back in 1865 when Fort Buchanan was taken by seventy-five Chiricahua warriors. But that had been a mere skirmish, and the nine defenders had put up a token resistance and then fled. Fort Concho was a much more valuable prize, and its destruction could endanger the whole of West Texas. By comparison, the Patterson stage was insignificant, hardly worth the attention of a mighty warrior like Ilesh.

Red Ryan made up his mind. "All right, everybody, back in the coach," he said.

Stella Morgan smiled and said, "Red, are we continuing our journey to Fort Bliss?"

Ryan saw the look of triumph on Carter's face, and much as it troubled him to do it, he said, "Yes, Stella, we are."

The woman got up on tiptoe and kissed Red on the cheek. "Thank you, Red. You're a brave, wonderful man."

"Thank Buttons," Red said. "This is his idea."

Buttons Muldoon swung the stage away from the charnel house that was the bloodstained northern slope of Ketchum Mountain. Red Ryan looked back at the scattered bodies of the troopers, tangles of blue against stone. How still they were, how quiet and un-complaining in their endless night . . . dead men don't bewail their cruel fate. That is a luxury reserved only for the living.

His heart heavy, Red lowered the rim of his derby against the sun and turned his attention to the trail ahead, aware of the rhythms of the horses and the creaking coach.

Four hundred miles to Fort Bliss.

He tried not to think about it.

CHAPTER SEVEN

The four Roper brothers were scavengers who feasted on the misery and bad luck of others. So far, apart from one isolated farmhouse, their hunt for plunder had been disappointing. Behind them they'd left a dead sodbuster, his young wife who'd begged for death long before the Ropers finished with her, and a baby boy abandoned to die in his cradle. Pickings had been mighty slim, twenty-three dollars and eighteen cents in cash, a nickel watch, a shotgun, a gold wedding band, and a woman's flowered straw hat that Barney, the youngest Roper, took a fancy to and wore in place of his ragged peaked cap.

"Seth, I say we head back to El Paso," Eldon Roper said, addressing the oldest brother. "There's nothing for us out here."

"There's nothing for us back in El Paso either, except a noose for Jake," Seth said.

"She was only a whore," Jake Roper said. "Hell, she told me she liked it rough."

"But not so rough that you broke her damned neck," Seth said. "You don't know your own strength, boy." He reached into his saddlebags and brought out a bottle. After taking a swig he gave it to Barney. "Pass it around."

Barney took a drink, wiped his mouth with the back of his hand, then said, "Seth, you reckon them rumors we heard about Apaches are true?"

"You seen any?" Seth said. A mirror image of his brothers, he was a tall, heavily built and handsome man with hard, black eyes and the predatory instincts of a lobo wolf.

"You know we ain't seen any," Barney said.

"Folks say all kind of things that ain't true," Seth said. "Do you recollect the story of the boy who cried wolf? How many times have we heard somebody say, *'Run! Run! the Apaches are out!'* and it was all a pack of damned lies?"

"So, what do we do, Seth?" Barney said.

"Keep on going until we reach the Brazos. Bound to be settlements around there, and maybe sodbusters ready to be picked clean."

"Ranches too," Eldon said.

Seth shook his head. "No, you damned fool. Remember what I've always told you, that we steer well clear of ranches. Ranches mean punchers and punchers mean guns. Heed what I say, we don't want to get into a shooting scrape with a tough rancher and a bunch of riled-up Texas waddies. Just no future in it."

Seth grabbed the bottle from Eldon and put it back in the saddlebags. "The way my thinking is inclined, is to find us a nice, fat farm, one with women on it, and winter there," he said. "Come spring, we get rid of the women and ride on."

"Sounds reasonable to me," Eldon said. "Barney, Jake, what about you?"

The brothers nodded, and Jake said, "Hell, we only need one woman, come to that."

"One like that last little gal, you mean?" Seth said. "Share and share alike, that's the motto of the Roper brothers, ain't it?"

Jake grinned, let loose a wild rooster crow, and yelled, "Share and share alike, that's—" Whatever the man was going to say was choked off as, a stupid expression on his face, he looked down at the feathered arrow that had entered his throat just above the Adam's apple and protruded three inches out the back of his neck.

With a patience and endurance alien to a white man, the eight Mescaleros had been lying in wait for two hours, fully aware that the four men riding good horses would eventually come to them. A distance away, in the hollow between a pair of shallow hills, two of the younger warriors stayed with the war ponies and would not take part in the ambush.

Short, stocky men with broad faces and barrel chests, the Apaches seemed to rise out of the ground, out of the blasting heat that was a living thing . . . out of the depths of hell.

An arrow took Eldon, a bullet smashed into Jake, killing them both, and to save his own skin, Seth Roper gave Barney to the Mescalero.

Without a moment's hesitation, he shot the youngster's horse out from under him and then savagely rowel-raked his own mount into a wild gallop. The sudden move surprised the Indians, and by the time they recovered and shot at Seth, he was bent over in the saddle beyond their range. The warriors didn't pursue . . . not when there was good sport to be had close at hand.

When Barney's horse fell, he jumped clear and landed on his feet. He saw Seth gallop into the distance, trailing dust, and knew with a spike of anger mixed with terror that his faithless brother had sacrificed him. Barney turned and ran, stumbling through the long grass in the high-heeled boots he'd once taken from a murdered puncher. Made on a narrow last, the boots were for riding, not walking, certainly not for running. He staggered on, screeching his fear, cursing his faithless brother.

The grinning Apaches thought this splendid and teased him mercilessly, driving him around and around in circles. The young warriors ran alongside Barney Roper, beating him with their bows and riding quirts, and when he tripped and fell they kicked him to his feet again. Barney's first serious wound happened when he tried to draw his gun, unhandy in the pocket of his ragged Union army greatcoat. As he fumbled the Remington clear, a young Mescalero slashed at his hand with the razor edge of a hunting knife. Barney shrieked as he saw his severed right thumb and forefinger fall to the grass at his feet. That shriek, torn from the white-hot depths of his pain and terror, was destined to be the first of many.

Finally tiring of the chase, the Apaches settled down and worked on Barney for a long, long time with fire and hooks and pincers and red-hot steel, and after seven hours of torture that took him to the screaming, screeching, gibbering pinnacles of torment, he died cursing his brother, his God, and the mother who bore him.

Later the Mescalero talked among themselves for a while and agreed that the white man had died badly. They were sorely disappointed because no power had been gained from Barney Roper's cowardly death.

CHAPTER EIGHT

Red Ryan watched the rider appear from out of a dancing heat haze and swing his horse toward the stage. The team was resting, and the passengers stretched their legs, the women walking back and forth through the long grass, talking.

"You see him, Buttons?" Red said.

"I see him. White man. Civilian. Maybe one of Colonel Grierson's missing scouts."

"Could be," Red said. "Well, let him come and hear what he has to say."

"Keep your scattergun handy," Buttons said. "He may be a road agent."

Red smiled. "He's a bold one if he is."

Lucian Carter stood beside Red, and his eyes searched into the distance.

"Somebody coming," he said.

"We see him," Buttons said.

"Apache?" Carter said.

"No. He sits his horse like a white man."

"So how does a white man sit his horse?" Carter

said, displaying the sneering, superior smile that set Red's teeth on edge.

"He don't have the same confidence in his mount as an Indian has," Buttons said.

"And it shows," Red said. "At least some of the time."

"Like now," Buttons said. "And that is one tuckered-out hoss the feller is riding."

Red Ryan cradled his Greener in his arms as the rider came within talking distance and drew rein. "Howdy," Red said, prepared to be sociable, but he didn't like the look of the man. He'd seen frontier trash before . . . and looked into the cold eyes of killers . . . and this man was both.

"And a howdy right back," the man said. "Name's Seth Roper, and I'm headed for the Brazos. Got kinfolk there on my Ma's side."

"On a lathered hoss, huh?" Buttons said.

"Ran into Apaches a couple of miles back. Had to make a run for it," Roper said. His eyes roamed, dismissed the two army wives, and settled on Stella Morgan. "See you got some mighty fine womenfolk with you."

Red ignored that and said, "Which way were those Apaches headed? We figured they were raising hob well east of here."

Roper shrugged. "Hell, I don't know which way they were headed, and I was too busy running from them to care."

Red gave the rider a second look, measuring the man. Roper wore a black frock coat over a collarless shirt, gray with ingrained dirt around the neck, and pants shoved into the tops of expensive boots. He carried a holstered Colt on his hip, a Winchester under his knee and looked as though he knew how to use both.

In all, Seth Roper cut an ominous, dangerous figure, black hair, black eyes, and in Ryan's snap judgment, black heart.

But apparently, that was not how the man appeared to Lucian Carter.

"We're headed for Fort Bliss up El Paso way," Carter said. "With the Indians on the warpath and all, you're welcome to ride along. We can always use another gun."

"That may be true, but, mister, it will cost you two hundred dollars to ride in the stage," Buttons Muldoon said.

"He can ride on top until his horse is rested," Carter said.

"Fifty dollars to ride on top," Buttons said. "One mile or four hundred, it don't make no difference. That's the policy of the Patterson company, and I am its agent."

Seth Roper stared at Buttons, the cold, fixed stare one man gives another before the draw and shoot. But Buttons had been up that trail a time or three before and would not be intimidated.

Finally, Roper said, "All right, I'll ride along part of the way with you. I'll let my horse rest a spell here and catch up."

Prepared to take the man at more than face value, at least for now, Red said, "Nolan's Station is forty miles ahead of us and we should reach it before dark. Maybe Emmett Nolan will trade horses with you."

"Mister, nobody takes this horse," Roper said. "Not now, not ever."

"Just a suggestion," Red said, the man falling in his estimation again.

Roper swung from the saddle, lit a cigar, and then walked his horse to where Carter stood. The two of them drew off a few yards and immediately began a whispering conversation.

"Them two got cozy right quick," Buttons said to Red.

"Yeah, seems like."

"Wouldn't you like to know what they're saying?"

"None of my business."

"Maybe it is your business."

"No, the safety of this stage is my business, and right now I'm more worried about Apaches than I am about conversations."

"Red, you really think the Apaches will hit us?" Buttons said.

"I wish I knew the answer to that question, but I sure as hell don't," Ryan said.

He turned to the passengers. "Everybody back in the stage. Next stop Nolan's Station. Antelope steak and beans for dinner, I'm sure, but Nolan's wife makes the best bear sign in Texas."

CHAPTER NINE

Tired horses and hilly country slowed the stage, and by the time Nolan's Station came in sight Buttons Muldoon had lit the side lamps against the fading daylight. Seth Roper had caught up an hour before and rode point. The man seemed as concerned about Apaches as Red Ryan was, and he carried his Winchester upright, the butt on his thigh, his head moving constantly.

Suddenly Roper raised his arm and called a halt.

Buttons drew rein on the team and said, "What the hell . . ."

Roper turned his horse, rode back to the stage and said, "Something is happening at the station, and it don't look good."

"Hell, there's always happenings at a stage stop," Buttons said, scowling at the man.

But Red Ryan's gaze reached across distance and he said, "It's Apaches, Buttons. Looks like they're looting the place."

"Have they seen us?" Buttons said.

"Not yet, but they will," Red said. He made up his

mind, bent over in his seat, and called out, "Carter, climb up here on top. You ladies get down between the seats. Roper, you lead us in. We'll charge at a gallop right down their damn throats."

Seth Roper was a frontier ruffian, but he was smart. He knew very well that the stage couldn't outrun the Apaches and it would be a disaster if they were caught out in the open. Attacking with only four fighting men didn't seem like a good idea either. Roper thought about making a run for it on his own, but dismissed the idea. He'd very quickly reached an understanding with Lucian Carter, one desperado to another, and the stakes were too high for him to turn his back on the money involved.

"Ready when you are, Ryan," Roper said. "I hope you've got the belly for a fight."

"When it comes to fighting, you can try me any time, Roper," Red said, irritated by the man's arrogance.

Roper laughed and said, "One day I might just take you up on that."

The stage rocked as Lucian Carter climbed on top. He braced his legs against Stella Morgan's large steamer trunk, drew his guns, and said, "Ryan, I hope you know what the hell you're doing."

Buttons hoorawed the horses into motion and yelled over his shoulder at Carter, "No, he don't!"

The Apaches were preoccupied, three with Nolan's woman, four others leading horses out of the barn, and they didn't heed the stage until it was right on top of them. One of the Indians with the horses whooped in alarm when he saw the thundering, dust-clouded coach bearing down on him. He snapped off a shot from his rifle . . . and the fight was on.

Buttons hauled the team to a shuddering halt and immediately a tall warrior with a broad, painted face came at Red Ryan through the following dust cloud, a Colt in his fist. The Apaches were not noted revolver fighters, and the Indian's shot missed, splitting the air close to Red's left ear. Red let the man have both barrels of the Greener in the face, and the Apache's features instantly disappeared in a scarlet mess, like a raspberry pie dropped on a bakery floor. Red threw down his shotgun, drew his Colt, and jumped from his seat. Events flickered fast around him, a real-life magic-lantern show that revealed images for just a fleeting moment before they were gone. Red saw an Apache fall to Carter's roaring guns, and then another . . . damn, the man was good! Roper fought his rearing horse and then fired at a half-naked warrior who'd just rolled off Mrs. Nolan. Surprised by the attack, dulled by his lust, the Apache grabbed his rifle, climbed out of the wagon bed, and staggered to his feet. Roper shot the man down and then spurred his mount toward a couple of warriors who stood in the doorway of the barn, both of them firing, making a fight of it.

Red left those two to Roper and met a pair who'd been ravishing the now-unconscious woman. The range was close. A bullet burned across the meat of Ryan's left shoulder and another kicked a startled exclamation point of dust inches from his boots. Red Ryan's name was always mentioned when men talked about shootists and the new breed of Texas draw fighters, and that evening at Nolan's Station he proved himself worthy of his reputation. At a range of just five yards, he thumbed off two shots and dropped both Apaches. One was dead when he hit the ground, the second, part of his left cheekbone torn away by Red's bullet, gamely tried to work his Winchester but the effort proved too much for him and, his black eyes glittering with hatred, he spat his defiance at Ryan, kneeled, and waited for the bullet . . . that never came.

The young warrior had sand and Red was willing to let him die on his own terms.

But Buttons Muldoon didn't see it that way.

As far as he was concerned a wounded Apache buck with a rifle close by was an imminent danger, and three bullets from his revolver hammered the Indian into the ground.

"Taking chances, ain't you, Red?" Buttons yelled, his Remington trailing smoke.

"I guess I'm getting soft in my old age," Ryan said.

"And you only thirty-five," Buttons said. "Don't get any softer, not when Apaches are around."

Red took in the gunsmoke-shrouded scene, his gun ready in his hand. But the Battle of Nolan's Station, as it would come to be called, was over. Six Mescaleros were dead and one wounded. That quickly became seven dead when Lucian Carter put a bullet though the head of the injured warrior.

Then Seth Roper called out, "Ryan, you better come over here."

The gunman stood beside the wagon where Maud Nolan lay on her back. As he walked toward the woman, Red saw that she was plump, pretty . . . and out of her mind.

CHAPTER TEN

The two army wives kneeled one on each side of the raving Maud Nolan and wrung their hands.

"Oh . . . what do we do?" the older woman wailed. Her name was Rhoda Carr, a respectable forty-year-old who'd never before faced the realities of the savage Indian wars, where killing and rape had become commonplace.

Edna Powell, ten years younger than Rhoda and usually a rosy-cheeked mirror image of her companion, sat stunned, staring at Maud Nolan with horrified eyes, her plump cheeks no longer rosy but ashen gray.

Rhoda looked up at Red Ryan with pleading eyes and said again, "What do we do, Mr. Ryan?" She'd pulled down the woman's dress so that the others would not see her nakedness.

Red had no answer to that question. He felt helpless, lost. He kneeled beside Maud, took her work-calloused hand in his, and said, "Maud, you're going to be all right. You'll be just fine."

Recognition dawned in the woman's eyes and she

said, "Red, where is Emmett? Don't let him see me like this."

Ryan looked at Seth Roper. The big gunman shook his head.

"Emmett will be along presently," Red said. "Everything is going to be fine."

Maud grabbed the sleeve of his shirt. "Red," she whispered, "kill me and end my disgrace. Will you do that for me . . . as a kindness?"

Red gently squeezed the woman's hand, his mouth working.

Dear God, give me the words. Tell me what to say that will make this better.

After a while, he said, "You'll be all right, Maud." He was sick at heart that God had failed him and that a young woman he knew and liked had been raped and abused and teetered on the ragged edge of madness.

The sanity of a woman who lived on the vast, empty Plains was always a fragile thing. Often, she succumbed to what doctors called Prairie Madness, brought about by isolation and harsh living conditions. Sometimes, driven over the edge by the never-ending wind that rushed through the long grass, forceful and pitiless, the alien heartbeat of an enemy more powerful than anything she'd known in her previous life, her mind gone, she'd stand outside the cabin and scream and scream until she could scream no longer.

Now Maud Nolan was screaming . . . but inside . . . and she was in a dark place from whence she might never return.

In the past, in lonely army outposts on the rim of nowhere, Rhoda Carr had birthed babies and buried the hurting dead. Now, after a tremendous effort, she gathered her strength and stepped into the void.

"Edna, we'll take Mrs. Nolan into the cabin and bathe her and dress her in clean clothes," she said.

Edna Powell managed a nervous smile. "Yes, that might help. No, it will help, Rhoda, won't it?"

The older woman shook her head. "I don't know. I just don't know," she said. Then, "Say a prayer, Edna. Sometimes a prayer works when all else fails."

Red Ryan stood aside and let the women carry Maud Nolan into the cabin. It was then that he saw Stella Morgan for the first time since the fight began. She stood with her back against the stage, as though she felt reassured by its solid bulk. Stella had done nothing to help Mrs. Nolan, keeping her distance. But her beautiful face was pale, her eyes haunted. Rape is one of the most terrible crimes on earth, and the young woman had witnessed it firsthand. The vestiges of its savage violence still whispered darkly in her mind.

Then Buttons Muldoon stepped beside Stella and said something that forced her to smile, and she hugged him, briefly, his sturdy presence an anchor that helped her hold fast to her own faltering courage.

Sprawled Apache bodies lay scattered around the station, and the spare team they'd tried to steal had spread out and grazed as though nothing had happened.

Despite his own efforts, the battle had been won by the revolver skills of Lucian Carter and Seth Roper, and Red did not try to pretend otherwise. Had the fight been a rifle clash at distance, the result might have turned out otherwise, but up close at spitting range, bucking Colts in the hands of two skilled gunmen had been a decisive factor, and together they'd inflicted great slaughter.

Unbidden, the thought came into Ryan's mind that if he ever had to face both Carter and Roper in a gunfight, the odds would not be in his favor.

"You done good, Ryan." Seth Roper stepped beside Red. "For a spell there, it was a close-run thing." He glanced at the blood on Red's shoulder. "I see one of them winged you."

Ryan nodded. "It's not serious. I saw you get your work in, Roper. You killed your share and then some."

The big man shrugged. "Look at them, all young bucks. Green as hell, they knew nothing. How's the woman?"

"Bad . . . not good . . . I don't know."

"Pity about that. They say Apaches are hard on white women."

"Seems like."

"Come, I've got something to show you."

Roper turned on his heel and Ryan followed him into the barn.

"He was lucky. He had time to shoot himself," Roper said. Then, as a disinterested aside, he pointed to his own left temple and said, "Shot himself right there. He was a left-handed man."

Because of the Mescaleros' fear of a suicide, Emmett Nolan's body was untouched and his gun was still in his hand.

"He knew enough to kill himself before the Apaches captured him," Roper said. "Had he fit Indians before?"

"I don't know," Red said. "But I guarantee he knew

what Apaches do to a man. He didn't want to face that, and I don't blame him none."

Roper shook his head. "Too bad." He glanced around the well-kept barn. "Looks like he understood his business."

"Emmett Nolan knew horses," Ryan said.

And that would prove to be the dead man's only epitaph.

After the dead Mescalero were dragged out of the station by Red Ryan and the other men and dropped a mile away among the long grass, two women sought out his company.

The first was Rhoda Carr, her round, homely face grim. In answer to Red's inquiry about Maud Nolan, she said, "She won't talk. We bathed her all over and dressed her in her best clothes and she let us do it without saying a word. And Mr. Ryan, she's pregnant. I'd say three months."

"Are you sure?" Red said.

Rhoda made a face. "Have you any idea how many pregnant women I've seen in my time?"

"Yeah, I reckon you have," Red said, way out of his depth. "We'll take her to Fort Bliss. There are doctors there."

"Right now, she doesn't need a doctor, she needs her husband."

"Emmett Nolan is dead," Ryan said. Then, a small lie that he intended to repeat in the hope that it might ensure a Patterson and Son pension for his widow. "The Apaches killed him."

"Oh, poor Mrs. Nolan, with the baby coming and

all," Rhoda said, wringing her hands as was her habit. "What is to become of her?"

Ryan placed his hand on the woman's plump shoulder. "We'll take good care of Maud," he said, fully aware that all he could do was put her in the stage and take her to a doctor.

Rhoda Carr was not convinced, but she was old enough and experienced enough to know that the big, redheaded man with the kind green eyes could not pull miracles out of a hat. Well, they needed only one miracle, a miracle that would make Maud Nolan well again . . . but there was a dire shortage of those on the frontier.

"Red, how is the woman?" Stella Morgan said.

"I'd like to say that she's fine, but she isn't," Ryan said.

"What happened to her . . . the Apaches . . . I'd never recover from that," Stella said.

"I think maybe Maud won't get over it either," Red said.

The woman's face was very pale, her full lips almost white, and strain lined her face. "It could have been me," Stella said. "I've been thinking about that, thinking about it constantly, and for the first time I'm really scared."

"We hurt them, hurt them bad," Red said. "The Mescalero are few and the deaths of seven young warriors is a big loss. They may not try us again."

"But is there a chance they will?" Stella said.

"I don't know," Red said. "The Apache is the most notional creature on earth, and there's no telling what he will or will not do. All I can say is that I think there's a good chance they'll leave us alone and go after easier prey."

Stella thought about that and then said, "If the Apaches come again and it looks like we're about to be overcome, I asked Seth Roper to put a bullet in my brain." She gave a slight smile. "He said he'd be happy to oblige."

"Yeah, he would say that," Red said. Then, again stating something he didn't believe himself, "It won't come to that."

"But there are no guarantees," Stella said.

"When it comes to Apaches, there never are. Why don't you go see Maud Nolan, Stella? Try and talk to her. Maybe you can help."

The woman shook her head. "No, I don't want to go anywhere near her. I don't want to touch her. I won't want to look at her defiled body and think, *I could be you.* I'm not strong enough for that. I'm not Joan of Arc. I don't wear armor."

"No, I guess none of us do," Red Ryan said.

CHAPTER ELEVEN

Buttons Muldoon decided to keep his own team and set the Nolan horses loose to fend for themselves. He told Red Ryan that even tired, the six in his hitch were better than the others.

"Nolan's wheelers were always too small and I told him that a few times," he said. "But he never did listen and learn. Well, it's too late to teach him anything now, ain't it?"

"You're the boss, Buttons," Red said. "Now grab a couple of shovels from the toolshed, we've got a burying to do."

"What about them other two, Red?" Buttons said, his voice whiny. "Can't they do some digging?"

"If you were Emmett Nolan, would you want to be laid to rest by the likes of Seth Roper and Lucian Carter?"

"No, I guess not. But I got to eat afterward. Here, you think them women will rustle us up some grub?"

"I doubt that they're in the mood, Buttons. But I'm a fair hand with a skillet."

Buttons was surprised. "I never knew you was a cook."

"I'm not. But I know how to make coffee and burn an antelope steak."

"And that sounds good enough for me," Buttons said.

"I figured it would be," Red Ryan said.

To Red's surprise Seth Roper grabbed a shovel and pitched in, but making a hole for Emmett Nolan was not easy. The ground was root-bound and there were rocks as big as buffalo skulls. The work was so hard that after an hour of steady digging Buttons Muldoon spat on his hands and said, "Damn, this is like plowing a wet field behind a drunk mule."

Waist deep in the hole, Red leaned on his shovel and said, "Buttons, when did you ever plow a wet field, or a dry one, come to that?"

"Never. But if I ever did, this is what it would be like."

Like so many Western men, Emmett Nolan was buried without much ceremony. Stella Morgan was at the graveside as were the other army wives and Carter and Roper. By the amber light of oil lamps, they all joined Muldoon in singing "Shall We Gather at the River," or as much of it as they remembered, and then it was over. In the course of time, prairie grass would cover the scar on the earth made by Nolan's grave, and his last resting place would be lost forever . . . and only the wind would remember and keep its secret.

* * *

Red Ryan stood watch throughout the night while the others slept, and at first light he mounted Nolan's saddle mare and rode out to where the Apache bodies had been left. As he expected, they were gone.

"And that means the Apaches are still around," Buttons Muldoon said.

"Seems like," Red said, using a fork to scramble eggs in the hot fat left by the bacon.

Buttons watched Ryan's culinary skills with more than passing interest, sipped his coffee, and said, "Red, I got a bad feeling."

"What kind of bad feeling?"

"An all-over bad feeling and the rheumatisms in my hands are paining me like they always do when hard times are fixing to come down."

"Apache hard times, you reckon?" Ryan said, filling plates with eggs, bacon, and fried sourdough bread.

"Right in the here and now, is there any other kind?"

"I guess not," Ryan said. "Go give the passengers a holler for breakfast. Tell them to come and get it or I'll throw it out."

Seth Roper and the two army wives ate heartily, but Stella Morgan picked at her food, and Lucian Carter complained that his eggs were greasy.

"I'm a shotgun guard, not your personal chef, Mr. Carter," Red said.

"Hey, Carter, you gonna finish them eggs?" Roper said.

"Hell, no. Here, take them."

"Thank'ee," Roper said. Wielding his fork like a shovel, he dug in with a will and then raised his eyes to Red and said, "You're a good cook."

"Thank you," Red said. And then to Rhoda Carr, "I boiled a couple of eggs for Mrs. Nolan. Do you want to take them to her?"

"Yes, I'll do that now." The woman dabbed her mouth with a blue and white checkered napkin and rose to her feet.

"There's some buttered toast to go with the eggs," Ryan said.

Rhoda Carr came back a few moments later, her eyes as round as coins, her face pale. "I dropped the eggs," she said. "Oh, dear me, I dropped the eggs."

The woman was in shock, and Red said, "Steady, Mrs. Carr, what has happened?"

"She's gone."

"Mrs. Nolan?"

Angry at himself—who the hell else could it be?— Red dashed past the woman and hurried to the cabin. The bed was empty and there was no sign of Maud.

"Red, how did she get past us in the dark?" Buttons said. "How did she do that?"

"I've no idea, but she did," Red said.

"Apache bodies gone, Maud Nolan gone, everything is vanishing around here," Buttons grumbled. "I've never seen the like."

Red swung into the saddle of the mare, a tall, rangy horse with a lot of Thoroughbred in her. "Buttons, gather up what supplies you can and then load the passengers. Once I find Maud I'll catch up with you on the trail."

Lucian Carter and Seth Roper stepped beside Ryan, and Roper said, "You lost the crazy woman?"

"I'll find her," Red said.

"Careless of you all the same, Ryan," Carter said, stepping in front of the horse.

Red kept his quick temper in check. "She can't have gone far," he said. "Now, will you give me the road?"

He kneed the mare forward, roughly bumped Carter aside, and Buttons put his hand over his mouth to hide his giggles.

CHAPTER TWELVE

Red Ryan could find no tracks leading from the station, and when he scanned the distances around him nothing moved but the wind rippling the prairie grass with the sound of waves breaking on a shingle beach.

Ryan swung the mare south and at a distance of a quarter mile made a loop around Nolan's Station. He saw no sign of Maud Nolan. He tried the same route, this time a half-mile out. As he rode the northern flank of his loop, the stage drove out of the station, Buttons Muldoon up on the box, handling the reins with his usual practiced ease. The wheels kicked up ribbons of dust, and the coach was soon lost behind a tan-colored cloud.

Red Ryan resumed his hunt, each loop expanding the distance between himself and the station, but there was no life on the land, only endless grass and the vast, turquoise bowl of the sky.

In the end, after two hours of searching, it was a Mescalero who led him to Maud Nolan.

Red had drawn rein, telling himself that the hopeless search was over. A small, slender woman could easily lose herself in such an immense, rolling plain. She might even be close, hiding like a hunted animal in the long grass, watching him with mad eyes, seeing not Red Ryan, but yet another male . . . another enemy.

The sun was high, and sweat trickled down Red's back under his buckskin shirt. The mare's head hung, and her glossy chestnut flanks were stained black. Red stepped out of the saddle and took his canteen from the saddle horn. He let the horse drink from his cupped hand and then drank himself. It was as he lowered the canteen that he saw the Apache.

Ryan had earlier dismissed what he'd seen as a notched rock formation in the distance, and it was only now when he saw it with rested eyes that he could make out an Indian. The man stood, holding the reins of his horse as he stared down at something in the grass, and Ryan knew with certainty that it could only be Maud Nolan.

Red swung into the saddle. He'd left his shotgun with Buttons, but he slid Emmett Nolan's Winchester from the boot under his knee and kicked the tired mare forward. On the plains, under a burning sun, the eyes can play tricks, and even a hardened desert warrior like the Apache stared at Ryan for a long time before he shielded his eyes with his hand and took a closer look. After a moment, the Indian made up his mind. A mounted white man riding toward him meant only one thing . . . a bitter foe to be dealt with.

The Mescalero immediately dropped to one knee, threw a rifle to his shoulder, and fired. The bullet kicked up dust twenty feet in front of Ryan's horse, and at the same time Ryan heard the distinctive, sharp bark of a Springfield. The range was more than a hundred yards, but Ryan dusted off a few shots with the Winchester, all of them misses. But the young Apache, armed with a single-shot weapon, decided he didn't like the odds. He jumped onto his paint pony, raised the Springfield above his head and yelled at Ryan probably the only white-man insult he knew, "Son of beech!" The young buck then sped away, his galloping mount trailing a farewell of dust.

Red figured the Apache had been hunting, stumbled on Maud Nolan by accident, and wasn't really looking for a fight. The Mescalero were like that. They'd only get into a scrap when they felt like it—though they felt like it most of the time—and always when the odds were in their favor. It didn't make them any less brave. It was just their traditional, raid-and-run approach to warfare.

Red Ryan kneed his horse forward. Now he could see the skirts of Maud Nolan's dress lifting in the wind, fluttering like pale blue moths. He rode closer, his mouth dry, a sense of dread cold in his belly. Was she alive or dead?

The answer to that question came when he dismounted and walked to where the woman lay. Maud was dead . . . and she'd taken her own life. Red couldn't even begin to imagine the strength of will it must have taken for the woman to plunge a butcher's knife into her own chest between her naked breasts. Judging by the almost serene expression on her face, she'd died quickly and gratefully, and Ryan figured that such a death had surely been one of God's tender mercies.

Red Ryan buried Maud Nolan beside her husband, uniting them in death and with their unborn child. It was a task that took him well into the afternoon, and by the time he rode away from the station the daylight was waning. Buttons had swung the stage to the northeast, its passage through the prairie grass as obvious as a railroad track.

A single star hung in a blue steel sky when Ryan encountered wagon tracks that had come in from the west and then swung into the path left by the stage. The lost C Company cavalry patrol? Unlikely. With fast, hard-hitting Apaches on the warpath, a wagon would be too much an encumbrance, and Red had seen no wheel tracks around Ketchum Mountain. Frightened settlers fleeing for the safety of Fort Bliss was the more obvious answer.

Ryan dismounted and studied the wagon tracks. Four wheeled, drawn by four small horses or mules. Judging by the depth of the wheel ruts, the wagon was fairly heavily loaded and it looked like three, maybe four people walked alongside. Red straightened and looked ahead to where the paths of both vehicles gradually disappeared into the crowding murk. It seemed that settlers driving a wagon, no doubt piled with furniture and Aunt Minnie's spinet, followed the stage in hopes of gaining its protection. Red's smile was grim. Their chances of catching up with Buttons's speedy team with a heavily loaded wagon were slim to none.

"But good luck to you whoever you are," Ryan said aloud. "I reckon you're going to need it."

CHAPTER THIRTEEN

Red Ryan decided not to attempt to outrun the darkness and settled for a night on the prairie. He ate a supper of the venison jerky he'd found in the station's kitchen, smoked several cigarettes, and then spread his blankets on the grass. Tired from his newly discovered calling as gravedigger in chief, he slept soundly, waking with the dawn and a gun muzzle pushed into his face.

"Ain't a watch-keeping man, are you, mister?"

The ranny behind the Winchester was young, tall, skinny, and shabby with a slack-mouthed, inbred face and eyes the color of muddy swamp water.

Red blinked, blinked again, and then said, "Who the hell are you?"

"Name's Billy Buck, and I'm the man that's gonna kill you just as soon as you saddle that there hoss of your'n."

"Saddle your own damned hoss," Red said.

"Cain't do that, on account of my bad back," the man said. "Now do what I tell you or I'll scatter your brains right now."

Then Billy Buck, his frayed hat pushed to the back of his head, took an aggressive step forward, his Winchester at the ready. Billy was not long on smarts and he'd just made a major mistake.

Red turned on his side and at the same time swung his powerful right leg like a scythe, sweeping the man's legs out from under him. Billy Buck's mouth opened in a startled O of surprise, and he hit the ground hard, falling heavily on his bad back. Ryan jumped to his feet and caught Buck with a tremendous straight right to the chin as the man tried to scramble to his feet. Irritated at Billy Buck for giving him such a scare, Red was merciless. He followed up the right with a left uppercut that slammed into Buck's belly and dropped him, all flailing arms and legs, like a puppet that just had his strings cut. The man got to his hands and knees, gasping for breath, his mouth stringing blood-streaked saliva, and Red Ryan, never a stickler for the Marquess of Queensberry Rules, booted him hard in the ribs. Red picked up the Winchester, pointed it at Buck and said, "On your feet."

Billy staggered to his feet and squealed, "For God's sake, don't shoot me, mister."

"I ought to blow your damned guts out," Red said. And then, "Where the hell did you come from?"

Buck pointed to the wagon tracks. "With the wagon just ahead of you. I'm with my Ma and my brothers and them."

"Who's 'and them'?"

"Three womenfolk, Mildred, Minerva, and Molly, they're sisters that jumped the broom with my brothers."

"You got a wife?"

Billy Buck shook his head. "No woman will have me. I got a bad back."

"Could be you got a bad attitude," Red said.

"Women told me that very thing afore." Buck rubbed his chin. "You hit hard, mister."

"Well, maybe you should find another line of work, Billy boy. Bushwhacking a man sure don't fit your pistol." He took stock of the youngster and then said, "Seems like I got two options with you, Billy Buck. I can drill you right where you stand or take you back to your ma. What's it to be?"

"Hell, mister, one's as bad as t'other."

"What's worse than dying?"

"My ma with a hickory switch."

"Good, maybe she can beat some sense into you," Red said.

He used the rope from Nolan's saddle to truss up Buck like a chicken and once mounted, tethered him behind his horse. After a mile with Buck constantly complaining that walking hurt his back, Red turned his head and said, "Your ma know the Apaches are out?"

"Nobody told us that. We come up from the border country, and we ain't seen no Apaches or anybody else either."

"Around these parts, if you see Apaches, you're already a dead man. You better warn your ma."

"Our wagon is just a little ways ahead," Buck said. "You can warn her your ownself. She won't believe me, she never does."

"Well, somebody should tell her, I guess," Red said.

He thought he saw a sly look flit across Billy Buck's face, but he figured he was imagining things. As a responsible employee of the Patterson & Son Stage and Express Company, he considered it his duty to warn Ma Buck about the Apache uprising, a thing he could not trust her son to do.

And so it was that Billy Buck had made his mistake earlier . . . and now it was Red Ryan's turn to make his.

The Buck family wagon was parked on the long grass and its four-mule team were out of the traces, grazing. The wagon was a canvas-covered Conestoga that showed considerable wear, its weathered side-boards held together by baling wire and twine. The ribs of the underfed mules stood out like rows of fence poles, and their scarred flanks revealed whip abuse.

When Red Ryan rode closer, his prisoner in tow, four women and three men stopped what they were doing and watched him come. The men wore belt guns over their dingy rags and one of the females, who Red at first took to be a man wearing a woman's dress, carried a rifle. A blackened cooking pot hung over a stingy campfire, and a coffeepot bubbled on the coals. A rank smell hung over the camp, deriving from the wagon, from the people themselves, or both.

Ryan summed up the Bucks as a two-by-twice outfit, the younger women wild-haired and slatternly and the men unshaven and dirty, dressed in whatever pants and coats they'd been able to scrounge or steal. None looked intelligent, or even aware, as they stared at Red with the flat, empty, button eyes of rag dolls.

A wretched, poverty-stricken bunch and no mistake, Red thought. No one is happy to be destitute, and Red had seen and admired plenty of poor people as they struggled to make a better life for themselves in the

West, but the Bucks seemed content to wallow in their own filth, like pigs in a sty, and that he could not forgive.

Red reminded himself that he was not there to pass judgment, but to warn the folks of the impending Apache danger, and he was prepared to be sociable.

He drew rein, touched the rim of his derby, and said, "Howdy," and hauled Billy alongside his horse. "I believe this is yours," he said.

A shove in the back from Ryan's boot propelled Billy forward. The man tried to keep his footing but fell flat on his face in front of a heavyset, older woman with close-cropped hair and hard, mannish features that Red took to be Ma Buck.

Red saw the question on the woman's face and said, "He tried to steal my horse."

The woman was not in the least surprised. "Oh, he did, did he?" she said. Her voice was harsh, the words formed in the back of her throat. She rushed to the wagon, lifted the canvas, and found what she wanted, a supple hickory wand about an inch around and four feet long.

Billy Buck fell on his knees, his face paralyzed by fear. "No, Ma, don't," he said. "Don't beat me."

Wielded with the full force of her strong arm and to the grinning delight of the Buck family, Ma's hickory wand slashed across Billy's head and shoulders, the vicious, cutting strokes sounding like a string of firecrackers. Blood poured from the man's scalp and a thin gash opened up on his cheek. Billy shrieked and begged for mercy but the hickory wand rose and fell, ripping, slicing, tearing, blow after savage blow.

But Red Ryan had seen enough. He swung out of the saddle, crossed the distance to the woman in a couple of wide steps, and wrenched the wand out of her hand.

"Damn it, woman, you're beating him to death," he said.

Ma Buck's face was a mask of rage, and when Red looked into her red-rimmed eyes he caught a glimpse of hell. The woman visibly fought a battle with herself, and gradually her breathing slowed and the insane fury left her face. She turned away from Red and stood over her whimpering son like a vengeful colossus. Then, in a voice like a murmur from the tomb, she said, "When you want to steal from a man what is his'n, kill him first. You hear me, kill him first. What did I teach you, you stupid, ungrateful, whoremaster's whelp?"

"Beat him some more, Ma," one of the grinning sons said.

"You shut your trap, Enoch," Ma said. She looked down at the bleeding, cowering Billy. "Now will you heed what I tell you?" She waved a hand in Red's direction. "He shouldn't be here, only his horse."

"I'll remember next time, Ma," Billy said. "I swear I will."

Ma Buck turned to her inhuman brood. "Anybody else need a lesson on when to kill a man . . . or a woman, come to that?"

No one answered. Then one of the sons spoke up, "Ma, can I have his fancy shirt with all that Injun stuff on it?"

"Maybe, Gabe. I'll study on it," Ma said. Then to Red, "Unbuckle that fancy gun rig, drawfighter. Let it drop and don't make any fancy moves."

"The hell I will," Red said. But then something

cold, hard, and double-barreled shoved into the back of his neck and a voice said, "Do as Ma says, Tex."

Red Ryan's reeling brain snarled at him. *You damned fool, you lost track of one of the brothers.*

He unbuckled his gunbelt and holster and let it drop at his feet. A moment later a shotgun butt crashed into the back of his skull, and he plunged headlong into darkness that had no beginning and no end . . .

CHAPTER FOURTEEN

The soul of Ilesh the Mescalero was dark, his grief scalding him as though he'd drank molten metal. The screams of the two Mexican sheepherders being tortured by the women would have pleased him yesterday or the day before, but not today.

The news of the death of his youngest and much-loved brother at the hands of white men had just arrived, brought by a sorrowful messenger on a fast pony.

"Men riding in a stagecoach killed Yuma," the messenger said. "His body will be brought to you."

"Where is this stagecoach?" Ilesh said.

The messenger waved a hand. "To the west of this place."

"Then we will find it and kill every one of the white men, but before they die they will beg us for death," Ilesh said.

Woe to the bringer of bad news, and the messenger was so afraid he trembled. But Ilesh gave him a fine blanket and sent him away.

Many of the lodges were dark as the people mourned

for their dead, and Ilesh spent a day and a night by himself, grieving for Yuma, a brave warrior and a singer of songs. Then, on the second day he emerged from his wickiup and spoke to the young men. Ilesh reminded them of Yuma's prowess in battle, how the as yet unwed woman smiled at him as he passed and crowded around him when he sang his songs or played his flute.

The young warriors smiled and slapped each other on the shoulder, pleased that they remembered Yuma so well and had held him in such high esteem.

Then Ilesh told them of the white men in the stagecoach and he said that they must wreak a terrible revenge. He told them that the attack on Fort Concho must wait until Yuma's death was avenged, and with this the warriors agreed.

Ilesh was greatly pleased with his young men and how they'd loved Yuma, and he ordered a mule be slaughtered and for the woman to prepare a great feast. Then Ilesh said that only the deaths of a hundred white men would atone for the death of Yuma, and the warriors must kill without mercy.

All this the young men heard, and their hearts were light that they were going to war against the white beasts in the stagecoach and they sang the Mescalero war song and Ilesh listened and planned . . .

The death of Yuma would soon be avenged.

CHAPTER FIFTEEN

Red Ryan woke with a thumping headache and opened his eyes to darkness. Slowly, as his senses returned, the full seriousness of his predicament dawned on him. His wrists were roped to a huge rear wheel of the Conestoga, and his ankles were tied. His shirt and boots were gone and so was his derby hat, bullet-holed now, but bought new only a couple of weeks before.

Red cursed under his breath. He'd fallen in with thieves.

A horned moon hung high in the night sky surrounded by the clustered stars. The wind restlessly prowled around the wagon and rocked it gently, soothing its snoring occupant that Ryan guessed was Ma Buck, the formidable matriarch of her mangy clan.

As coyotes yipped out in the long grass, Red tried moving his wrists, but they were securely bound to the wheel and didn't budge. He gave up and looked around him. The blanketed Bucks lay sleeping around the low, guttering campfire, one of the women muttering in uneasy slumber. Beyond the somnambulists, neatly piled on a white-streaked chicken cage, were Red's clothes, his gunbelt, still with his Colt in the holster, on top. It seemed that Ma Buck had not yet decided to whom would go the spoils, deciding to wait until daylight to determine who among her brood was the most deserving.

Red stared at his gun . . . if only . . .

Not a chance. When the Bucks tied a man to a wagon wheel, they tied him good.

And then a thought: Why the hell was he still alive?

Red couldn't figure that one.

Unless . . . torture was a possibility. He shook his head. Nah, white folks didn't torture people. Did they? Of course not. Red dismissed the thought, but then hit on the obvious . . . Ma Buck would kill him at her leisure, probably come morning after breakfast and before she and her clan moved out.

Well, there was no dismissing that possibility, and Red moved it forward in his mind from probable to dead certain. He smiled to himself. He hadn't even warned Ma about the Apaches, and that served her right. She was no better than an Apache herself.

Ryan sighed over his perilous plight and then dropped his head and dozed.

He woke up with a start, thinking that it was morning, but the night was still dark, and the moon remained in her heaven and Ma Buck continued to snore in the wagon. Red tried his bonds again, a futile struggle that only hurt his wrists and deepened his despair. No matter how he cut it, he was doomed and that was a natural fact.

Then, a whisper in the darkness, not a voice but the soft rustle of booted feet moving through long grass . . . followed by silence. Ryan's eyes searched the gloom. He saw nothing. Heard nothing. His heart sank. He was imagining things. One of the Buck men snorted, turned over on his side and then lay still. Long seconds passed . . .

Wait, there it was again, louder now, making more noise than even the clumsiest Apache ever would. It could only be a tangle-footed white man trying to injun closer.

Buttons Muldoon emerged from the murk, a rifle in his hands and an uneasy look on his face. He looked around, saw Red, and sneaked toward him with all the stealth of a longhorn bull in a brothel. Buttons took a knee beside Red, put a finger to his lips and said, "Shh . . ." so loud that it sounded like steam escaping a burst boiler.

Red looked around him in a panic, but the Buck family still slept and Ma's steady snoring reassured him.

Buttons produced a barlow, opened the blade, and sawed on the rope binding Red's left wrist. In a moment, his arm was free. Then the right . . .

Ma Buck stopped snoring and the ensuing silence was as ominous as a skeleton dangling in a cotton-wood tree.

Urgently now, Buttons slashed the rope away from Ryan's ankles and whispered, "Let's go."

"My duds," Red said.

"Leave them," Buttons said.

"The hell I will," Red said.

"Oh my God, we're all gonna be killed," Buttons said.

On sock feet Red tiptoed past the sleeping Bucks, put on his derby, then grabbed his gunbelt, boots, and shirt and followed Buttons into the sheltering darkness.

But then an unexpected disaster . . .

Ryan yelled, "Owww! Damn it! Damn it! Damn it!"

Buttons turned and saw Red hopping around on one leg, his face twisted in pain. "What happened?" he said, no longer bothering to whisper.

"I stubbed my toe on a rock!" Ryan wailed. "I think I broke it!"

Rifles roared and bullets buzzed through the air like angry hornets.

Buttons said, "That was a damned fool thing to do!"

"It's dark," Red said. "I didn't even see the damned rock. I think it's broke. I'm sure my big toe is broke."

"Well, no matter, you'll have run on it. We need to get out of here," Buttons said.

Then Ma Buck's voice, echoing into the darkness like the hoarse cawing of an enraged crow, "Get them! Kill them!"

More shots shattered into the night, one so close that it almost trimmed Red's mustache. "The hell with this," he said. He pulled his Colt from the holster and dusted off five shots in the direction of the dim glow of the Buck firelight. Then to Buttons, "That will keep them honest for a spell."

"Go, go, go!" Buttons said. "Follow me."

Red followed, hobbling on his tormented left foot, his every step accompanied by a painful, "Ow! Ow! Ow!"

Buttons made his way through the gloom that was once again getting punctured by shots, and then, grazing in a patch of moonlight was a ground-tied horse, one of the big, strong wheelers from the stage stripped of its harness except for a bridle. With surprising alacrity, Buttons jumped on the horse and pulled Red up behind him. "Ow!" Red said. Buttons kicked the horse into a flat-out run, and he and Red were pursued by a few parting shots from the outraged Bucks . . . but they fired blindly into the darkness and came nowhere close.

CHAPTER SIXTEEN

Stomping through the thin light of dawn, Lucian Carter was riled up, and Red Ryan was the target of his anger.

"Damn it, Ryan, get this show on the road," he said. "We've wasted enough time already because of your foolishness."

Red ignored the man, looked at Buttons Muldoon, and said, "I got my boot on, but I don't know if I can get it back off." And then, shaking his head, "A busted toe is a considerable misery."

Buttons nodded, glaring at Carter. "And if that wasn't enough, Red, now you got a pain in the ass to contend with."

"Yeah, very funny," Carter said, his eyes tight and mean. He wore his guns butts forward under his armpits. "I want to reach Fort Bliss this side of Christmas, so you two do something about it."

Red sighed and said, "You ladies please get in the stage. I'm sorry you'll have to forgo breakfast, but the Mountain Meadows stop is just five hours ahead of us, and they serve lunch." Red smiled. "There's no mountain and no meadows but you'll meet some personable folks there, and Stan Evans is a good cook."

"More rancid salt pork and beans, you mean," Carter said.

Red smiled, determined to be a model Patterson & Son employee. "It's the specialty of the house," he said.

Seth Roper tied his mount to the back of the stage and then took his position on top. He looked down at Red. "What happened to your hoss?"

"Those Bucks I was telling y'all about took it," Red said.

"Seems to me that you and Muldoon should've killed them all and took it back," Roper said.

"We were a tad outgunned, you know, and then I broke my toe."

"A busted toe is a sorry excuse for letting a bunch of raggedy-assed rubes steal your horse," Roper said.

Red held his temper in check. "I'm sure you would have done better, Roper."

"Damn right I would," the man said. He studied the sky to the north. "Looks like a big storm is headed our way."

"Sooner or later, I'd say," Red said.

Roper smiled and nodded, knowing exactly what the other man meant.

The thunderstorm hit when the stage was still an hour out from the Mountain Meadows station. Red Ryan and Buttons Muldoon donned their slickers and Seth Roper was allowed to sit inside at no cost.

Yelling above a howling wind, Buttons called down

to the passengers, "Hold on, folks. We're in for a bumpy ride!"

He gave the horses their heads and the stage careened through the roaring day under a turbulent sky that was as black as midnight.

Thunder bellowed, and lightning scrawled across the sky like the signature of a demented god as the stage rolled into the station. Stan Evans and his four gangly sons were there to greet Muldoon and his tired, battered passengers.

The team was quickly unhitched from the stage and led to the barn, and the hungry travelers quickly herded into the warmth and shelter of the cabin.

About twenty-five yards distant, built on a shallow rise, stood a slender wooden structure about three stories high, a platform on top fortified on all four sides with sod walls topped by timber boards nailed to posts. Spaces had been left between the boards for riflemen to shoot from cover under the Confederate-banner flying proudly from a tall flagpole. Evans called his tower The Citadel and claimed it had never been taken by Apaches, Comanches, or by outlaws either.

Red Ryan thought the structure vulnerable to fire, but he'd never told Evans that, and he secretly harbored a doubt that the Citadel had ever beaten off an attack by determined Indians of any tribe or outlaws of any stripe. Seth Evans would tell folks otherwise, but he was prone to big windies, probably to set at ease the minds of nervous stage passengers.

Thunder crashed and lightning shimmered in the murky interior of the cabin as Evans had the ladies stand around the stove to dry their damp clothes. Red noticed that Seth Roper stood very close to

Stella Morgan, closer than propriety allowed, but before he had time to study on that, Evans called everyone to table.

The food was surprisingly good, salt pork and beans as Ryan had predicted, but the staple stage station fare was accompanied by good sourdough bread, a crock of butter, and buttermilk to drink, courtesy of the cows that Evans kept in an enclosure near the barn, and there was a generous soda-cracker pie for dessert.

After eating, Red Ryan excused himself and stood on the narrow porch outside the cabin, built himself a cigarette, and then stared at the teeming rain falling from a bruised sky. Hanging on the inside of a support post was a Patterson & Son stage schedule that covered mostly East Texas routes, but the Fort Concho to El Paso run wasn't mentioned, and that indicated to Ryan where he and Buttons stood with the company . . . pretty damned low on the totem pole.

Red lit a second cigarette and watched the rider come.

The man wore a slicker and a wide-brimmed hat and rode a mouse-colored grulla horse. Oblivious of the downpour, the rider drew rein at the porch, studied Ryan from the toes of his boots to the crown of his derby and then said, "Howdy."

"Howdy right back at ya," Red said. "Kinda wet, huh?"

"Seems like," the rider said. "I got to say that I don't much cotton to lightning when I'm the tallest thing on the prairie." He was a young, blue-eyed man but his great dragoon mustache made him look older, and that might have been its purpose.

"Name's Red Ryan. I ride shotgun for the Patterson stage."

"Pleased to make your acquaintance, Red. My name is Josh Gentry, make that Sergeant Gentry of the Frontier Battalion, Texas Rangers."

Red touched the brim of his hat. "A pleasure, I'm sure. Ran into Rangers a time or two."

"Uh-huh," Gentry said, a comment that could have implied anything. Then, "Is Evans inside?"

"He sure is. Supper's over, but I'd guess that there's plenty left."

"Send Evans out here," Gentry said.

Ryan summoned Evans to the porch and he and the Ranger exchanged greetings. "Come inside and set, Josh," Evans said.

"Don't have the time to get comfortable," Gentry said. "I have to pick up a prisoner in Niceville. Sack me up some grub, Stan, while I take care of my horse."

"There's oats in the barn," Evans said. "Cost you two bits a scoop, though."

"I'll write you a Ranger scrip for the oats and the grub," Gantry said.

"I was afraid of that," Evans said, his face falling.

The Ranger waited until a crash of thunder rolled across the sky and then said, "Apaches are out, Stan."

"I know," Evans said. "And I'm more than ready for them."

"Saw some of their handiwork south of here," Gentry said. "It wasn't pretty."

He swung his horse away and headed for the barn. On a hunch, Red Ryan stepped into the rain and followed him.

Red waited until Gentry forked hay for the grulla and then scooped oats into a feed bucket. The Ranger said, "He ain't much to look at, but this little horse will go from cain't see to cain't see without a complaint."

"Good hoss," Ryan said. "What did you see south of here?"

"What did I see? I saw dead people, or what was left of them."

"Four women and the same number of men?"

"Sounds about right," Gentry said. He found a piece of sacking and began to rub down the grulla.

"That was Ma Buck and her brood," Red said.

"Is that a natural fact? Well, it's good to have a name for my report," Gentry said. "Seems that nowadays Rangers do more writing than riding." He turned to Red. "Them Bucks kinfolk of yours?"

"No." Then, unwilling to speak ill of the dead, Red said, "I met them on my way here. Were they—"

"The Apaches took their own sweet time with them," Gentry said. "That answer the question you were about to ask?"

"Yeah, I guess it does."

"There was a lot of anger there. I could tell from the state of the bodies. I've seen the results of Apache torture before, but it seemed to me that them hostiles were mad as hell about something." Gentry managed a ghost of a smile. "If there's a heaven, then those folks are in it. They sure spent their time in hell."

"That bad, huh?"

"Worse than you can ever imagine, shotgun guard." The Ranger's blue eyes turned to ice. "Now let it go. Some things a man has seen are best forgotten and not talked about."

"I can't find fault in that thinking," Red said. Then, to firmly change the subject, "The town you mentioned, Niceville, I never heard of it."

"That's because it isn't a town. Well, maybe it's part of a town," Gentry said. "If you consider a hotel that doubles as a saloon and cathouse, a blacksmith forge, a general store, and a livery is a town, then it's a town. If you don't, then it's just another robber's roost frequented by outlaws and other frontier trash. Niceville's only claim to fame is that one time Clay Allison stayed overnight at the hotel. Heard of him?"

"Yeah, a fast draw out of Colfax County in the New Mexico Territory. Does some ranching but runs with a hard crowd."

"I don't know how fast Allison is," Gentry said. "But if I ever catch up with him I guess I'll find out."

"What about your prisoner in Niceville," Ryan said. "He a badman?"

"Bad woman, according to the wire the army sent us. It was a cutting by a whore. Seems like a feller lost all claim to manhood while he was passed out drunk."

"That sets my teeth on edge," Ryan said.

"Mine too." The Ranger saddled his horse, tightened the cinch, and said, "Well, it's been good talking with you, Red." He smiled as lightning flickered in the barn. "I guess before I go I should mention that the Rangers don't hold the killing of Brazos Bob Benson against you."

Red was surprised. "How did you . . ."

"It took me a while, but then I remembered your name," Gentry said. "The shooting scrape was in Galveston, wasn't it?"

"Yeah, in front of the Orphans Home," Ryan said.

"Brazos Bob was not a reasonable man, and he drew down on me."

"He needed killing, or that's what I heard."

"You heard right. At the time, I was working for C. Bain and Company as a guard on the San Antone to Fort Concho route. Benson held up my stage a day out from San Antone, wounded me, and killed one of my passengers. As soon as my wounds healed, I went after him and tracked him down to Galveston, and me and him had it out in the street. Brazos Bob was nasty and mean as all get-out, but he wasn't as fast on the draw as he thought he was."

Gentry said, "Learned that the hard way, didn't he?"

"Yeah, I read to him from the book that day."

"Well, like I said, Ryan, just so you know, there's no hard feelings as far as the Rangers are concerned. Let bygones be bygones." He led his horse out of the stall. "Now, will you give me the road?"

Red stepped aside and said, "Good luck, Ranger."

"Yeah, you too, shotgun guard. Good luck."

Stan Evans had no overnight accommodation available for stage passengers, so the ladies commandeered the cabin, and Buttons Muldoon and Lucian Carter, lugging his carpetbag, stretched out inside the stage. Red Ryan thought he'd try his luck in the barn. The thunder was gone but the rain persisted, a steady drizzle that soaked everything and turned the trampled ground in front of the cabin to mud.

Buttons's stentorian snoring punctuated the night quiet as Red walked in the direction of the barn. He stepped around an enormous sleeping hog and then passed a malodorous, pyramid-shaped dung pile. A frontier stage stop would never be mistaken for the Ritz. Then a sound halted Red in his tracks. Ahead of him he heard a woman moaning, a series of little, gasping groans, of pain or pleasure, he couldn't tell. He pulled his Colt and walked forward on cat feet, his wary eyes probing the darkness. Then what he saw brought him to another halt and made him blink in surprise.

Stella Morgan, her dress hiked up around the waist, her bodice unlaced, stood just inside the barn with her back to the wall. Seth Roper was jammed against her, moving, his mouth hungrily on hers. The woman kept up her steady chorus of moans and Roper, breathing heavily, grunted in tune.

Red backed away. He'd seen enough to know this did not bode well . . . it spelled trouble with a capital T.

CHAPTER SEVENTEEN

Red Ryan spent an uncomfortable night on Stan Evans's porch under a leaky roof and in the company of an agitated packrat. The rain cleared shortly before breakfast that Stella Morgan attended, telling the concerned army wives that she'd spent the night in the barn. Seth Roper showed up a short time later, ate his bacon and beans, and went out again. He didn't speak to anyone and studiously ignored Stella.

Buttons Muldoon kept his strong, experienced wheelers but changed the rest of his team and then sought out Red. "We're ready to hit the road," he said. "The horses are rested."

Red finished his coffee and said, "We need to talk. Outside."

They stepped away from the cabin, and Red told Buttons what he'd seen in the barn.

"And here I thought Carter was the only one sparkin' Miss Stella," Buttons said.

"And I bet so does Carter."

"You mean Roper has taken his place?"

"Seems like, don't it?"

Buttons shook his head. "Red, this kinda thing always leads to a shooting."

"Yeah, you're right about that. So we got to make sure it doesn't happen, not on this run. What Carter and Roper do in Fort Bliss is their business and no concern of Patterson and Son or its employees."

"I don't like it, Red. I don't like it one little bit," Buttons said.

"I don't either. But in the meantime, we got to live with it."

Buttons's homely face took on a puzzled expression. "Why do folks love to muddy up the water and make their lives so durned complicated? Take you and me, now. I drive a stage and you ride shotgun, an' that's it. Nothing knotty about us."

Red smiled. "We're shining examples of simple men, Buttons."

"Damn right we are," Buttons said. "Now round up the passengers and let's be on our way. As far as I'm concerned, the sooner we reach Fort Bliss, the better."

Rolling under a burning sun, the stage was two hours out from Evans Station when the Apaches emerged from a shimmering heat haze, thirty mounted warriors painted for battle, led by a young man on a beautiful paint pony.

At first the Mescalero and their Chiricahua allies were content to ride parallel to the stage, well outside of effective rifle range. Then ten warriors separated from the main band and galloped ahead of the stage before deploying to their left while keeping a distance of a hundred yards between themselves and Buttons's cantering team.

The Indians had seen Seth Roper on top with his rifle and Red Ryan up in the box, cradling his shotgun, but they didn't know how many other guns were inside, and for the moment they were wary. Red figured that the Apaches must soon test the stage's defenses. The younger warriors would make feints, all sound and fury, to draw fire while the older men counted the defending guns. Sizing up your enemy before a big fight was a tried-and-true strategy that had worked well for the Apache in the past.

Red leaned over and called out, "Carter, you see them?"

"See them? I can't hardly take my eyes off them," the man answered.

"When the Apaches attack, get down and don't shoot," Red yelled. "They want to count guns, and I aim to surprise them. You're my ace in the hole, Carter, understand?"

"Yeah, I got it," Carter said. "How will I know when it's the real attack?"

Red's smile was grim. "Believe me, you'll know," he said.

Buttons Muldoon held the team to a fast trot. If he had to make a run for it, he didn't want the horses exhausted, though he knew full well that the lumbering coach couldn't outdistance the tough Apache ponies at any speed.

"They're coming!" Seth Roper called out from his perch on top. "Ryan, get ready!"

"I'm ready," Red yelled. And then to Buttons, grinning, "As I'll ever be."

A dozen warriors detached themselves from the

flanking group and charged at an angle, aiming to cut off the stage's forward progress. Roper saw the danger, and his rifle roared three times as quickly as he could work the lever. The range was far, his targets moving fast, and he scored no hits. A few of the Apaches returned fire, shooting their Winchesters from the shoulder, but a galloping horse is not a steady gun platform, and their shots went wild.

More confident with a scattergun than he was with a rifle, Red Ryan gripped his Greener tight and bided his time. He didn't have to wait long. An Apache swung his mount and rode directly at the stage. When the warrior was close enough, Red saw the blue and yellow stripes across his nose and cheekbones that marked him as a former army scout. The Apache's intention was to kill the guard, and at a distance of twenty-five yards, he fired. A miss. The bullet plowed into the sideboard at Ryan's feet. Twenty yards . . . the buck cranked his rifle . . . fifteen yards . . . ten . . . the Mescalero and Red triggered at the same time. Two barrels of buckshot slammed into the Apache's chest, causing fatal damage, as the warrior's own shot went yards too high. The Apache's horse shied away from the rocking stage, and its rider was thrown from its back, a dead man before he hit the ground.

As Red fed shells into his shotgun, Roper dropped a speeding warrior at a distance of fifty yards and then a second. "Good shooting!" Ryan yelled, but he didn't know if the man heard him above the din of the hurtling stage and the roar of gunfire. Moments later the Apaches peeled away and returned to the others on the flank. The attack had been a success in that it identified only a driver and two fighting men aboard the stage . . . but the butcher's bill had been high.

Unlike the Sioux or Cheyenne, the Apaches were never a numerous tribe and the deaths of three young warriors was a loss grievous enough that it stung Ilesh and the Mescalero elders.

The young war chief would attack again, but next time he would use more caution.

Aware that a cat-and-mouse game had begun, Buttons Muldoon slowed the team to a walk while Red Ryan stepped down and checked on Lucian Carter and the women. The two plump army wives looked pale and frightened, but a small Hopkins & Allen .32 revolver lay on Stella Morgan's lap and her eyes betrayed no fear. As far as Red could tell, Carter had not drawn his guns, so the man had listened.

"Will they attack again?" Stella said.

"Depend on it," Red said.

"Do we have a chance?" the woman said. "Any chance at all?"

"Yes, of course we do," Red said. He walked beside the stage, his hand on the door.

Stella frowned. "That was a lie, Mr. Ryan, now tell me the truth: Do we have a chance?"

Red looked at the Apaches riding ahead of them and the ones on the side who were getting worked up into a frenzy by the shouting young warrior on the paint.

"Not much of one," he said. Then he added what he knew was an empty platitude, "But a Patterson and Son stage always gets through."

Stella picked up her gun. "Good, then it's settled.

I will not let myself be taken. I saw what they did to Mrs. Nolan."

"It will not come to that," Ryan said. "You can never tell about Apaches. If they lose more young men they may decide the prize isn't worth the cost."

Buttons yelled, "Red! Here they come!"

"What about me?" Carter said.

Yelling over his shoulder, Ryan said, "Sit tight. I'll tell you when."

Red Ryan climbed into the box, pointed at the Apaches ahead of them and said, "Buttons, straight into them at a run!"

Buttons slapped the team into a gallop, the two big wheelers, steady as rocks, setting the pace for the leaders. The stage drove into the Apache charge, splitting it in half . . . then followed a cartwheeling melee of broad, painted faces, roaring guns, and wild, yipping war cries. Red blasted a warrior who tried to skewer him with a lance made from a cavalry saber, its steel head a foot long. The man fell away, screaming, but Ryan didn't see him drop. Behind him, Roper, bleeding from a forehead wound, fired steadily, scoring hits. Then the stage was through and there was open ground ahead. But immediately an attack came from the right, the Apaches keeping their distance as they galloped parallel to the stage, firing. Bullets slammed into the coach, splintering blue-painted wood, and Red heard a woman scream. The young warrior on the paint and the line of a dozen warriors suddenly wheeled their mounts and charged directly at the stage.

"Carter! Now!" Red yelled.

Lucian Carter reacted at once. The Apaches were close, coming on fast, well within revolver-fighting range. Carter's blazing Colts hammered death. Shooting through the open top of the stage door, a revolver in each hand, he killed men rapidly, his big .45 bullets punching great holes in chests, shattering skulls.

Red Ryan, fighting for his life with his own belt gun, heard Carter's fusillade and wondered at its speed. But only for a second. The young warrior on the pinto galloped straight as an arrow for Red, his Winchester extended as though he held a pistol. The Apache's features were contorted into a mask of hatred, but he never got time to shoot. Buttons's whip snaked through the air and cracked like a lightning bolt across the warrior's face. The man momentarily reeled in pain and shock, blood streaming from a slash across his right cheek. It was all the time Ryan needed. He shot the Apache high on the man's chest, fired again, a killing bullet that entered under the chin and plowed into the brain. The Mescalero screamed, threw up his hands, and fell backward off his horse . . .

And in that instant the tide of battle turned.

The warriors close to where Ilesh fell from his paint cried out to each other in alarm, and one by one the Apaches streamed away from the battle. Their young war chief had been killed, and it was a bad omen . . . today was not a day to fight.

Roper fired a few parting shots to speed the Mescalero on their way, and a sudden silence descended on the plain, broken only by the moans of the Apache dying and the soft sobs of one of the army wives.

The sprawled bodies of nine young warriors lay around the stage, three of them wounded and those were quickly dispatched by Roper's Colt.

Red Ryan's immediate concern was for his passengers.

Edna Powell's left shoulder had been burned by a bullet, and Rhoda Carr held the woman in her arms and cooed her sympathy. Stella Morgan was unharmed, her revolver still on her lap. A round had grazed Seth Roper's head, but it was only a scratch, and Lucian Carter's coat sleeve had been torn by an arrowhead.

"You all right, Buttons?" Ryan asked the driver.

Buttons smiled and nodded. "Red, I got nine lives, and I reckon I used up half of them in the last few minutes."

"Four-and-a-half to go," Red said.

"Seems like that's what I recollect from my school day ciphers," Buttons said. "But what does a man do with half a life?"

"Spark half a woman, eat half a pie, work for half wages and shave just half of your face." Red grinned. "How about that for a start?"

"Sorry I asked," Buttons said.

CHAPTER EIGHTEEN

The Apaches would retrieve and mourn their dead, and Red Ryan had Buttons Muldoon drive the stage a couple of miles from the battle site before he told him to stop so he could talk with the passengers.

"Normally, we'd drive on through to Fort Bliss," he said, "but there's a settlement ahead they call Niceville, and I recommend we stop there and rest the horses." He smiled. "And yourselves."

"And there will be grub," Buttons said.

Lucian Carter looked out across an endless expanse of prairie and said, "How far to the fort?" Mrs. Morgan is most anxious that we get there with all due speed."

"Two days, I reckon," Red said. "We've got enough grub to last us that long."

"But we're low on ammunition," Seth Roper said. He stood close to Stella. "What if the Apaches decide to come back?"

"I don't believe that will happen," Red said. "The way the Apaches broke off the fight I think one of their dead was Ilesh, their war chief. We'll be at Fort Bliss long before they stop mourning him."

"You sure about that, Ryan?" Roper said.

"As sure as a man can ever be about Apaches," Red said.

"If Ilesh is dead, they'll return to the reservation," Buttons said. "The Apaches are leaderless, and they won't stay on the warpath. It's not their way. They'll sulk on the San Carlos for a year or two until a new leader appears."

"Buttons has it right," Red said. "The Apaches are done for a while."

"We only got your word for that, Ryan," Carter said.

"And Red's word is good enough for me," Stella said. "If Niceville has a hotel, I'd like to have a bath and then sleep between sheets for a night."

Red was surprised at that. Stella was so anxious to reach Fort Bliss she'd been willing to risk being caught up in an Apache uprising to get there. Now she was in favor of a delay. Why? Red had no answer to that question, and it troubled him.

"Where is this settlement, Ryan?" Roper said.

"I don't know for sure, but the Ranger told me it was north of here. I don't think it will be difficult to find."

"In this damned wilderness?" Carter said. "We could go right past it."

"Roper, if you lend me your horse I can scout ahead of the stage," Red said.

Roper shook his head. "Nobody rides my horse but me. I'll do the scouting."

"Suit yourself," Red said. He smiled at the two army wives. "Does stopping for an overnight stay at Niceville suit you ladies?"

"Is that what the place is called, Niceville?" Edna Powell said. Part of her petticoat had supplied a fat bandage that Rhoda Carr had applied to her arm.

"That's what the Ranger called it," Red said.

"Then it sounds a happy place for an overnight stay. Does it not, Mr. Ryan?" Edna said.

"I'm sure it is," Red said. Then, to himself, *It's a robber's roost and God forgive me for lying to innocent ladies.*

Red's reasons for stopping in Niceville were twofold . . . the horses needed a rest since there were no more stage stops between the Mountain Meadows station and Fort Bliss, and a good meal and a proper bed would calm everybody down after the ordeal of the Apache attack. He owed it to the passengers because that was the Patterson & Son way. And then there was a third reason . . . he wanted to know why Stella had left Carter and chosen Seth Roper as her new man. And where did that leave the soon-to-be-retired Major John Morgan and his plan to settle with Stella in Washington?

Red had more than enough questions . . . and he feared the answers.

Buttons Muldoon drove the stage in a northwest direction, allowing the team to walk. Seth Roper had ridden ahead and was no longer in sight, and since about four hours of daylight remained, Rhoda Carr and Edna Powell expressed the hope that they still might sleep in Niceville that night.

After half an hour on the trail, Stella stuck her head out the window and asked Red if she could join him up on the driver's box. Red hesitated, since that was strictly against company policy, but considering what the woman had been through earlier, he relented.

"This once," Red said. "And only because Buttons isn't exactly an entertaining companion."

"I've got the croup because of them damned Apaches," Buttons said. "You try to be an entertaining companion when you got the croup." Stella sat between him and Ryan, and Buttons gave the woman a sharp look. "Getting to be a tight squeeze up here."

Ryan smiled. "I don't mind a bit."

Buttons thought about that for a few moments and then said, "Now I study on it, neither do I."

Stella's eyes constantly scanned the distance in front of them and Red figured she was watching for Roper. To put her to the test, he smiled and said, "I guess you're looking forward to getting reacquainted with your husband, huh, Mrs. Morgan?"

The woman's lovely face showed no reaction, and then she shrugged and said, "John is a good deal older than I am."

Red thought that an odd thing for the woman to say, though Buttons stepped into the breach and grinned, "There's many a good tune played on an old fiddle, Stella."

"But not too old a fiddle, Mr. Muldoon," the woman said.

Red tried a different tack. "You'll settle in the Capital?"

This time Stella smiled. "Yes. John . . . Major Morgan . . . inherited a great deal of money and property, including a town house in Washington, when his dear Mama died, and I'm sure he'll want to make it our home. Oh, look! A jackrabbit!"

Red looked where Stella pointed but didn't see anything but wind in the grass.

"Ah, it's gone," Stella said. "You missed it."

But what Red didn't miss was that Stella Morgan stood to inherit a fortune if her husband died. It could be a motive for murder . . . and might explain her newfound attraction for a gunman and killer like Seth Roper.

Stella spoke again, "Do you think Seth will find Niceville?"

"Depends on how good a scout he is, ma'am," Buttons said.

"I'm sure he's a fine scout," Stella said.

"Then he'll find Niceville," Buttons said.

It seemed that Lucian Carter was not of the same opinion. As Stella had done earlier, he shoved his head out the stage window and said, "Hey, Ryan, where the hell is Roper?"

"I don't know," Red said.

"Well maybe we should see if this stage can go faster than a walk and head directly for Fort Bliss," Carter said.

"Red, tell him the team's beat and one of my leaders took a bullet to a leg. He's stumbling a tad," Buttons said.

Red said, "Carter, Buttons told me to tell you—"

"I know what Buttons told you to tell me," Carter said. "You boys ought to learn how to drive a damned stage."

Carter pulled his head back inside and Buttons said, "What's his all-fired hurry?"

"I think Lucian is as anxious to board a train for Washington as I am," Stella said.

"Does he have to be such a pain in the neck about it?" Buttons said.

"I don't know Lucian very well, but he can be impatient at times," Stella said. She inclined her head toward Buttons and looked at him from under the dark fringe of her eyelashes and said, "Mr. Muldoon, don't push him too hard. Lucian can be a very quick-tempered man."

Red said, "I saw him use his guns. Good shooting for a bank clerk."

Stella smiled slightly. "Lucian wasn't always a bank clerk."

Then Buttons said, "Rider coming in. Looks like Roper."

And Red lost his chance to question Stella further.

But there was something at the back of his mind, a vague, nagging whisper of a memory. *Lucian wasn't always a bank clerk.* What was it about the name Carter and some kind of an association with New Orleans, or was it Baton Rouge? Try as he might, he could not remember . .

CHAPTER NINETEEN

"Niceville is an hour from here, due north," Seth Roper said as he rode beside the stage.

"What's it like?" Red Ryan said.

"It's Texas's own little corner of hell."

"You mean it isn't safe for my passengers?" Red said.

"I didn't say that. It's got a hotel and a saloon, but it's a rough-looking place. Only face I recognized was Hamp Becker and four of them outlaw guns he runs with. I got to say that ol' Hamp's wanted dodgers don't do him justice. He looks a sight meaner in person."

"I heard Becker was dead, hung by the citizenry up Amarillo way," Buttons Muldoon said.

"Then you heard wrong. A high-line rider like Hamp Becker takes a power of killing."

"Buttons, where do we go from here?" Red said. "Push on through to Fort Bliss or take a chance on Niceville?"

Roper smirked and said, "You got me with you, Ryan, and I saw Carter use his guns. The young man is fast, as fast as I've seen. Bottom line is, between me and him we can protect you."

Red refused to be baited. "I can take care of myself, Roper," he said. "But I've got three women passengers to look out for. The policy of the Patterson and Son Stage and Express Company is that the safety and comfort of its passengers must be the employees' first concern."

Roper's smirk stretched into a grin. "Real company man, ain't you Ryan?"

"They pay my wages," Red said. Then to Buttons, "All right, Buttons, the horses are tired and one of them's wounded, and the women are tired and so am I. We'll take a chance on Niceville being nice enough."

Buttons nodded. "Whatever you say, Red. And don't it make you feel good all over that Roper will be there to protect us?"

Roper's smile was razor thin. "You're a joking man, driver. I shot a man for that one time. After the third good joke came out of his mouth, I shut it for him permanent."

"Any time you feel like hobbling my mouth then have at it, Roper," Buttons said. He looked like an ornery ol' longhorn bull. "The entire Yankee army couldn't kill me, the Comanche tried and so did the Apaches, and three times in my career I've buried road agents by the side of the trail." Buttons was a man who stood with his feet solidly planted on the ground, a man with no fear in him, ready and willing to burn powder, and Roper was no fool. He knew Muldoon couldn't match his gun skill, but the driver would take his hits and shoot back. He was a sturdy man, and he'd be hard to kill.

"Just so you know," Roper said. "I don't take to joking men."

Red allowed the gunman to save face. "Buttons, time to wake up the horses," he said. "Maybe we can find us a steak in Niceville."

"Two inches thick and done to a crisp," Buttons said. "Like my sainted Ma used to make." He grinned and rubbed his belly. "That lady sure knew how to burn a steak and bake a pie."

Roper already forgotten, Buttons was his old self again.

Red Ryan figured that whoever christened a hotel, general store, livery stable, and blacksmith's forge Niceville had a wicked sense of humor, either that or he was drunk at the time.

He said as much to Buttons Muldoon, who said. "Maybe it was ol' Clay Allison his ownself. They say he's crazy anyway."

The rickety, three-story hotel, like the rest of the buildings, rose out of the prairie like a rotten tooth and a faded, painted sign over the front door proclaimed:

EXCELSIOR HOTEL
~ Poke Farrell, *prop.*

It was a such grandiose name that it seemed to Red that Poke Farrell, prop., was the one with the wry sense of humor.

The hotel's ground floor was taken up by the lobby and a saloon with batwing doors that were presumably never locked. When the stage jangled to a halt outside, voices could be heard from within, the loud talk of men who'd gotten among the whiskey and the practiced shriek of women pretending to be amused by their witty remarks. A tinpanny piano played "Over the Hills and Far Away" as Red climbed down and checked on his passengers.

Edna Powell, timorous by nature, inquired if they were in the right place and was Mr. Ryan quite sure that this was Niceville. Red assured her that it was, but added that the inside of the Excelsior was no doubt much more comfortable than its dilapidated exterior would suggest. Rhoda Carr seemed indifferent, expressing the hope that the beds were clean. Stella Morgan's interest was not on the hotel but on Seth Roper, who'd tied his horse to the hitching rail and then held open the stagecoach door. Lucian Carter seemed irritable and mean, his angry blue eyes slanting to Roper, and his hands were all over Stella's slender back as she stepped down into the street.

The hotel door opened and a tall, bearded man who'd obviously hurriedly thrown a threadbare frock coat over his shabby pants and rumpled shirt stood on the porch. He picked out Seth Roper and said, "Don't have many stages stop here anymore. Where are you headed?"

"Up Fort Bliss and El Paso way," Roper said.

"You planning to stay the night?"

"I guess that's the plan." Roper pointed to Red Ryan. "But you better speak to him. He's the shotgun guard."

Red joined the bearded man on the porch, and said, "Are you Poke Farrell, prop?"

The man nodded. "That would be me."

"Name's Ryan. I have three lady passengers who'd like to stay the night, and one gent," Red said. "The two ladies you see over there by the stage can double up. The other woman is an officer's wife, and she'll need her own room and so will the gent."

Farrell nodded and looked wise. "Three rooms then." He nodded in Roper's direction. "What about him?"

"He can fend for himself. Me and the driver will bed down in the livery."

Farrell frowned, making a quick calculation, and said, "That will be six dollars for the rooms. Dinner tonight will be a dollar a head and breakfast an extry fifty cents per person. Mr. Ryan, that will be a total of twelve dollars, not counting you and the driver."

"Expensive, ain't you, Farrell?"

"A man can afford to be expensive when he's the only game in town."

"Then I'll give you a Patterson and Son Stage and Express Company scrip," Red said.

"No, you won't. I need cash on the barrelhead."

Roper had overheard and now, his spurs ringing, he stepped beside Farrell. "Ten dollars for everything. And the sheets better be clean."

"I run a clean house here," Farrell said, bristling.

"You run a damned saloon and brothel," Roper said.

Farrell looked angrily into Roper's eyes, caught a glimpse of hellfire, and backed off. "All right, ten dollars it is," he said. And then to salvage a hatful of pride, "But that does not include beverages."

CHAPTER TWENTY

After dinner and a traumatic day, the two army wives elected to retire early. Red Ryan had already inspected the beds, a couple of iron cots with corn-shuck mattresses, and declared them passable.

Edna Powell was so impressed by Red's concern for the comfort and safety of his passengers that she vowed to write to Abe Patterson and commend Mr. Ryan as a crackerjack employee. Rhoda Carr agreed that a letter of commendation was a grand idea, especially since, almost singlehandedly, Red had fought off a whole tribe of bloodthirsty savages. "We'll see that you get promoted to driver in short order, Mr. Ryan," she said.

And Red made a point of profusely thanking them both.

Buttons Muldoon suggested to Red Ryan that they cut the trail dust and have a nightcap in the saloon. It seemed to Red a good idea at the time . . . but violent events would very soon prove that it was not.

Red and Buttons bellied up to the bar and ordered whiskey with a beer chaser. A sullen Poke Farrell used a wet cloth to wipe down a small patch in front of them and then allowed that the whiskey was tarantula juice and the beer was warm.

"We've probably drank worse," Buttons said. "So set 'em up."

"Your funeral," Farrell said.

The beer was warm and flat, but Red thought the whiskey wasn't so bad, more like panther piss than tarantula juice. He built and lit a cigarette and looked around the saloon, a single room with a knotted wooden floor and a collection of tables and chairs randomly clustered around a small dance floor. Above this was a balcony where there were several cribs, each screened from prying eyes by an army blanket. A couple of bored whores leaned on the banister and looked down at the proceedings with disinterested eyes, and the piano player, a reformed drunk named Milo, belted out a credible rendition of "The Boatman's Dance."

Stella Morgan sat at a corner table with Lucian Carter and Seth Roper, neither of the men looking happy. Somebody had sprung for champagne, or what passed for it in Farrell's humble establishment, but it was obviously potent enough to give Stella the giggles.

By the time he'd smoked his cigarette, Red Ryan saw the trouble building . . . gunsmoke-colored storm clouds on the horizon.

A couple of the tables were occupied by armed men. Near the piano, two young punchers nursed beers and talked in low voices. Red had earlier dismissed the pair as saddle tramps riding the grub line, and he sensed no danger from them.

However, the five men who sat at another table were an entirely different breed, outlaws who were prospering.

Their duds, boots, and gun leather were all of good quality, expensive, more than the grub-line waddies could ever afford, and their arrogance was the kind that reaches out, grabs lesser folks by the throat, and squeezes. Loud, profane, not giving a damn whether anyone disapproved of them or not, they laughed, cursed, and made the entire saloon their own.

That night they took over the Excelsior saloon lock, stock, and barrel, and one of them, big, brawny, and bold, decided that his ownership extended to Stella Morgan, who looked fresh and lovely, in contrast to the grubby, worn-out whores on the balcony.

Red Ryan watched closely as the big man rose to his feet and stepped to Stella's table. Seth Roper looked up at the man and said, "Howdy, Hamp. It's been a while."

"Hell, I thought it was you I saw earlier," Hamp Becker said.

Roper nodded. "I just stuck my head in the door and then left."

"I heard you'd been hung," Becker said. He wore a pearl-handled Colt in the holster of a finely tooled gunbelt.

"Heard the same about you, Hamp," Roper said.

"Small world," Becker said.

"Ain't it, though," Roper said.

"How are your brothers? One of them was simple, wasn't he? What was his name again?"

"They were all simple, and they're all dead, killed by Apaches," Roper said.

"You don't seem too cut up about it, Seth."

Roper shrugged. "I never did find out what inbred rube sired them. But whoever he was, he wasn't my pa. So, no, I'm not too cut up about it."

"A man can't choose his relatives," Becker said. "That's what I always say."

The big outlaw glanced at Lucian Carter, dismissed him, and then said, "How much for the woman, Seth? I'll give you two hundred dollars."

Roper went along with that, grinning. "Hell, Hamp, I can get six hundred for her in Old Mexico any day of the week."

Like a poker player reading the cards, Red studied Roper and Carter, trying to decide if either of them would be willing to make a play. Right then, it didn't seem likely.

"Yeah, well, this is Texas, Seth," Becker said. "And I'll only pay Texas prices." He looked over at the piano player, who was flipping through a pile of sheet music. "You, Milo, play something."

"Play what?" the man asked. He was small and thin, his nose and cheekbones a crimson network of broken veins.

"I don't know. Something me and the little lady here can dance to, a waltz maybe."

"I don't wish to dance," Stella said.

Becker's smile was unpleasant. "Little lady, you'll dance because I'm telling you to dance."

This brought cheers from the three men sitting at the table and one of them said, "You tell her, Hamp."

Emboldened by the approval of his companions,

Becker grabbed Stella by her upper arm and proceeded to drag her out of the chair.

Red Ryan's angry yell stopped him.

"Mrs. Morgan is a passenger of the Patterson and Son Stage and Express Company, and I will not allow her to be handled in that way," he said.

"You shut your trap," Becker said.

Red crossed the floor and pushed the big man away from the table, but then Becker surprised him when he swung a hook at Red's chin. The outlaw telegraphed the punch, and Red saw it coming. He feinted to his left, took most of the blow on his shoulder, then countered with a powerful straight right that connected with Becker's chin and rocked him back on his heels.

Becker was a big man, and strong, and he could have come back swinging, but he was a practiced gunman, and his fast draw was his ultimate answer to any violent situation. He shucked his Colt, but before he could bring it level, Red drew and shot him in the belly.

Becker gasped in pain and shock and staggered back several steps, his suddenly ashen face disbelieving. He thumbed off a shot that missed, and Red shot him again. The big outlaw's back slammed so hard against the wall that Buttons would later claim the entire rickety hotel shook to its foundations. Becker slid down the wall, leaving behind a crimson snail trail, coughed up black blood, and died.

Gunsmoke drifted, a ringing silence descended . . . and then all hell broke loose.

One of the men at the table, a tall, lanky towhead with reckless eyes, yelled, "Damn you!" at Red and went for his holstered Colt. The man never cleared leather. Several shots slammed into him, jerked him around like a ragdoll, and he crashed backward onto the tabletop. His three surviving companions jumped out of the way of the falling body and then two of them cut loose, swapping lead with the advancing Roper and Carter. The third hotfooted it for the door. The two who'd decided to shoot it out were good, very good, but no match for Roper's speed and accuracy and the rapid, rolling thunder of Carter's hammering Colts. Both went down, shot to pieces, dying hard. After downing Becker, Red hadn't fired another shot and now he watched as Roper swung around, two-handed his gun to eye level, drew a bead on the man running to the door, and shot him in the back. The man fell headfirst through the batwings and sprawled onto the porch outside . . .

And then it was over.

Roper, Carter, and Red still stood on their feet, unscathed, guns smoking in their hands after twenty-three seconds of hellfire. Four dead men littered the floor, weltering in their blood, staring into eternal night with horrified eyes. In 1926, an aging Buttons Muldoon would tell New York newspaper reporter John N. Howard that the gunfight at Niceville, Texas, was won when Roper and Carter advanced on their enemies shooting, in those moments gaining a mental advantage as they became aggressors, not victims. "It was the way of the gunfighter then as it still is today," Buttons said.

Poke Farrell stood behind the bar, staring open-mouthed at the carnage, and then broke the silence, saying the first thing that popped into his reeling head. "I hope you haven't wakened my guests."

Roper looked at the man and said, "What did you see?"

"A gunfight," Farrell said.

Roper's words gritted in his throat. "What did you see?"

"They drew down on you first, mister," one of the young punchers said. He looked scared as he tried to head off another shooting.

"I'm asking this man, not you," Roper said, his eyes cold and hard on Farrell. "What did you see?"

After a moment's hesitation, the man said. "Becker and them drew down on you. I seen that. Four of my best customers lost in less than a minute." He shook his head. "Don't that beat all."

"Times are tough all over," Roper said.

Red holstered his gun and crossed the floor to Stella. "That was a terrible thing to see, and the same day as the Apache attack," he said. "Are you feeling all right, Mrs. Morgan?"

The woman reached across the table, picked up Lucian Carter's untouched whiskey, and downed it in a gulp. "I am now," she said, smiling. "Ah, just in time the two washerwomen have arrived to save the day."

Dressed in threadbare robes, Edna Powell's hair in paper curlers, the two women timidly entered the saloon from the side door off the lobby. Rhoda Carr's gaze went to the dead men, and she immediately reached out and covered her companion's eyes with her hand. "Don't look, Edna," she said.

"I've already looked," Edna said. She was close to tears, her round face flushed. "So many dead people on this journey . . . so many. Corporal Powell will be horrified." She saw Red standing at Stella's table and said, "Oh, Mr. Ryan, I'm so glad you're safe." Then, "Oh dear, I feel quite faint."

Red stepped quickly to Edna's side and put his arm around her shoulders. "Let me take you to your room, Mrs. Powell," he said. "As a representative of the Patterson Stage and Express Company, I won't let anyone hurt you. And that goes for you too, Mrs. Carr."

As Red helped Edna navigate the dark stairs, Rhoda said, "What happened, Mr. Ryan? We heard all the shooting."

"We ran into four men who didn't want to keep their six-shooters holstered," Red said. "There was a fight."

"Did Mrs. Morgan see it?" Rhoda said.

"Yes, I'm afraid she did."

"Oh, the poor thing," Edna said. "She must have been scared out of her wits, and her an officer's wife."

"Yes, she was quite upset," Red said, telling the lie.

"Mr. Ryan, please inform her that I have a bottle of Dr. Jacob's Nerve Tonic for Anxious Ladies if she'd care to make a trial of it. I'm sure it will help calm her."

"I certainly will, Mrs. Powell," Red said. "But I think Mrs. Morgan has a bottle of her own."

"Well, if she doesn't, tell her she can have some of mine and welcome," Edna said. At the door to her room, the woman held Red's shirtsleeve and said, "I'm sure I won't be able to sleep tonight. I'm very afraid, Mr. Ryan."

Red smiled. "You and Mrs. Carr are my passengers, and it is my sworn duty to protect you from harm. Sleep peacefully, Mrs. Powell. I'll be on guard all night."

The woman got up on her tiptoes and kissed Red on the cheek. "You're so good to us, Mr. Ryan. You saved us from Apaches and now dangerous outlaws. When I tell Corporal Powell about you, he will be very grateful."

"Well, that's good to know," Red said. "Now sleep tight, Mrs. Powell."

"We both will, Mr. Ryan," Rhoda Carr said. She sighed. "You are our very special hero."

CHAPTER TWENTY-ONE

"Who's going to do the burying?" Poke Farrell said. "I'm shorthanded here."

Red Ryan forked up the last piece of his breakfast salt pork, chewed for a few moments, then said, "You are the undertaker, Farrell. You get to keep their horses and traps. That's enough reward for a little spadework."

Farrell scowled across the table at Red. "Them boys were riding mustangs. I wouldn't give you a hundred dollars for all four of them."

Buttons Muldoon said, "A mustang will keep going miles after your big American stud has pulled up lame. He knows where his feet are, and that makes him a surefooted mountain hoss. And he's as savvy as a bunkhouse rat. He can scent trouble in the wind and give a warning better than any lobo wolf and that's why outlaws ride them."

"If mustangs are so great, why the hell ain't they hauling your stage?" Farrell said.

"Because the mustang is too light and he don't take well to the traces," Muldoon said. "Now, even a big mule weighs only about a thousand pounds, but he works well as part of a team. A mustang just ain't that way inclined."

"I've never had much truck with mustangs," Red said. "But now they're yours, Farrell."

"I bet there's a big reward out for Hamp Becker," Seth Roper said, speaking for the first time since he sat down to breakfast. "Farrell, before you plant him, cut off his head and keep it somewhere cool. Next time a Ranger comes along, show him the head and claim your money. I reckon the reward could go as high as five, six thousand dollars."

"Must we talk about cutting off heads at breakfast?" Lucian Carter said, dropping his fork onto his plate.

"Man's got to show proof, and the head is the best," Roper said. He grinned. "At least that's been my experience."

Carter got to his feet. "Ryan, it's been daylight for an hour. High time we were moving."

Buttons grinned. "Fort Bliss, here we come. The team is hitched and we're ready to go." He looked over at the army wives. "At your convenience, ladies. And you too, Mrs. Morgan."

If Stella took that as a slight, she didn't let it show. "I'm ready," is all she said.

Red Ryan thought the woman seemed preoccupied, as though her thoughts were elsewhere, perhaps with her husband waiting at the fort . . . but he doubted it.

"Hey, don't leave yet. What about me?" Poke Farrell said.

"What about you?" Ryan said.

"I got four dead men laid out on my front porch," Farrell said.

"Then bury them decent, Farrell," Lucian Carter said. "You've got their horse and guns."

"I told you, I'm shorthanded," Farrell said, his voice a high whine.

Roper, seemed slightly angry, a man at the end of his patience. "You got yourself, two strong whores, and a Chinee in the kitchen. That's enough to dig a hole someplace."

"Damn you, it ain't near enough and—"

Suddenly Roper shoved the muzzle of his Colt into Farrell's belly and pulled the trigger. The gun roared, and Farrell stood upright for a moment, his face shocked, unable to believe that he'd been killed, and then slumped to the floor.

"I can't stand a complaining man," Roper said, looking down at Farrell's writhing body. He holstered his gun, turned on his heel, stepped into the kitchen. Roper returned, pushing ahead of him a small, terrified Chinese man by the scruff of the neck. He shook the little man like a terrier with a rat and said, "You speakee American?"

The Chinese nodded.

"Good. You see the man on the floor? He'll be dead soon and you're the new proprietor—you know what proprietor means? You do? Good. Then you're the new proprietor of this establishment. Understandee?"

"I understand," the Chinese said.

"What's your name?" Roper said.

"Huan."

"All right, Huan, a damned heathen name if you ask me, when Farrell dies, you'll have five men to bury. Can you do that?"

The little man nodded. "Yes, I take them far, far away from here."

"I don't give a damn where you take them. Some folks here want them buried, understand?"

"Mr. Farrell not dead yet," Huan said. He put his fingers in his ears and said, "He making big row."

"Yeah, he is, ain't he?" Roper said. He drew his gun and fired a shot into Farrell's head, and the man's pained shrieks stopped. "Now he's dead."

"Damn you, Roper, you murdered that man," Red Ryan said.

"You care, Ryan? He wasn't a Patterson employee, just a saloonkeeper and pimp."

The army wives were sitting in stunned silence, their eyes as round as coins. Lucian Carter had an arm around Stella's shoulders as though to comfort her. She looked like she didn't need comforting, her speculative gaze fixed on Roper.

"The man was unarmed," Red said.

"That was Farrell's problem, not mine," Roper said. "He should've armed himself."

"When we reach El Paso, I'll press a murder charge," Red said.

"And I'll deny it, and nobody in El Paso will lose any sleep over the death of a two-bit pimp who turned up his toes at the ass-end of nowhere."

Stella Morgan said, "It looked to me that Farrell was going for a hideout gun. I'd swear that on a stack of Bibles."

"Carter, what about you?" Roper said.

The man hesitated for a moment, and then Stella whispered something to him, and he nodded and said, "The pimp had a sneaky gun on him. I'm sure of that."

Roper grinned. "You still going to press charges, Ryan?"

"I will, and I'll make them stick," Red said. "What I saw was cold-blooded murder."

Suddenly Roper was tense and a hollow silence descended on the room . . . waiting to be filled by whatever came next.

"Since I'm an accused murderer, maybe you want to take my gun away from me, Ryan," Roper said. He was primed . . . ready for the draw.

Red had been there before, and he knew how fast he was, quicker with the gun than most. "I reckon I will," he said.

"No!"

Stella Morgan leaped from her chair and got between the two men.

"Let's settle this in El Paso," she said. "Mr. Muldoon, how far to Fort Bliss?"

"We're two days out," Buttons said.

"Two days out, and there's still Apaches around," Stella said. "You fools, this is no time to be killing one another."

Edna Powell had the same idea because she rushed to Red's side as fast as her dumpy legs would carry her. "Oh, Mr. Ryan, please don't fight." She glared at Roper. "Mr. Roper, you're a dreadful, violent man. I thought you very brave when you fought the savages, and I still do, but now I'm very disappointed in you."

"And that goes for me too," Rhoda Carr said. "You can rest assured that Corporal Carr will hear of this."

Roper grinned, swept off his hat, and made a leg. "Ladies," he said. He brushed past Ryan and walked out of the room.

Buttons took Red aside and whispered, "Sooner or later, you're gonna have to kill that man."

"I reckon I'll let the law do that," Red said.

Buttons shook his head. "No, that's not how it will happen. The law won't act, and it will be down to you."

Red smiled. "You have a crystal ball, Buttons?"

"Nope, I don't need no crystal ball. I have something better."

"What's that?"

"The Irish gift, Red . . . the Irish gift."

CHAPTER TWENTY-TWO

Because of the simmering tension between Red Ryan and Seth Roper, Buttons Muldoon made it clear that he'd decided to forgo sleep and drive directly for Fort Bliss without any further stops.

"Buttons, there aren't any more stage stops between here and the Franklin Mountains," Red said.

"I know that," Buttons said. "My plan is a halt just long enough to rest the horses and let the passengers stretch their legs." He took his eyes off the trotting team and turned his head. "You still aim to turn Roper over to the law?"

"Just as soon as we reach El Paso," Red said.

"Pity Dallas Stoudenmire is no longer with us," Buttons said. "He had a way of dealing with the likes of Roper. He'd just shoot him." He called out over his shoulder. "You hear that, Seth?"

From his perch on top of the stage, Roper said, "Hear what?"

"That if ol' Dallas Stoudenmire was still El Paso city marshal he would shoot you on sight fer a scoundrel."

"Stoudenmire couldn't shade me, not on his best

day, he couldn't," Roper yelled above the rumble of wheels on the sun-baked ground.

"Easy to say now he's dead," Buttons said.

"What about you, Ryan? Do you reckon I could've shaded Stoudenmire?"

"I know you can shoot an unarmed man in the belly, Roper," Red said. "And that's all I know."

Roper laughed. "You're a funny man, Ryan, a very funny man."

Muldoon didn't like where the conversation was headed. He hoorawed the team into a canter . . . and fifteen minutes later he saw the Apache.

"Ahead of us, Red," Buttons said.

"I see him," Red said. "He's watching us."

The Apache sat his pony just out of rifle range. He wore a soldier's blue coat with corporal's chevrons on the sleeves and carried a Winchester, the butt resting on his thigh.

Red grabbed his shotgun and said, "Drive straight at him, Buttons. Let's see what he does."

"Right now, he's not doing anything," Buttons said. "Ah, and now he's made a liar out of me."

The Indian yipped, swung his horse around, and rode back the way he'd come.

"Slow down, Buttons," Red said. "He might be trying to lead us into an ambush."

Buttons slowed the team to a walk as Lucian Carter stuck his head out the stage window and said, "Ryan, what's happening?"

"Apache," Red said.

"How many?"

"Just one."

"And one's enough," Buttons said.

Red heard Edna Powell say, "Oh dear no, not again," exactly expressing his own thought.

"Ryan, where do you want me?" Carter said. "You're the general here."

"Stay where you are," Red said. "If we're attacked again, you'll protect the ladies."

But the attack never came.

When the Apache showed again he rode with a buffalo soldier cavalry patrol led by a white captain wearing a fringed buckskin jacket with Cheyenne beadwork. The officer led his men to the stage and drew rein.

Buttons had halted the team and now he said, "What can I do for you, Cap'n?"

"I'm Captain James Moore, Company L 9th Cavalry," the soldier said. "I've been ordered to find and escort an officer's wife to Fort Bliss. We were informed by wire from Fort Concho that she left several days ago. Is she on this stage, driver?"

"Would that be Mrs. Stella Morgan?" Buttons said.

"It would," the captain said.

"The lady is inside," Buttons said.

Captain Moore kneed his horse to the side of the stage, looked inside, and said to Stella, "You are Mrs. Morgan, I presume."

Stella smiled and fluttered her lashes. "Indeed I am."

"Captain James Moore at your service, ma'am." He bowed in the saddle. "I am here to escort you to Fort Bliss."

"You are very *gallante*, Captain," Stella said.

"Your obedient servant, dear lady." Moore looked at Edna and Rhoda. "And you women are?"

"I'm the wife of Corporal Powell," Edna said,

smiling. "And my companion is the wife of Corporal Carr. Our husbands are serving with the 15th Infantry."

"Ah yes, I was told a couple of enlisted men's women might be on the stage," the captain said, dismissing them.

Stella said, "For a moment there I harbored the brief hope that Major Morgan would be with you, Captain."

"Alas, dear lady, the major was wounded in a skirmish with some hostiles," Moore said. He read Stella's face and said, "Nothing serious, a slight inner leg wound, but enough to keep him out of the saddle for another week or so."

"Then I'll count the hours until I can be at his side," Stella said.

"And that's what I would expect to hear from an officer's lady wife," Captain Moore said. "I hope that when I enter into the state of matrimony I find a bride who will display such love and devotion." He glanced at Lucian Carter, touched the brim of his forage cap, and then swung his horse away.

"Judging by the bullet holes in the coach, you've been under attack," Moore said to Red Ryan.

"Yes, Captain, we had a brush with Apaches," Red said.

"Well, I have good tidings. The latest news we have on the wire is that the war chief Ilesh is dead and that the Chiricahua are already drifting back to the San Carlos," the soldier said.

Red wanted to say, "I know he's dead, because we killed him," but he decided against it. Captain Moore wouldn't believe him anyway. He settled for, "That's good to hear."

"Indeed, it is," the captain said. "Probably Ilesh and

his band ran into a punitive column from Fort Concho, and they killed the rascal."

Buttons looked at Red from the corner of his eye, but said nothing. Roper was also silent, no doubt because he didn't wish to draw attention to himself. The army exerted real power on the plains and with Ryan's threat of a murder charge hanging over him, the last thing he wanted was to deal with any kind of legal authority.

Buttons said, "You plan to ride straight through to the fort, Cap'n?" Buttons said.

"No, driver, we'll camp tonight and reach Fort Bliss by tomorrow evening," Moore said. "It will be good for Mrs. Morgan to get out of the cramped stage for a while and enjoy the stars."

"And the other ladies will too," Red said.

"What other ladies?"

"Mrs. Powell and Mrs. Carr."

"Oh, yes, of course, and them too," Captain Moore said.

When night fell and Captain Moore and his buffalo soldiers made camp, the troopers made a fire big enough to boil coffee and fry bacon. Buttons Muldoon was amazed. "Cap'n, we're surrounded by nothing but grass, how do them black boys find the makings for a fire?" he said.

"I don't know," Moore said. "But I swear they could start a blaze on top of an iceberg."

The night passed uneventfully, apart from one incident that puzzled Red Ryan and made him wonder at Stella Morgan's thinking. She sat close to Captain

Moore, her firelit eyes on the scout. "He is an Apache, isn't he?" she asked, nodding in the Indian's direction.

"Yes, he is," Moore said. "His name is Nascha and he's a Jicarilla."

"Bring it over here," Stella said.

Moore looked puzzled but he spoke to the scout in his own tongue and the man stood near Stella. After a while she reached out a hand and the tips of her fingers lightly stroked the smooth skin of the Apache's brown, muscular thigh. Stella's tongue touched her top lip and she shuddered, her breath coming in little gasps. Finally she withdrew her hand and said, "Send it away, Captain Moore. It smells."

The officer did as Stella asked, then he and Ryan exchanged glances. Moore looked as puzzled and ill at ease as Red did.

CHAPTER TWENTY-THREE

When Buttons Muldoon drove the Patterson stage into El Paso, the town was booming, thanks to the arrival of the Southern Pacific and the Atchison, Topeka and Santa Fe Railway. Set in a green valley with a nearly perfect, year-round climate, the city attracted merchants, entrepreneurs, and more than of its fair share of young men on the make. But a myriad of undesirables arrived with the professionals. El Paso was a haven for gamblers, gunmen, thieves, murderers, and whores who frequented the town's scores of saloons, dance halls, gambling establishments, opium dens, and brothels that lined its main streets.

For a while Dallas Stoudenmire had kept order with his shoot-now-ask-questions-later method of law enforcement, but Stoudenmire was six months in the grave, and the town that Red Ryan saw around him was wide open and raring to go.

The stage's side lamps were lit as Buttons followed the cavalry escort to nearby Fort Bliss and pulled up outside the headquarters building in the evening light. Captain Moore went inside and when he returned he was accompanied by a colonel, several junior officers, and a handsome major with gray in his hair who leaned heavily on a cane.

A soldier opened the stage door and assisted Stella Morgan down and then Edna and Rhoda, who seemed a little confused . . . in contrast to Stella's poise and dazzling smile as she saw her husband. But she stayed where she was, making Major Morgan, despite his wound, limp to her. The couple embraced, the major's smiling face revealing his obvious delight at the reunion, though Stella seemed stiff and remote and she finally pushed her husband away, gently, but still a definite, if genteel, shove.

If Major Morgan was disappointed at his wife's reaction, he didn't let it show, and he was still smiling broadly when he introduced Stella to the colonel.

"I'm so glad to meet you at last, Mrs. Morgan," Colonel David Anderson said, bowing over Stella's hand. "Major Morgan has often spoken of your beauty, and now I find that it was no exaggeration." He smiled. "You bring your own light to illuminate our dreary surroundings."

"You are most kind, Colonel," Stella said, playing her role to the hilt. "I confess that the major and I have been separated for too long."

"And my only regret is that we will not long have the pleasure of your company," the colonel said. "Major Morgan's retirement takes effect tomorrow at noon and then you are off to Washington. Is that not so?"

"Indeed, it is so, Colonel Anderson," Stella said. Her smile was perfect, that of a dutiful, loving wife. "Both John and myself consider the rail journey the first step of a great life adventure."

"Then I am delighted, and wish you all the very best for your future," Anderson said. Then, in a conspiratorial whisper, "I have planned a ball in your and Major Morgan's honor for tomorrow evening."

Stella said, "That is most gracious, Colonel."

"You will be the belle of the ball, dear lady," Colonel Anderson said. "I fear you will outshine all the other officers' ladies."

Stella fluttered her eyelashes. "La, Colonel Anderson, you do flatter me so."

"Flattery where flattery is deserved, my dear," the colonel said, beaming.

Red Ryan heard and remembered the night in the Stan Evans barn when he'd seen Stella and Seth Roper in the throes of passion. It occurred to him that the woman said all the right words to Colonel Anderson . . . but to Red she sounded as false as the chime of a cracked bell.

"And we've been invited to the ball," Edna Powell said. "Mr. Ryan, isn't that wonderful?"

Red smiled. "It sure is. And after all that's happened, make sure that you and Mrs. Carr enjoy yourselves."

"Oh, we will, Mr. Ryan," Rhoda Carr said. And then, "Corporal Carr, do you have something to say to Mr. Ryan?"

Corporal Carr was a small, slender man with chevrons on the sleeves of his blouse. "I want to thank you for saving my wife from the savages, Mr. Ryan," he said. "It was most . . ."

". . . most heroic of you," Rhoda prompted.

"Yes, most heroic of you and . . . and . . ."

"I am in your debt forever," Rhoda said.

"In your debt forever," Corporal Carr said. He looked relieved that his ordeal was over.

Red was amused. It seemed that Corporal Carr had been coached by his spouse. "You're most welcome," Red said. "But it was my duty as an employee of the Patterson and Son Stage and Express Company to see to the well-being of my passengers."

"Corporal Powell, do you have something to add?" Edna said to her husband.

In contrast to the small Corporal Carr, Corporal Powell was a big-bellied man with a round, good-humored face. He spared Red a speech, but put his arm around Rhoda's ample waist and grinned. "Mr. Ryan, you're true blue on account of how you brought the purdiest li'l gal in Texas safely home. Tomorrow night, she's gonna be the belle of the ball."

"I think there will be two belles of the ball," Red said. "I can't see any other gals being prettier than Edna and Rhoda, and that's a natural fact."

As Edna blushed and Rhoda smiled, Corporal Powell grinned and stuck out his hand. "Put it there, Mr. Ryan. Y'all just said a natural fact we can surely agree on."

Red Ryan left the enlisted married men's quarters and walked through moonlight toward downtown El Paso, which was ablaze with thousands of newfangled gas lamps and the siren song of the raucous saloons luring the unwary and those who preyed on them. Red's destination was a stage depot, originally built by the Butterfield company, but now shared by half a dozen different carriers, including Patterson & Son.

He figured that Buttons Muldoon was still there, shooting the breeze with other drivers, and hopefully he'd lined up passengers for the return trip to Fort Concho and points east.

Ryan walked through a bottle-strewn alley between a lumberyard and dry-goods stores and into a plaza crowded with promenading couples and Mexican street vendors. Then, a voice behind him stopped him in his tracks.

"Hold up, Ryan, I want to talk with you."

Red turned and saw Seth Roper. The man had acquired a new white shirt with a celluloid collar, and his broadcloth coat looked as though it had been cleaned and pressed. He carried a Colt in his waistband, but his gun hand was busy with a cigar, implying no threat.

Red said, "Roper, you'll do your talking to the law."

"That's harsh," the man said.

"So was murdering Poke Farrell."

"If it wasn't for me, your hair could be hanging in some Apache lodge right now," Roper said.

"I'm aware of that," Red said. "You did well, fought bravely, and I will mention it at your trial. But it doesn't excuse your murder of Farrell."

Roper's cigar glowed scarlet in the gloom as he took a puff and then he said behind a cloud of smoke, "Ryan, why the hell do you care? I mean, explain to me why you give a damn over the death of a damned pimp."

"Because when Poke Farrell fed and supplied sleeping accommodation for my passengers, I considered him a temporary employee of the Patterson and Son Stage and Express Company. It's my duty to care."

"Duty? Hell, Ryan, did you go to West Point?" Roper waited for a reaction, got none, then shrugged and said, "All right, let's go talk with the law right now."

"Suits me," Red said. "Roper, I'll take it hard if I see your hand go anywhere near your gun."

"I'll give it to you. Left hand, two fingers, Ryan. That set all right with you?"

"Slow. I mean like molasses in January."

"You're a careful man, Ryan."

"Live longer that way."

"Suppose I decide to draw down on you?"

"Then I'll kill you, Roper."

"Hard talk. Big talk."

"Keep this up and my talking will be done." Red pushed away a Mexican boy who was anxious to see how the gringo standoff would end. "You, git," he said. "Go back to your ma."

The boy stuck out his tongue and then disappeared into the crowd.

"Two fingers, Roper," Red said.

"I've never let a man take my gun before," Roper said.

"There's a first time for everything," Red said.

Red's hand dropped to his gun and he tensed for the draw as Roper's flexed fingers moved slowly toward his Colt. He grinned, then eased the revolver out of his waistband and passed it over.

"Satisfied, Ryan?" Roper said.

"No, I won't be satisfied until I hear the sheriff charge you with murder."

Roper smiled and said, "His name is T. C. Lyons, and he ain't really a sheriff, he was an El Paso fireman. But he's tipped to be the chief of police when the city sets up its own department."

"Who told you all this?" Red said, feeling a vague disappointment.

"Soldier feller at the post who'd no more liking for the law than I do."

"When does it all happen? This police department?"

"Hell, I don't know," Roper said. "A year or two maybe." He smiled. "This T. C. Lyons feller ain't a shootist, he puts out fires. He never once in his life drew a gun on a man. I bet he never saw the likes of me, huh, Ryan? Or you, come to that."

"If he knew Dallas Stoudenmire, he saw the likes of you, Roper. Now let's find this marshal, and keep in mind that if you figure on running, I'll shoot you."

"I ain't running anywhere," Roper said. "I got nothing to fear and that's why I've gone along with you this far. But I have a word of warning for you, Ryan, don't get in over your head. There's big doings coming down and a fortune at stake. Maybe you should stick to your stagecoach."

"You care to explain that, Roper?" Red said.

"No, not to you, because it's none of your damned business."

Acting El Paso city marshal T. C. Lyons was a small, neat man with a trimmed goatee and bright, intelligent eyes. His movements were quick and jerky, and he put Red Ryan in mind of an overgrown squirrel.

"I've heard with interest what you have to say, Mr. Ryan, but my jurisdiction extends only as far as the city limits," Lyons said. "Pressing a murder charge against Mr. Roper is a job for the county marshal."

"And where can I find him?" Red said.

"Nowhere at the moment, on account of how we

don't have one," Lyons said. "An appointment should be made soon, maybe a month or two from now. He'll be sworn in right here in this office." His eyes went to Roper. "You say you have witnesses who are willing to testify that you shot . . . what was his name again?"

"Poke Farrell," Ryan said.

"Refresh my memory. He was a pimp. Is that correct?"

"He ran a hotel," Red said.

"And a brothel," Seth Roper said.

"And, you say you shot him in self-defense, Mr. Roper? Your witnesses will testify to that fact?" Lyons said.

"Yes, they will. Farrell had a sneaky gun on him."

"Were you drunk at the time, Mr. Roper?"

"No, I was sober."

"Pity," Lyons said. "Sometimes a jury will consider drunkenness as a defense, since the accused wasn't fully aware of what he was doing."

The marshal sat back in his chair, steepled his fingers, and was silent in thought for a few moments. Then he said, "What manner of men are your witnesses, Mr. Roper?"

"One man and a woman, Marshal," Roper said.

"And, where are they?"

"At the fort. The woman is the lady wife of Major Morgan and—"

"John Morgan?"

"Yes."

"He's a fine man, is Major Morgan, and I'm sure his wife is a perfect lady."

"Oh, she is, Marshal," Roper said. "She most certainly is. My other witness is a bank clerk who was Mrs. Morgan's traveling companion and protector. He's in El Paso to further his banking career."

"A sound move, in my estimation," Lyons said. "El Paso has need of ambitious, intelligent young men."

"And Mr. Lucian Carter is both of those things," Roper said. "El Paso will not be disappointed in him."

"What is your occupation, Mr. Roper?" Lyons said.

"I'm a cattle buyer, but currently I'm acting as financial adviser to Mrs. Morgan, helping her settle the affairs of her late mother's estate."

"Very commendable of you, I'm sure," Lyons said, studying Red from the crown of his derby hat to the scuffed toes of his boots. He did not seem impressed. "And you, Mr. Ryan, what is your calling?"

"Mr. Ryan is a stagecoach shotgun guard," Roper said,

Lyons nodded. "Ah, yes, by your garb, I took you for a person engaged in . . . shall we say? . . . one of the *wilder* Western occupations."

Red let that go and said, "Marshal Lyons, what is your decision?"

"On Mr. Roper?"

Who else, you damned squirrel?

Red bit his tongue and said, "On his murder of Poke Farrell."

"In view of the fact that Mr. Roper has two sterling witnesses, including the wife of a fine army officer, who say the dead man was armed, I cannot charge him with the murder of the unfortunate pimp, especially when the alleged crime took place outside of my jurisdiction."

"Farrell ran a hotel," Red said.

"Mr. Ryan, it boils down to your word against Mr. Roper's and his sterling witnesses and I do not believe that your accusation would stand up in a court of law. Also, I'd like to remind you that you are a shotgun messenger. That gives you no status as an officer of the law, and you cannot press charges against anyone. On your part, to think otherwise would be presumptuous."

"The Texas Rangers might differ with that opinion." Red said.

"Perhaps, but the Rangers have their hands full with the Apache outbreak, and I don't think they will take any interest in the death of a pimp."

"He ran a hotel," Red said.

Lyons clapped his hands together and said, "Now, is there anything else I can do for you gentlemen?"

"Yes, Marshal, I'd like you to order Mr. Ryan to return my weapon that he confiscated," Roper said. "Mrs. Morgan may be in peril in such a rough town and in addition to being her financial adviser, I'm also her protector."

"Of course, Mr. Roper, I fully understand. But please tell the lady that I will guarantee her safety for as long as she is in El Paso." Lyons's bright eyes turned to Red. "Mr. Ryan, return Mr. Roper's weapon." He frowned. "Instanter!"

Seth Roper stood on the boardwalk outside the sheriff's office, a triumphant smile on his face. "You wasted my time, Ryan," he said.

Red Ryan waited until some noisy revelers passed and then said, "It's not over until the Rangers say it's over."

"Another waste of time," Roper said. "You never learn, do you?" He looked down the bustling street, the windows of the gaslit saloons and dance halls casting rectangles of bluish light, their competing tinpanny pianos getting their tunes tangled, and said, "Well, I thought about buying you a drink, Ryan, but I don't think I will. Fact is, I only drink with friends, and I don't like you that much."

"The feeling is mutual, Roper," Red said.

"Then better luck next time," Roper said.

"Go to hell, Roper," Red said.

Red Ryan made his way to the stage depot and was greeted by a commotion at the door, about two dozen men and a few soldiers in animated talk. Buttons Muldoon saw Red coming and paced hurriedly toward him. "Where the hell have you been, Red?" he said. "I've been looking all over for you."

"With the marshal, trying to hang Seth Roper," Ryan said.

"And will he?"

"Will he what?"

"Hang him?"

"No. He says Roper is innocent."

"Then you haven't heard the news?" Buttons said.

"What news?"

"Major Morgan is dead. Murdered. They say an Apache did it."

CHAPTER TWENTY-FOUR

"It's an Apache knife, all right," Marshal T. C. Lyons said. "Major Morgan got it right between the shoulder blades. He didn't stand a chance."

"It's an English-made trade knife," Red Ryan said. "Plenty of those around, carried by white men and Indians alike. And the ground shows only boot tracks, no moccasin prints."

"Booted men have been stomping all over this area for the past hour or so, that's why you don't see moccasin tracks. A white man didn't commit this murder, Ryan," Lyons said. He held up his oil lantern so that the light shone on Red. "And why the hell are you here?"

"Major Morgan was the husband of one of my passengers," Red said. "I feel a certain responsibility."

"Your responsibility ended when you delivered Mrs. Morgan, now the widow Morgan, to this post," Lyons said. "I suggest you leave and be about your business."

"No, let Mr. Ryan stay," Colonel David Anderson said. "He has a keen eye, and the more people we have investigating this murder, the better."

"How many Apaches are on the post, Colonel?" Lyons said.

"At the moment, only one. The Jicarilla scout Nascha. But he wouldn't—"

"Then he's the killer," Lyons said. "I'm willing to bet a month's pay on that."

"But Nascha had no reason to kill Major Morgan," Anderson said. "He's always been a loyal scout, and he received a medal for his excellent service during the Victorio campaign."

"An Apache doesn't need a reason to kill a white man, Colonel," Lyons said. "He saw the major leave the sutler's store, followed him here to the black-smith's shop, and stabbed him in the back. It was a crime of opportunity and pretty cut and dried, I'd say."

Lyons had deputized a couple of townsmen, and now he told them to arrest the Apache. But Colonel Anderson objected. "The murder happened on a United States army post, and Nascha will remain here until such time as he goes to trial."

"I've got no problem with that," Lyons said. "Just so long as you keep him locked up. I'd rather not transfer him to my jail, since I don't want his Apache friends to try breaking him out."

"I'll see that he's held securely under guard," Anderson said.

"See that you do, Colonel," Lyons said.

When Stella Morgan took center stage, the curtain rose on the second act of the tragic play that was the death of her husband . . . as Red Ryan knew it would.

Wearing a cavalry yellow dress, Stella hiked up her skirts, ran across the parade ground like a candle flame, and threw herself on her husband's bloody body. She turned her eyes to the dark sky, uttered a shriek of torment and grief, and stained the major's face with her own salt tears.

Had there been a classical scholar among the gathering of soldiers, he might have considered Stella's performance worthy of the Trojan woman Andromache lamenting the death of Hector, but since there was not one present, it fell to Red Ryan to think that the woman's display of sorrow was a tad overdone. And what Stella said next reinforced that opinion.

"Oh, John, John, what have they done to you?" she wailed. "The Apaches have murdered you at last."

Colonel Anderson, visibly distressed, coaxed Stella to her feet and said, "You've suffered a terrible shock, dear lady. I suggest you lie down and let Captain Murdoch, the post doctor, attend you. Perhaps he can give you a sleeping draught."

"Colonel, why did the Apache murder my husband?" Stella said. She sobbed, "Why? Why? Why?" And then, looking brave, "But . . . but I know why."

"What do you know, dear lady?" Anderson said, a man in anguish. "Tell me what you know."

"The Apache scout, the one called Nascha, Major Morgan caught him . . . caught him . . . no, I can't go on . . ."

"Caught him doing what?" the colonel said, being kind, his arm supporting the fainting Stella.

"John . . . he caught the Apache they call Nascha peering in my bedroom window as I changed garments."

"And what happened?" Anderson said. He shook his head. "This is most distressing."

"John . . . Major Morgan . . . rushed outside and caught Nascha in the act. My husband, he was such a forgiving man, warned the Apache that if he engaged in such behavior again he'd thrash him within an inch of his life. Nascha said . . . he said . . . oh, Colonel . . . it was terrible."

"Dear lady, what did Nascha say?" Anderson asked.

"He said that he would kill John . . . and . . . and leave his body for the buzzards."

Major Morgan had been a popular officer. That last comment drew growled threats against Nascha from the throats of the soldiers, and Anderson had to call them to order. Then he told a sergeant to take a squad and arrest the Apache. "Put him in the guardhouse and detail two sentries."

The sergeant left, replaced by Rhoda and Edna, curlers in their hair and tears in their eyes. The women rushed to Stella and cradled her to their substantial bosoms.

"I know how you loved the major," Edna said. "I'm heartbroken for you, Mrs. Morgan, and Corporal Powell is very upset." It was only then that Edna saw the major's body being carried away by four cavalry troopers, and she cried out in alarm. "Oh, what a horrible thing to have happened. I hope that murdering Apache hangs."

Rhoda noticed Red Ryan in the crowd and she said, "Isn't this just awful, Mr. Ryan?"

"Yes, it is," Red said.

"Corporal Carr says he'd like to pull the lever on the Indian himself," Rhoda said.

"I think there's a lot of people around here who would like to do just that," Red said.

"And who can blame them?" Rhoda said. "Major

Morgan dead at the hands of a savage is just too horrible to contemplate."

Hearing that, Stella began to wail and cry again, and Colonel Anderson said to Edna and Rhoda, "If you women will take Mrs. Morgan to her quarters and remain with her, I'll send the doctor to visit."

"Yes, Colonel, we'll do that most willingly," Edna said as Rhoda led the stricken Stella away. "Poor thing, besides a surfeit of grief, I believe that Mrs. Morgan is suffering from female hysteria and a wandering womb. I'll let the doctor know."

"I'm sure Captain Murdoch will be most grateful for your help," Colonel Anderson said, his face unreadable.

It was almost midnight when Red Ryan and Buttons Muldoon walked to their hotel through the still-roaring streets of El Paso.

"Buttons, there's nothing we can do for the Apache," Red said. "He's already a dead man."

"You really reckon he didn't do it, Red?" Buttons said.

"I know he didn't do it. Hell, Nascha's knife was still in its sheath when they arrested him."

"Maybe he had a spare," Buttons said. "I mean, that's possible."

"Maybe. But it don't seem likely."

"Well, if the Indian didn't kill Major Morgan, who did?" Buttons said.

Red stepped to the side as a brewer's dray trundled past, the stacked beer barrels thumping. Day or night, the thirsty saloons must be resupplied. He didn't answer Buttons's question, at least not directly.

"Seth Roper told me that something big was coming down and a fortune was at stake. What did he mean by that?"

"Hell, if I know," Buttons said.

"I do know this much," Red said. "Now her husband is dead, the widow Morgan inherits his estate. As of tonight, Stella is a very rich young woman."

Buttons stopped in his tracks, his hand on Red's arm. "Here, you ain't saying it was Stella punched the major's ticket?"

"No, she didn't stick a knife in her husband's back, but she could've had it done."

"You mean by Roper? Or that Carter feller?"

"Either one, Buttons, either one."

"And now Stella is willing to see another man swing for what she done?"

"The killing made her rich, and the man who'll hang is only an Apache," Red said. "It's easy to pin a murderer tag on an Indian because nobody much gives a damn."

Buttons shook his head. "It just ain't fair."

"I reckon so. But life isn't fair," Red said.

A split second later Red Ryan realized just how unfair life can be when a rifle blasted from the darkness and put a second bullet hole in his almost-new derby hat.

CHAPTER TWENTY-FIVE

Buttons Muldoon yelled, "What the hell?" as Red Ryan's hat flew off his head. But Red was already on the move, sprinting toward an alley where a drift of gunsmoke gave away the bushwhacker's position.

Colt drawn, Red slowed down and warily entered the alley, a dark, narrow passageway between a furniture warehouse and the New York Hat Shop. His own breathing loud in his ears, Ryan slowly entered the alley, which was littered with bottles and other garbage and as black as ink. Ahead of him a cat let out a shriek of pain and surprise, and a man cursed. Red's smile was grim. If you're going to ambush a fellow, don't step on a cat's tail.

Red fixed the rifleman's position, but didn't shoot. He'd be firing blind, and the flash from his revolver would dazzle him momentarily, leaving him vulnerable. Instead he stepped forward, his eyes searching the gloom.

BLAM!!

A rifle flared at the far end of the alley, and a bullet whined an inch past Red's head. Instinctively, he snapped off a shot and was rewarded by a yelp as his round burned the ambusher.

Behind him a man took a step into the alley and yelled in a drunken slur, "Now then, that won't do!"

"Get the hell away from here!" Red said.

Another rifle bullet split the air, missing badly, but close enough to draw a shriek from the frightened drunk, who scampered away yelling, "Murder! Murder!"

Then footsteps thudded in the darkness ahead, and Red followed at a run, empty bottles clanking around his feet.

The alley ended at a narrow footpath that fronted the rear, corrugated iron wall of another warehouse. The worn pathway ran east and west, and there was no indication of what direction the bushwhacker had taken.

Red stood still, his Colt up and ready, and listened into the night.

He heard voices from somewhere in the street behind, Button's excited Texas drawl and the irritable high-pitched yells of T. C. Lyons as he asked questions of anybody and everybody.

What was that?

Red's head snapped to his left as he heard the sound of what could be an empty wooden crate hitting the ground. Another alley cat or the man who had tried to kill him? There was one way to find out. Red stepped in the direction of the sound.

The path widened to about a dozen feet wide and ahead of him, just visible in the feeble moonlight, a pile of crates was stacked up behind a workshop of some kind. The one that had fallen lay across the pathway.

"Come out with your hands in the air," Red said.

"I'm with a dozen deputies here, all well-armed and determined men."

T. C. Lyons was in the alley. Red heard him call his name, ordering him to cease and desist. But in no mood to listen, Red stepped forward through a night now filled with the shouts of wary men . . .

He moved steadily toward the pile of crates, his Colt waist high and ready. The darkness closed around him, his visibility down to just a few murky yards. Somewhere a saloon piano played "Ol' Dan Tucker," its notes made tinny by distance. Red Ryan, his mouth as dry as mummy dust, walked on . . .

Suddenly a shadowy figure leaped up from behind the stacked crates, a rifle at his shoulder. He and Red fired at the same time. The bushwhacker's bullet went wild, Ryan's did not. The man cried out, "Oh, I am hit" when the big .45 round crashed into his chest, dead center, a killing shot.

The man fell, crates tumbling around him, and he was dead when Red reached him. A moment later something cold and hard pressed into the back of Red's skull and T. C. Lyons's voice said, "Drop your gun, Ryan, or by God, I'll scatter your brains."

Red opened his fingers and let his Colt fall to the ground. Lyons quickly scooped it up and shoved it into his waistband. "What's going on here, Ryan? You've shot up half of the damned city."

Red motioned to the sprawled body. "He tried to kill me, took a pot from the alley when I was standing in the street talking to my driver."

"Is he dead?"

"As he's ever gonna be."

Lyons took Red's derby from one of his deputies, a middle-aged man named Lou Hunt, "Were two of these caused by the shot?" Lyons said, waggling his fingers through four bullet holes in the crown, entrances and exits.

"Yeah, but I don't rightly know which two," Red said. "But I sure set store by that hat. It was almost new."

"Seems like other folks don't like the hat as much as you do, Ryan. Lucky you didn't get your fool brains blown out," Lyons said. Then he said to the gray-bearded deputy, "Lou, bring the lantern up here. Let's take a look at the dead man."

Lou raised the lantern and then said, "Hell, Sheriff, that there is Sam Glover as ever was."

"You sure?"

"Sure as there's dung in a donkey."

Red said, "Who is he?"

"Who was he, you mean," Lyons said. "He was a chicken and pie thief and a damned nuisance. He should've been hung years ago just on principle."

"Any wife and young 'uns?" Red said, fearing the answer.

Lou said, "Nah. Worked as a swamper and lived in a shack behind the Hipflask saloon. Drank whiskey when he could, kerosene when he couldn't, and never had two pennies to rub together in his entire life."

Red kneeled, tried the man's pockets, and came up with three double eagles. "Well, somebody gave him sixty dollars to rub together," he said.

Buttons Muldoon pushed his way through the crowd and said, "Red, you're still alive and kicking. For a spell there I thought for sure you were a goner."

"I'm still kicking, but no thanks to the feller lying at your feet, Buttons. His name was Sam Glover, and it seems like somebody paid him sixty dollars to dry gulch me."

Buttons bent down and picked up a beat-up .44-40 Henry. "This his rifle?" he said.

Red nodded. "Yeah, that's it. Brass tacks all over the stock. Looks like an Indian owned it at one time."

"An Apache owned it," Buttons said. "And an Apache owned the knife that killed Major Morgan. Now where did this man get a rifle like this?"

"My guess is that the party that wants me dead gave it to him to do the job," Red said. "Trouble is he . . . or she . . . hired a tinhorn who couldn't even shoot straight."

A bright idea dawned on Buttons, lighting up his face. "Red, somebody could've picked up this rifle and the knife after those scrapes we had with the Apaches out on the long grass."

"Could be," Red allowed. "But I didn't see anybody do it."

"As I recollect, you were busy and so was I," Buttons said. "Easy enough for Seth Roper or that Carter feller to stash a rifle and knife in the stage."

T. C. Lyons said, "Could be somebody gave an Indian rifle to Glover. But the Apache who killed the major would have his own knife."

"Then why leave it in Morgan's back?" Red said. "An Indian sets store by a good fighting knife, and Nascha was still wearing his when he was arrested. I reckon somebody used a trade knife to make it seem obvious that an Apache was the killer."

"Maybe Nascha had two knives," Lyons said.

"That's what Buttons said, but it ain't real likely," Red said.

"Don't forget that the Apache did threaten to kill the major," Lyons said.

"Yeah, we have Mrs. Morgan's word for that," Red

said. "And now that she's a very rich widow, I guess we have to heed what she says."

Lyons was in the process of lighting his pipe, but he stopped in thought and let the match burn down in his fingers. He tossed the match away and after a while said, "All right, Ryan, some things just don't add up. I'll need to take time to walk through this."

"What about Nascha?" Red said.

"As a civilian scout, I've decided that he'll be transferred to the city jail, where I'll be responsible for him," Lyons said. "I still believe the Apache murdered Major Morgan and that there's a logical explanation for all your objections. In the meantime, Ryan, study on who would want you dead."

Red nodded. "I'll do that."

"And so will I," Lyons said. "One thing, though, don't call out Seth Roper. He wouldn't hire somebody to kill you, he'd do it himself. And if he did hire an assassin, he'd pick somebody a sight better than Sam Glover."

"Could be that whoever hired Glover knew he wasn't near good enough to kill me," Red said. "Maybe it was meant as a warning . . . to scare me the hell out of El Paso."

"What we got here is a heap of could be and maybe," Lyons said. "When you come up with something definite, come see me, Ryan. Until then you're just a rooster crowing on a dung pile. And another thing, unless you have some natural facts to tell, stay the hell away from me, huh?"

CHAPTER TWENTY-SIX

As the grandfather clock in the lobby chimed midnight, Red Ryan and Buttons Muldoon were the only patrons of the La Scala Hotel's bar. A bored mixologist polished a glass and looked forward to the one o'clock closing time, and over by the piano an equally bored saloon girl used a forefinger to pick out the melody of a Chopin nocturne.

Buttons had opened his mouth several times to say something and then shut it again. Finally, Red said, "Out with it, Buttons. What's on your mind?"

Muldoon raised his whiskey to his lips, decided against it, and laid the glass back on the table. "All right then, here's what I think . . . the major was murdered because Stella Morgan wanted to be a rich widow. Either Roper or Carter did the killing and used an Apache knife so the scout would be blamed. Red, you made a lot of noise about Nascha not being the murderer, and that made you a danger to Stella's plans and a marked man. Somebody then paid Sam Glover to kill you, tried to do it on the cheap, and hired a greenhorn who spent his life seeing double and couldn't shoot worth a damn. Are you with me so far?"

"I'm listening," Red said.

"Good, because here's where I sum it all up . . . none of this Stella Morgan stuff is any business of ours. I say we hitch up the team, take the stage back to Fort Concho, and then let the Rangers handle it."

"And in the meantime, the Apache hangs and Stella takes the train to Washington and enters high society, well away from Texas Ranger jurisdiction. Of course, Roper and Carter go with her as strong-arm bodyguards and provide the muscle for her further criminal ventures. After all, if you're a beautiful woman who can murder an army officer husband and get away with it, you might believe that you can bump off another wealthy husband and become richer still. So, how does that set with you?"

"Like I said, that's all well and good, but it's still got nothing to do with us. Red, you're a shotgun messenger, I'm a driver, so let's get back to what we know best. As far as I'm concerned, we shake the dust of El Paso off our boots and never come back. Red, we can pick up passengers along the way for points east as far as New Orleans. Hell, ol' Abe Patterson will be so pleased, he'll give us a bonus."

Suddenly, Red Ryan's face creased in thought. Then he said, "New Orleans . . . Buttons . . . hell . . . yeah . . . that's it!"

Buttons grinned. "Red, I'm as happy as a pig in a peach orchard that I've talked some sense into you at last."

"No, it's not about picking up passengers, it's about Lucian Carter."

"Huh?"

"Lucian Carter. I just remembered what I heard one time. Listen, do you recollect the name Elijah Carter? The newspapers called him Old Man Carter or Killer Carter on account of how he ran a murder-for-hire business out of New Orleans."

Button's puzzled face told Red that his driver had drawn a blank.

"Well, he did, and over the course of twenty years he signed up some of the fastest guns in the business to make the kills," Ryan said. "Yeah, it's all coming back to me now. At Carter's trial, the prosecutor said that Bill Longley did a job for Carter, so did Cullen Baker and Dallas Stoudenmire and a dozen other named gunfighters, but none of that could be proved, and the gunslingers never stood trial. But Elijah Carter was found guilty of contracting out seven murders for hire by person or persons unknown, though the real number was at least twenty times that."

"So, what happened to him?"

"They hung him. But here's the thing . . . Elijah Carter had two sons, both of them stone-cold killers who did a lot of their Pa's dirty work, but, like the other gunmen, there was not enough evidence to convict them. The older brother was soon shot dead by a deputy sheriff in Abilene, but the other disappeared. I think the missing son is Lucian Carter, and Stella Morgan hired him in San Antonio around the time Major Morgan's mother died."

"And left him all her money," Buttons said. "You think Carter murdered the old lady?"

"That seems logical to me," Red said. "You saw Lucian Carter shoot. He's no bank clerk, lay to that."

Buttons stifled a yawn, and the saloon girl left the piano and walked past Red, her hips swaying, but her heart wasn't in it, and she kept on walking to the bar and ordered a rum punch.

"Red, who told you all that stuff about the Carters?" Buttons said. "Maybe somebody was spinning you a big windy."

"Do you mind I told you that a few years back I rode shotgun for the Dexter Brothers Mining Company up the Montana Territory way?" Red said. "Well, us shotgun guards and some muleskinners got snowed in for three weeks in the winter of 1880 and all we had to do was talk. One of the guards was out of New Orleans, a nice Cajun feller by the name of Alan Belanger, and one day we got to talking about gunslingers and sich, and he told me about old Elijah Carter and them. Now Belanger was a religious feller, much given to saying his prayers and all, so he wasn't the kind to tell a big windy." Ryan shook his head. "He got killed by holdup men the following spring, and I took that hard when I heard it."

Buttons sat in silence for a while, drained his glass, and replaced it on the table. "Well, it's me for my bed," he said. Then, standing, "Red, the story about the Elijah Carter feller changes nothing. What Stella Morgan does or doesn't do is still none of our business."

"Maybe you're right, and that's the case. I don't know," Red said.

"We're well out of it," Buttons said.

"They did try to kill me," Red said. "I'd say that makes it kinda personal."

"And who is *they*?"

"Stella Morgan, Seth Roper, and Lucian Carter, that's who they are."

Buttons shook his head. "Sleep on it, Red. Maybe you'll see things in a different light come morning."

"Buttons, it's all about righting a wrong, isn't it?" Ryan said.

"Yeah, Red, I'm right, you're wrong. Now, good-night to ye."

After Buttons left, Red Ryan stepped to the bar and said to the girl, "Can I buy you a drink?"

She smiled, showing crooked teeth. "Yes, I'd like a bottle of champagne."

"Bartender, a rum punch for the lady and a whiskey for me," Red said.

"Cheapskate," the girl said. "If you were ugly I'd walk right on out of here."

"If you were ugly, so would I," Red said.

"And ugly or not, you're both out of here at one o'clock," the bartender said.

CHAPTER TWENTY-SEVEN

On what would be the last day of his life, the Apache named Nascha was taken in chains from the Fort Bliss guardhouse to the El Paso city jail, a log structure with a dirt floor behind the marshal's office that was due for demolition.

At the same time across town, Red Ryan woke with a pounding headache, and beside him was a girl with crooked teeth who'd looked a sight prettier seen through the amber prism of last night's whiskey glass.

Ryan swung his legs over the side of the bed, groaned, held his head in his hands, and suffered . . . and a few moments later his torment was made worse by a demanding and determined pounding on the hotel room door.

"Go away," Red whimpered. "I'm dying here."

"Open the door, Red," Buttons Muldoon said. He sounded just fine, almost jolly. "I found us a job."

Red's lamentations were loud and many, but he finally summed them up when he said, "I don't want a damned job."

The girl beside him stirred and said, "Wha . . . what's happening?"

"Nothing," Red said. "Go back to sleep."

Buttons hammered on the door again. "Red, it's a short passenger run to a ranch near the Franklin Mountains. Hell, we'll make fifty dollars."

Despite his hangover, Red was interested enough to ask, "What kind of passenger?"

"The female kind, a college student visiting her folks. She plans to be a doctor, and she's right pretty."

"I need a doctor," Red said.

"No, you don't," Buttons said. "You need coffee and some bacon and eggs, and Red, I want you with me riding shotgun. Now buck up and come back to the land of the living."

"Give me another hour or two, for mercy's sake," Ryan said. "Come back then. The college gal can wait for a spell."

"You got ten seconds to open this door, Red Ryan, or I'll break it down," Buttons said.

"All right, all right, keep your shirt on," Red said. "Hell, Buttons, you sure know how to plague a man."

He opened the door, and Buttons gave him a critical glance and said, "You look like the deadest dead man I've even seen."

"I know. You can hitch up the hearse anytime."

"Get dressed," Buttons said. "Did you pay the girl?"

"I don't think so," Red said. "I don't have any money left."

Buttons took two silver dollars from his pocket, laid them on the table beside the bed, and then shook the girl awake. "For you, young lady, he said.

The girl sat up, glared at the money, and said, "Is that all I get?"

"I don't know," Buttons said. He nodded to Red, who was struggling into his pants. "Why don't you ask him?"

"Don't ask me conundrums," Red said. "My brain stopped working sometime around one o'clock this morning."

"You're a damned skinflint," the girl said. "I knew that the minute I set eyes on you."

Red pulled on his boots, wary of his still aching toe, placed his holed hat gingerly on his pounding head, and said, "Buttons, where's the Greener?"

"You don't plan on doing yourself in with it, do you?"

"No. I need it for the run."

"Well, it's where it always is. With the stage. Now let's go."

Buttons opened the door, Red stepped into the hallway and behind him the girl with the crooked teeth yelled, "Skinflint!"

Ma's Kitchen, catering to the early breakfast crowd, was crowded, steamy, and hot and smelled of frying bacon and coffee. Red Ryan's stomach lurched.

"Over there, Red," Buttons Muldoon said, leading the way to a corner table, where a prim-looking young woman sat drinking coffee, a nibbled donut on a plate in front of her. When the girl looked up, Buttons said, "Miss Rachel Tyler, this is Red Ryan, the best shotgun guard in Texas."

"Then I'm in safe hands," the young woman said. Her pretty face concerned, she added, "You don't look very well, Mr. Ryan. I do hope you're not ill."

Red managed a smile. "My stomach is a little upset. I . . . ate some underdone beef last night."

"Ah, then that's the culprit," Rachel said.

Buttons and Red sat and ordered coffee. "You plan on becoming a doctor, Miss Tyler?" Red said.

"Yes, I do. An odd profession for a woman, to be sure, but I've dreamed about being a physician since I was a little girl. My father approves, more or less, but secretly I'm sure he'd prefer me to stay and help him around the ranch." The woman smiled, "My father owns the Rafter-T, the biggest cattle ranch in these parts. He won't admit it, but he's quite rich."

Buttons said, "You were born on the ranch, Miss Tyler?"

"Yes. My mother died giving birth to me. I don't think my father's ever gotten over it."

"I'm real sorry about that," Buttons said.

As Red spooned sugar into his coffee, feeling dreadful, he was suddenly attentive as the girl said, "A gentleman I spoke with earlier was very interested in buying my father's ranch." She smiled. "He said he was interested in acquiring property around El Paso."

Buttons took the words out of Red's mouth. "What else did this gentleman say?"

"Oh, he wanted to know where the ranch was, and how I was getting there. I told him by the Patterson stage, and he seemed very curious about that."

Ryan said, "Miss Tyler, what did this man look like?"

"Look like? Why, I hardly noticed."

"Try and remember," Red said.

"Well, he was tall and well-built, and he wore a re-volver. I will say that he did seem roughly dressed to be a property buyer, but then many rich men don't care what they wear. At the ranch, my father enter-tained some of the wealthiest men in Texas, some of them worth millions, but they looked as poor as church mice. Appearances can be very deceptive."

"Yes, they can," Red said. "Where is this man now, Miss Tyler? Is he here?"

"No, he left rather abruptly, said he had some business to attend to."

Red and Buttons exchanged glances, each knowing what the other was thinking . . . rich man . . . pretty daughter . . . kidnap . . . ransom . . .

Suddenly Red was sobering, his hangover only a hellish ninety percent of what it had been earlier. He still couldn't face bacon and eggs or even a soda cracker.

"Drink up," Buttons said, pushing Red's cup closer to him. "It's time we took Miss Tyler to meet her pa."

Red finished his coffee, and he and Buttons paid their bill and escorted Rachel Tyler out of the restaurant. On the boardwalk outside, the girl stopped, stood on tiptoe, and whispered into Red's ear, "Mr. Ryan, I've been around cowboys enough to know a rye whiskey hangover when I see one." She smiled. "Underdone beef, indeed."

The terrain between El Paso and the Franklin Mountains was a flat, high desert plateau covered in cactus, bunchgrass, and bright patches of yellow poppies. The sun rose higher in the bowl of the sky as Buttons Muldoon followed a wagon track across the sandy ground, the blue Franklins ahead of him, soaring seven thousand feet above the level.

Red Ryan, his hangover rapidly dissipating thanks to the clean morning air and the nearness of danger, as palpable as a man sensing the presence of a threat in a darkened room, sat with his shotgun across his thighs, his eyes constantly scanning the land around him. The stage startled a small herd of mule deer and once he thought he saw the glint of metal or glass in the distance, but it was there, then gone, and it could have been anything, even the sun catching an empty bottle tossed away by a careless puncher. But it troubled Red and honed his awareness to razor sharpness.

The team had given Buttons Muldoon trouble all morning, mainly because of the inexperienced wheeler he'd substituted for his own horse that had shown signs of lameness after it was wounded in the fight with the Apaches. Buttons had been quiet, concentrating on his driving, breaking his silence only now and then to curse at the green wheeler.

Now, when he turned his head and talked to Red, his voice was flat, matter-of-fact, a man who had accepted the inevitable. "Dust ahead, coming in from the north."

"I see it," Red said. "Road agents?"

"What else?" Buttons said. "We're carrying a valuable cargo."

"Maybe it's punchers driving a herd," Red said.

"At a gallop?"

"Should we turn around and make a run for it?"

"The team is balky, Red. Those boys would catch up to us pretty fast."

Red groaned. "Well, a man with a hangover doesn't need this."

"Neither does a man without a hangover," Buttons said.

"How many of them do you think?"

"Hell, I don't know. But I'd guess there's enough."

There were four of them, rough-looking men blocking the trail, all of them with rifles at the ready.

"Drive right through them, Buttons," Red said.

"I'd say them boys have done this afore," Buttons said. "They'll know all they have to do is shoot a leader and we're stranded."

"All right then, maybe I can talk our way out of this," Red said.

"Maybe, but I doubt it," Buttons said.

"You shut your damned yap and toss away the scattergun," the black-bearded man said.

Years later, when El Paso men discussed the Franklin Mountains holdup, the popular opinion was that whiskey fumes from the previous night clouded Red Ryan's judgment and that's why he yelled, "The hell with you!" and raised his shotgun. But all agreed that a single shot from a holdup man's .44-40 Winchester sent Red tumbling, senseless, off the stage.

He was unconscious when he hit the ground hard. The bullet had grazed his skull, but it had the same effect as a blow by a two-by-four upside the head, and although he regained consciousness quite quickly, he remained dizzy and disoriented.

Buttons Muldoon didn't like the odds and dropped the reins and raised his hands.

"Behave yourself, driver, and no one else gets killed," the bearded man said. "Is that clear?"

"Clear as mother's milk," Buttons said.

The bearded man turned his head. "Kyle, go fetch the girl. If she struggles, punch her hard and bring her to me unconscious."

The man named Kyle, a big, uncurried brute with

shaggy black eyebrows, grinned and said, "Hell, I'll give her more than that, Boone."

"No, you won't," Boone said. "I don't want her hurt . . . at least until after we get the money."

Kyle swung out of the saddle and stepped to the door of the stage. "You, git the hell out of there, girlie," he said.

Those were the last words Kyle ever said, because a .40 caliber ball from a Remington derringer hit him smack between the eyes and wrote FINIS at the bottom of the last chapter of his life.

The situation deteriorated fast after Kyle fell, and mistakes were made.

The black-bearded man named Boone made the first one.

He'd already badly underestimated Buttons Muldoon, by all appearances an affable, harmless gent. Buttons was affable all right, but he was far from harmless. Boone's mistake was to get angry as a hornet and go after the girl in the stage, and Buttons cashed in on it. As Boone dismounted, Buttons drew and fired, a well-timed shot that hit the bearded man in the belly and dropped him beside his horse.

Shocked at the violence of the past few seconds, the two other bandits hesitated . . . and hesitation kills men in gunfights. It was another fatal mistake.

The shot fired by Rachel Tyler and what it implied for his passenger had helped Red Ryan overcome his dazed stupor. Staggering a little, blood streaming from the left side of his head, he grabbed his fallen shotgun and rounded the rear of the stage, just as Buttons gut-shot Boone out of the saddle.

Red took in the situation at a glance and triggered a barrel at the man closer to him. The buckshot tore into the bandit's right side and did terrible destruction. With a scream *in extremis*, the rider collapsed on his mount's neck and then slid slowly to the ground. The surviving rider made the final mistake of the morning when he raised his arms and opened his mouth to yell his surrender. He never uttered the words because Rachel Tyler, mistaking the bandit's gesture as aggression, fired at him. She missed, but her shot forced the man to give up the idea of quitting, and instead he threw his rifle to his shoulder and turned to fire on Red. Buttons shot him out of the saddle and shot him again when he attempted to stagger to his feet. The second bullet put the road agent down permanently . . . and silence once again fell on the land.

Red Ryan's first thought was for his passenger. He warily approached the stage window and then stopped. "Miss Tyler, it's me, Red Ryan of the Patterson and Son Stage and Express Company."

"I know who you are, Mr. Ryan," the girl said.

Red stepped to the window, looked at Rachel and said, "You are not harmed?"

"No. I'm just fine."

Red glanced at the dead man with the bullet between his eyes. "Good shooting," he said.

"A girl can't grow up on a ranch without learning how to shoot," Rachel said. "I'm sorry I had to kill the man, but he had evil intentions and gave me no choice."

"He needed killing," Ryan said. "No doubt about that." He admired the girl's spunk. She had strength and fortitude, the attributes that would one day help her become a doctor in a profession dominated by men. Red saw Buttons walking among the other dead and said, "Recognize anybody?"

Muldoon shook his head. "They're all strangers to me. A rough-looking bunch."

"Mr. Ryan, I'm feeling a little faint. Can we proceed?" Rachel said.

"Of course," Red said.

"My father will make sure these men are buried decently," Rachel said.

"In the end, I guess that's all an outlaw can hope for," Red said.

CHAPTER TWENTY-EIGHT

Holt Tyler was a big, brown-haired man with wide shoulders and the lean, sun-bronzed face of the high-desert rider. If there was weakness in the man, Red Ryan couldn't see it. Tyler was tough, and judging by the much-used Colt on his hip, he would be sudden and dangerous when the occasion demanded. But the lines around his blue eyes hinted at remembered laughter, and when he looked at his daughter there was a tenderness in his expression that he reserved for her and her alone. He told Rachel she looked more like her dead mother with every passing year, had inherited all her sweet little mannerisms and that his heart swelled with joy and pride when he beheld her.

But toward Red Ryan and Buttons Muldoon he was much less sentimental.

"Why the hell did you two scoundrels put my daughter's life in such mortal danger?" he said.

Tyler spoke as a hard-bitten rancher who'd hanged a baker's dozen rustlers over the years and whose fast Colt had put seven others in the grave.

Red Ryan did not underestimate him.

"Mr. Tyler, we had a feeling that something might happen on the trail, but we weren't real sure," he said.

"So you took chances with my daughter's life?" Tyler said. "Is that it?"

At that moment, the sooty muzzles of Red's shotgun looked friendlier than the rancher's eyes.

Red said, "Mr. Tyler, it is the policy of the Patterson and Son Stage and Express Company that the safety of our passengers must be a priority. If we were responsible for a lapse in this policy, then I apologize."

"Lapse!" Tyler's face turned thunderous. "You call almost getting my daughter killed a lapse? Why, you—"

"Father, taking the stage was my idea," Rachel said. "I knew the Apaches were out and that we could possibly be waylaid by outlaws, but I insisted on leaving El Paso right away. Mr. Ryan and Mr. Muldoon saved my life, and poor Mr. Ryan was wounded by a desperado's bullet." The girl frowned. "I think both these gentlemen are to be praised for their gallantry, not ill-used in this way."

Tyler visibly grew calmer. "Was that the way of it, Rachel?"

"Yes, Father, that was the way of it."

"Then it seems that I owe you boys an apology," Tyler said. "Mr. Ryan, where were you wounded? Oh, wait, I see it now. The side of your head is bloody."

"It's just a graze," Red said. "I've got a hard head."

"Nonetheless it should be seen to."

Tyler stepped to a ranch house window, opened it, and called out to a passing puncher, "Deke, ask Leosanni to come to the house and tell her to bring her medical kit."

"Sure thing, boss," the puncher yelled.

Holt Tyler closed the window and then said to Red, "I apologize for my temper, Mr. Ryan. Sometimes it gets the better of me. One time when I was angry I hung a couple of boys just like you and Mr. Muldoon. I've always regretted that . . . lapse."

Red and Buttons exchanged glances, and then Rachel said, "I should warn you that Leosanni is an Apache. But please don't be alarmed, she won't harm you."

Red nodded. "Thank you, Miss Tyler. That's a relief to know," he said.

Leosanni was a plump Chiricahua woman with a kind face and gentle hands. His hangover now a memory, Red Ryan drank a glass of Holt Tyler's excellent bourbon as she bathed his wound, swabbed it with something that stung, and then bandaged his head so he looked like an Apache himself.

The rancher insisted that Red and Buttons stay for lunch, and after they'd eaten, he said, "If you boys are ready, I suggest we go take a look at the dead men and see if I recognize any of them. The county sheriff, when we get one, might want names."

Red and Buttons allowed that they were ready and thanked Tyler for feeding and watering the team. Before they left, Rachel kissed them both on the cheek and said that she might see them in El Paso before they left for Fort Concho.

"Real nice gal, that Miss Tyler," Buttons said as he and Red climbed into the box. "She'll make one hell of a doctor."

"She'll make one hell of a whatever she wants to be," Red said.

* * *

"This man is shot right between the eyes," Holt Tyler said. "Your handiwork, Mr. Ryan?"

"No, your daughter's," Red said.

Tyler beamed and nodded. "That's my clever little gal," he said.

After scanning the bodies, the rancher said, "Well, I only recognize one of them. The man with the black beard is Boone Whelan. In the past he's done some rustling and train robbing and probably a killing or two. For a while he was a lawman up in the New Mexico Territory, got into a couple of shooting scrapes and then came back to Texas. He ran with the Roper brothers for a year or so, and then they had a falling-out of some kind, and Boone went his own way."

Red's ears pricked up at the Roper mention, and he said. "Would one of those brothers be Seth Roper?"

"Sure would," Tyler said. "Let me see . . . yeah . . . Seth is the oldest and then there's Barney, Eldon, and Jake. I suspect that in the past they lifted some of my cattle, but I could never catch them at it."

"Seth Roper is in El Paso," Red said.

"Is that a fact? Well, I've heard that from time to time he poses as a cattle buyer," Tyler said.

"He's posing as a financial adviser to a rich widow woman," Red said.

The rancher shook his head and grinned. "Well, don't that beat all, the worst thief in West Texas telling a widow woman how to spend her money. I got to hand it to him, he's got gall."

Buttons Muldoon said, "Seems that right now

would be a good time to hang him, Mr. Tyler. For old time's sake."

The big man laughed. "When it comes to Roper and that breed sometimes I'm willing to let bygones be bygones if they aren't troubling me none, and now Rachel is home for a while I hanker for the peaceful life."

Tyler turned and called out to half a dozen punchers who were standing around a wagon, "Break out the shovels, boys. We've got some burying to do."

Buttons Muldoon lit the stage's side lamps when he and Red Ryan were still an hour out from El Paso. He handled the ribbons in silence for a while and then said, "Red, where do you stand on the extry hundred dollars Holt Tyler gave us for saving his daughter?"

"I'm not catching your drift," Red said.

"Well, here's the question . . . does it belong to us or Abe Patterson?"

"Us, of course," Red said. His derby hat balanced on the fat bandage around his head. "We did most of the gunfighting with the road agents, and I damned near got killed. Abe gets the fifty dollars for the fare, that's all."

"It's what I figured, but with you being such a company man an' all, I wasn't sure."

Red smiled. "Like it says in the Bible, 'Render unto Caesar the things that are Caesar's . . .'"

"Is that what it says?"

"It sure does."

Buttons nodded. "Then I guess that's why they call it the Good Book, huh?"

"I'd say so, Buttons. It tells us that we should keep

Holt Tyler's hundred bucks, and that's advice right from the good Lord's mouth."

"Hell, Red, I got to read that book more often," Buttons said. "What does it say about whiskey and whores?"

"My boy, read it and you'll learn," Red said, grinning.

On the outskirts of El Paso, on the bank of a dry creek, stood an ancient cottonwood, an unremarkable tree except for a heart carved into its trunk and inside the heart the date 1880 and under that the initials JW L EH proclaimed some lovelorn swain's undying devotion.

But what made Buttons Muldoon halt the stage was not the heart, but the hanged man swinging from one of the lower tree limbs, his moccasins only a few inches off the ground. Nascha the army scout had died hard. He'd strangled to death, slowly, the life choked out of him by the rough hemp of a noose.

"Well, they done for him at last," Buttons said, his face like stone.

Red Ryan nodded, shocked. "Seems like."

Under a copper-colored sky, he climbed down from the stage, found his barlow, and cut the rope. The Apache collapsed in a lifeless heap, and Red said, "Buttons, help me get him into the stage."

"What are you going to do with him?" Muldoon said.

"Leave him on T. C. Lyons's doorstep," Red said.

CHAPTER TWENTY-NINE

When Red Ryan and Buttons Muldoon drove into El Paso, the early-evening festivities were in full swing . . . as though the murder of the Apache had gone unnoticed.

Buttons drove to the sheriff's office, and the stage jangled to a halt. Scalded by anger, Red jumped down and opened the stage door to retrieve Nascha's body, then stopped as T. C. Lyons staggered out onto the boardwalk.

The sheriff had been badly beaten.

His face was bruised, his left eye swollen shut, and there was blood in his mouth. It looked like his left cheek had been scratched by a knife blade, and his clothing was ripped, the ends of his celluloid collar up around his ears.

Lyons glimpsed the Apache's body through the open door of the stage and said, his voice a harsh croak, "Damn you, Ryan, don't blame me none. I tried to stop them. I did my best to save him."

"Who did it, Lyons?" Red said. "Who lynched him?"

"Half the damned town. I couldn't fight off half the

town." Then, as though he couldn't believe it had happened. "They beat me, Ryan. My own town . . . folks I know . . . and they beat me."

Lyons took a step toward Red, and then groaned and fell heavily to the boardwalk.

"He's out, Buttons. Let's get him inside," Red said.

The four-man orchestra of the nearby saloon played "Oh! Susanna" and boots thumped on a timber floor as Red and Buttons half-carried, half-dragged Lyons inside and dropped him into the chair behind his desk.

"Where do you suppose he keeps his whiskey?" Red said.

"Try the bottom drawers of the desk," Buttons said. "Lyons is a bottom-drawer drinker if ever I saw one."

Red was sure there was Buttons Muldoon logic there someplace, but he did as the driver said, and sure enough in one of the drawers he found a bottle of Old Crow and glasses. He poured whiskey for Buttons and himself and then a glass for Lyons that he held to the man's lips.

"Drink this," Red said. "It will do you good."

Lyon's eyes fluttered open and he said, "I don't drink."

"You do now," Red said. He tipped whiskey into the sheriff's mouth.

Lyons lurched forward in his chair, coughing, the bite of Old Crow in his throat. "Enough!" he gasped.

"You back in the land of the living?" Red said.

"More or less. There's coffee. Bring me a cup."

Muldoon poured coffee from a pot on the stove and brought it to the sheriff. Red waited until the man had taken a gulp and then said, "All right, tell me what happened."

"Somebody riled them up, turned a crowd into a mob with free whiskey and wild talk," Lyons said. "They came for the Apache, and there was no stopping them."

"Recognize any of them?" Red said.

"Hell, Ryan, I recognized all of them."

"Good, then after they sober up you can arrest them for murder," Red said.

Lyons shook his head. "I got maybe two deputies I can count on. How are three of us going to arrest a hundred men? I try my best to uphold the law in this town, but I'm not about to commit suicide. The beating they gave me was a warning. Next time they'll shoot."

Buttons Muldoon said, "Sheriff, any idea who got the crowd so all-fired excited?"

"No, I don't. Somebody with a pile of money to spend and enough of a viper tongue to whip up a mob."

"I reckon that description could fit a few men in this town," Red said.

"Anybody in mind?" Lyons said.

"Yeah, I have. But for now, I'll keep my suspicions to myself."

"Somebody wanted that Injun dead real bad," Lyons said.

"You're right about that, and a rope was the best way to shut him up and avoid a trial," Red said. "For a spell there, your somebody was running just a little bit scared."

"Ryan, you should tell me what you know," Lyons said. "Maybe I can't arrest a lynch mob, but I can jail the ringleader."

"Later," Red said. "Right now, I know nothing. I still have some investigating to do."

"Damn it, Ryan, you think you're a lawman, don't you?" Lyons said.

"No, I don't. I'm a shotgun guard, but as such I am a representative of the Patterson and Son Stage and Express Company, and they would expect me to see justice done. The old Butterfield outfit always thought that way and so does Wells Fargo." Red lifted Lyons's cup from the desk and handed it to him. "Drink some more coffee, Sheriff. Earlier today, my driver and I were set upon by road agents, and we have a report to make."

Lyons stared hard into Red's face with his one good eye. "How many road agents?"

"Four."

"How many dead road agents?"

"Four."

Lyons shook his head. "You're a trial and a tribulation to me, Ryan."

"You want the report?" Red said.

"Did this encounter take place within the city limits?"

"No. It happened out near the Franklin Mountains."

"Thank God, then I don't need to hear your report. Tell it to the county sheriff."

"There is no county sheriff," Red said.

"I know," T. C. Lyons said.

CHAPTER THIRTY

Red Ryan and Buttons Muldoon ate a very early breakfast and then kicked their heels for a while until they figured it was time to rouse the town undertaker and arrange for Nascha's burial.

To their surprise, though it was still short of six in the morning, Thaddeus Wraith was already up and doing. Wearing the traditional black-as-a-raven's-wing frock coat and top hat of his melancholy profession, Wraith was a hopping little bird of a man with bright black eyes and a skin as white as parchment paper that never tanned in the Texas sun. The undertaker was washing his elaborate black and silver hearse when Muldoon drove the stage right into his front yard.

Wraith dropped the washing cloth into a bucket of soapy water, dried his hands on the skirt of his coat, and bobbed his way to the stage. He looked up at Red and said, "Good morning, sir, can I be of assistance? And may I say it's a fine morning to be alive."

"It's fine to be alive any morning," Red said.

"Just so," Wraith said. He smiled, revealing teeth as

big and yellow as ivory piano keys. "And what can I do for you this fine day?"

"I have a burying for you, undertaker," Red said.

"Ah, yes, of course. What other reason would you have for visiting the premises of Thaddeus Wraith? And the whereabouts of the deceased loved one?"

"In the stage, and we have to get him out of there," Red said. "I'm coming down."

Ryan climbed down from the box and opened the stage door. Wraith looked inside, hesitated a moment, then withdrew his head.

"Do my eyes deceive me, or is that an Apache gentleman?"

"Yes, Jicarilla."

Wraith looked pensive and then said, "There are few surprises in my profession, but being asked to bury a savage in the city's Concordia Cemetery must be listed among them."

"You don't want to do it?" Red said.

"Why, of course I want to do it, is that not my calling in life? Am I not the caretaker of the dead?" Wraith said. "Ah . . . judging by the deceased's face, his death was not a peaceful one."

"He was lynched by a mob yesterday," Red said.

"I heard a commotion and I knew something was afoot, but a lynching . . . how utterly horrible."

"So, you'll do the job?" Red said.

"Yes, I will, and at cost, dear sir," Wraith said. "At cost, mind you."

"Send the bill to Sheriff Lyons," Red said.

"That is most satisfactory," the little undertaker said. "Now it so happens, that I have a nice grave already dug, awaiting a lucky occupant. I believe it will fit the deceased most comfortably. Do you have a casket preference, Mister—"

"Ryan. Red Ryan, shotgun guard. And just joining us here is my associate and driver, Mr. Muldoon. We work for the Patterson and Son Stage and Express Company."

"And it's an honor to meet you both. I'm very fond of members of the stagecoach profession, especially shotgun guards. I've buried quite a number of them in my day. Now, about the casket, Mr. Ryan?"

"Pine box," Red said. He saw Wraith's face fall and added, "It's all Sheriff Lyons can afford."

"Here, undertaker, how come you have a grave all ready?" Buttons said. "Is it so you're always ready for future customers, huh?"

"Ah, no, stage driver. The vacant grave involves a morality tale that can teach us all a lesson about life and death," Wraith said.

"And what mought that be, if'n you don't mind me asking," Buttons said.

"Simply that you can flee the Grim Reaper, but you can't outrun him," Wraith said. He saw confusion in Button's face and said, "The gent who was to occupy the grave was thought to have died, and his wife had the hole dug and whiskey, rum, beer, and chocolate cake ordered for the wake. But, to everyone's surprise, the presumed deceased recovered consciousness, an occurrence the local Catholic priest called a miracle and the doctor called a damned mystery because he was sure the gent had been as dead as a doornail."

"And the wife asked you to plant him anyway, so not to spoil a good wake, not with all that whiskey, rum, and beer on order," Buttons said.

"Well, I can hardly bury a gent alive. But I must confess that the wife was not pleased by her husband's return to the land of the living," Wraith said. "By all accounts he was an abusive drunk and a whore-monger, as future events would soon show, but she didn't advocate burying her spouse alive. Oh, dear me, no, that would have been quite illegal."

"Yeah, I can see how the law could frown on that," Buttons said.

Wraith's face thinned into a solemn gray mask, and then he said, "On the morning of the day following his resurrection, the gentleman in question fled El Paso with an eighteen-year-old whore and all the money in his bank account. As a farewell, he gave his wife a black eye and then told me where to shove my grave. 'Beware,' I told him in plain English, just as I'm speaking to you now, 'Death always rectifies his mistakes.' But instead of heeding me and falling to his knees in prayer, Archibald Scratcher, for, unlovely as it sounds, that was the gentleman's name, said, 'I'm out of here. The grim reaper will have to catch me first.'"

Shadows shrank as the sun rose in a pale sky, and nearby among the pine trees songbirds greeted the new day. Wraith had stopped talking, and now Buttons urged him to start again. "So, what happened to Archie?" he said.

"Alas, the tale grows even more poignant," Wraith said. "And stranger, much stranger."

"I'm listening," Buttons said. "Ain't you, Red?"

Ryan's head was bowed, concentrating on the cigarette building in his fingers. Without looking up he said, "Every word."

"Well then, I will proceed," the undertaker said.

"Now, imagine five miles to the north of us a tall cottonwood tree, and imagine a beautiful young Mexican woman standing under that tree. Now listen to the testimony of a teenaged whore named Mattie Wells that she presented to the county coroner." Wraith reached into his frock coat and produced a paper that he unfolded and read, "'The woman was Mexican all right, wearing an off-the-shoulder blouse that showed most of her tits. Unlike mine, they were big, real big. Well, Archie took a look at the woman, studied her tits and then mine, and told me to get lost. He pushed me off the mule, and I landed on my ass. He rode to the woman and she smiled at him. Well, she put her arms around Archie's neck, kissed him, and a second later he dropped dead at her feet. The woman didn't move or anything, she just stood and stared at me, kind of friendly, as if we were kin or something, and all the time that son of a— I mean to say, Archie was lying dead at her feet, his face turning blue. I don't know what happened to the woman, because I grabbed Archie's wallet and then caught up the mule and lit a shuck back to El Paso. And that's all I can tell you about Archie Scratcher.'"

Thaddeus Wraith refolded the paper and put it back in his coat. "I'm keeping this testimony for my memoirs," he said. He placed a bony hand on Buttons's shoulder and said, "My friend, death comes in many guises, from ravening wolf to beautiful woman, be prepared and know that escape is impossible."

"Hey, what happened to Archie's body?" Buttons said. "Didn't you go looking for it so the widow could have the party?"

"In accordance with Mrs. Scratcher's wishes, yes, indeed I did," Wraith said. "Apparently, Mr. Scratcher had been torn to pieces, by wild animals or some other agency I know not which. I took a few scraps of bone and hair to the widow in a clock box, but she said she wasn't paying to bury a couple of ounces of dead husband and to throw it away, which I did."

Red Ryan said, "Well now a better man will lie in Archie's grave." He took a medal the size of a silver dollar from his pocket and handed it to Wraith. "Pin this on his shirt, he won it in the wars."

A small, mean-spirited man with thin lips clamped shut tight as a steel purse had drifted close to Red and overheard what he had just said. His name was Miles Landis, and he was one of Wraith's four assistants. At the first opportunity, he stole away in the direction of the saloons, determined to cause trouble.

And he did.

Chapter Thirty-one

The Platte River Saloon and Dance Hall was owned by a former rum and sugar, and slave importer by the name of Snow Jackson, a mean, violent lowlife who catered to others of the same breed. Of all the saloons in El Paso, the worst dive was the Platte, and more men had been rolled, stabbed, or shot in its adjoining alley than the town's other drinking establishments combined. It was a place for hard, dangerous men and, apart from the occasional rube attracted to its gambling, cheap whores, and cheaper whiskey, those were its clientele.

Big Jim Black, a moody, menacing, obscenely savage fist, boot, and skull fighter and named gunman, reigned as the dark lord of the Platte, feared by all, loved by none. Standing four inches over six feet, he was massive in the shoulders and chest, with huge hands and fingers like steel grappling hooks. His hair and eyes were the color of green slime, and his soul was a cesspit of mortal sin. There was no humanity in him, no pity, no love, no tenderness, just a scalding hatred for humanity, man, woman, and child, that ran

in his veins like liquid fire. In his thirty-five years of
life Big Jim had killed seven men with his bare hands,
crippled five more, shot a dozen other gunmen, one
of them Dawson G. Taylor, the famed Houston gunfighter and bounty hunter who'd boasted eight kills
and three shared. A whispered rumor persisted that
Black had murdered several women, all of them
whores he was pimping, but that was never confirmed,
and no one ever brought up the subject within his
hearing.

When Miles Landis slunk into the Platte, Jim Black
was partaking of his morning bourbon and cigars in
the company of Seth Roper. The two gentleman
gunfighters had similar interests, desires, and ambi-
tions, and they dominated the saloon with their mere
presence.

Landis sidled up to Black, and the gunman looked
down at him with distaste, as though he was studying
a louse. So great was the little undertaker's agitation
and eagerness to be seen as a person of importance
bearing urgent news, Landis spoke to Black first, a
severe breach of etiquette that was noticed even by
the hungover and insignificant morning crowd, the
more influential sporting set still abed.

"Mr. Black, did ye hear?" Landis said.

It took a while for Black to answer while Roper
stood aloof and a little irritated by the unwelcome
intrusion of a nobody.

"Hear what?" Black said, a volume of disrespect and
disdain in just two words.

"They're planning to bury that hung Apache in
the white folk's cemetery," Landis said. "I work for
Thaddeus Wraith the undertaker and overhead them
all talking about it."

Roper's ears perked up, and he said, "Who's planning to bury him there?"

"I don't know their names, but it's two stagecoach fellers," Landis said.

"Then I'm betting the farm that it's Red Ryan and Buttons Muldoon," Roper said, smiling.

"I dunno," Landis said. "Two stagecoach fellers, that's all."

Normally Big Jim Black wouldn't have given a tinker's cuss where the Apache was buried, but he listened to the outraged murmurs of the saloon patrons and wondered if it would be good for his reputation to get involved.

"Today redskins, tomorrow niggers," one half-drunk rooster said. "That's how it happens."

"My brother is buried in Concordia. I don't want him lying beside no damned Apache," said another man.

"Damned disgrace," said a third, slamming his fist on the bar for emphasis. "The Apache murdered an army officer at the fort and cut off his head is what he done."

Then, a rube in a celluloid collar and striped mustard and green tie said, "What we gonna do about it, Mr. Black?"

Two things pleased Black about that question. One was the respectful use of "Mr. Black," the other the unspoken acknowledgment that he was the leading citizen of El Paso.

Black considered his options, then made up his mind.

"There will be no murdering savage buried at Concordia," he said. "And I'll kill any man who tries."

This drew a cheer, but Seth Roper said nothing. He was highly amused. Lucian Carter had stuck a knife in

Major Morgan's back and then created the indignant uproar that had ended in the lynching of the Apache scout. By rights, Carter should bury the Indian. But Roper thought this a fine way to get rid of Ryan at no risk to himself. The redheaded shotgun guard had been a thorn in his side for too long.

From his towering height, Jim Black looked down at Landis and said, "What's your name?"

Flattered that the great man would ask him such a question, the little undertaker's assistant smiled and said, "Miles Landis, Mr. Black, but everybody calls me Landy."

"Landis, get back to the undertaker and when the Apache's body is about to leave for Concordia, come tell me," Black said.

"Be an hour or so, I think," Landis said.

"Come tell me," Black said. "Now get the hell out of here."

The railroad clock on the saloon wall claimed it was two minutes after ten when Miles Landis burst into the saloon and yelled, "They're on their way!"

Big Jim Black nodded, drained his whiskey glass, and pushed away from the bar. "Let's go," he said to the expectant crowd and, cheering, they followed him out of the saloon.

Seth Roper tagged along, grinning. This was going to be fun.

CHAPTER THIRTY-TWO

The main entrance to the Concordia Cemetery, where in 1895 John Wesley Hardin would be buried, is on Yandell Street, in Jim Black's day only a ten-minute walk from the Platte River saloon. Black gathered more gawkers as he walked purposefully toward the graveyard, and a few of the more excited, or drunk, fired shots into the air, announcing the coming of the man who would see justice done and the Apache lovers banished from Concordia and possibly El Paso itself.

Red Ryan and Buttons Muldoon had walked behind the hearse to the open grave, and now they watched as Thaddeus Wraith and a helper man-handled the pine box to the edge of the deep, rectangular hole.

Alerted by the random shots, Buttons looked toward the cemetery gate and said, "Red, we got company."

Red nodded. "Seems like. I didn't think the Apache was so popular."

Like a gunfighter Moses heading for the Red Sea, Jim Black led his raucous followers through the cemetery to the gravesite. The big gunman dismissed Wraith, considered Buttons for a moment, then settled on Red.

"You ain't burying that murdering savage here," he said. "Git the box back in the hearse and take him elsewhere."

"There is no elsewhere," Red said.

"The hell there isn't," Black said. "You got the whole of Texas to bury that animal. Go somewhere far and dig a hole."

"I got a hole already dug," Red said. "I don't need another." He turned to Wraith. "Bury him."

The undertaker hesitated, his fearful eyes on Black, who was unused to such open defiance and was on a slow burn. "Undertaker, try to put the savage in that grave, and I'll kill you," he said.

Wraith hopped back from the pine box, uncertain of how to proceed and now thoroughly frightened.

Red's own anger flared. "Hell, let me do it," he said.

"Touch that box and you're a dead man," Black said.

"And you go to hell," Red said.

A crowd of close to a hundred people watched the action, their excitement-hungry eyes moving expectantly from Ryan to Black and back again. A deadly insult had just been thrown by the redheaded man, and they knew Black would not let it stand. He did not disappoint them.

Big Jim considered going to the gun, but decided against it. When he outdrew and shot the redhead there were some who might see it as murder, and that would be inconvenient. Besides, the crowd wanted a show and Black wanted the insolent stagecoach driver, or whatever the hell he was, dead. Best do it with his hands. Black looked Red over . . . a little over six feet, good chest and shoulders, big, flat-knuckled fists that spoke of punching power . . . the man would be a handful, but he'd outfought and killed bigger, tougher men, and Black had no doubt he could beat the redhead. No, not beat him, pound him into a pulp, hit him hard again and again . . . and kill him with the final blow.

"What the hell is your Indian-loving name, mister?" Black said.

"Red Ryan, shotgun guard of the Patterson and Son Stage and Express Company."

"You've got a bandage on your head," Black said. "That supposed to get my sympathy?"

Red reached up, slid the bandage off his head, and tossed it away. "Any time you're ready," he said.

"Well, Mr. Ryan, it seems I have to beat some manners into you," Black said. He took off his coat and gave it to an onlooker, and then his cartridge belt and holstered Colt. "Do you have the sand for a fistfight or are you showing yellow, all wind and piss?"

Red didn't answer that question. He saw Seth Roper in the crowd and said, "Roper, are you taking a hand in this?"

The man shook his head. "Ryan, this is between you and Mr. Black. But, if you want my advice you'd better pick up your dead Apache friend and walk away from this. Jim is way too much for you with fists or a gun."

That last brought cheers and catcalls from the crowd, and somebody yelled, "Go get him, Big Jim!"

Black looked arrogant and sure, his knotty fists bunched, a fighting man confident in himself and his ability to maim and kill with his bare hands. He looked huge, a giant with enormous strength and ability who would absorb all kinds of punishment and still be standing when the fight was over and his opponent lay bloody and beaten at his feet.

Of course, what Black didn't know was that as a booth fighter, Red Ryan had taken on all comers and had fought men as big and mean as Black to a standstill. Red had not trained for years and had lost a step or two in quickness, but he was still a powerful puncher and as tough and durable as they come. And he had sand.

Red unbuckled his gunbelt and handed it to Buttons Muldoon, and the driver whispered, "Red, he's awful big."

"I know he is," Red said.

"Maybe we should take the Apache somewhere else."

"No, we bury him here," Red said. "He's already suffered one wrong, and I won't do him another."

"Red, I don't want to bury you here with him," Buttons said. "Hell, look at the size of that man."

"He's a man mountain, all right," Red said. "Well, I guess it's time to read to him from the book."

Red stepped forward, eager to get this uncertain thing over. As he came in, Black landed a stiff right jab to his face followed by a swinging left that missed. But the jab landed squarely on Red's chin and there was power behind the punch, cautioning Red that his opponent was a man to be reckoned with.

Red used his footwork, for the moment keeping his distance, but Black pressed the action. The big man missed with a right and Red countered with a jab, but a sudden, lightning-quick straight left by Black landed on the button and dropped Red like a felled oak. He landed on his back, his wounded head reeling, and

Black came in with the boot. With a sickening *thud* a vicious kick slammed into Red's ribs, and as he tried to roll away Black's boot swung again. The toe caught Red's left temple, a kick that rocked him, and searing lightning bolts flashed in his head. Grimly hanging on to consciousness, he tried to get to his feet and failed. Now he was down on all fours, vulnerable to another kick from Black, and the big man grinned and came in for the kill.

Buttons intervened and saved Red Ryan's life.

He ran to Red, grabbed him under the armpits, and hauled him to his feet.

Black, confident, sure of the fight, stood back with his hands on his hips and laughed, and the crowd laughed with him. But then the big man's face hardened, and he said, "Do that again, stagecoach man, and when this fight is over and he's dead, I'll beat your damned face in."

"Buttons, leave me be," Red said, angry now as he jerked out of Buttons's grasp. He raised his fists and covered up. "When you're ready."

Black shook his head and then yelled, laughing, to the crowd, "Well, you all heard the man. And I'm good and ready."

He came in swinging and connected with a hard right that rocked Red on his heels and made scarlet-stained saliva erupt from his mouth. Black smelled blood and grinned. He threw another hard right that barely missed, glancing off Red's head. Trying to drop Red again, a wild left hook by Black flew over Red's bobbing head and for a moment the big man was off balance. Red jabbed, a hard right and a left, and then quickly danced away. The crowd gasped. The unthinkable had happened. Black was bleeding heavily from a cut over his right eye. Enraged, the big man dashed away scarlet gore with the back of his hand and then came in swinging, looking for a knockout. Red avoided the wild punches and his straight right snapped Black's head back. And then another and another. The big man had been hit hard, and he knew it. And so did the crowd. Now there were a few people cheering for Red, and more joined them when Red threw a pair of hard lefts that connected, and his superior footwork paid off when Black caught air with his answering right and then gasped, openmouthed, when Red connected with a hard shot to the big man's belly.

Red Ryan had recovered from the beating he'd taken earlier. Now he was in his element, the boxing skills he'd learned in all those fights as a professional pugilist coming back to him. Hell, suddenly he was enjoying himself.

Black was fast running out of steam, and he knew he had to end this. It seemed that the redhead was made of iron. Black connected with a right to Red's forehead that the smaller man shrugged off, countering with hard lefts as Black backpedaled, seemingly with no answers to Red's punches. Red blocked the big man's powerful right-hand shot, a case of too little, too late, and then charged and landed two rights to Black's face. The big man hung tough and connected with a left hook that staggered Red, hurting him. But he recovered and nailed Black with a fast, powerful left to the chin that dropped him. The crowd gasped as the big man struggled to his feet, but Red Ryan was relentless. He nailed Black with another left that staggered him, but the big man countered with a flurry of punches that Red easily blocked. Sensing that Black was tiring, Red stalked the big man, and when Black telegraphed a looping left, Red stepped inside and nailed him with a massive right uppercut to the chin. The big man's legs went out from under him, and his lights went out. He sprawled unconscious on the ground and lay as still as a dead man.

Insanity in individuals is rare, but in a mob, it's the rule. The crowd's hero was down and now, out of its mind with adulation, it hailed his conqueror. In fact, many cheered when Red, hurting from the top of his head to his toes, said to Thaddeus Wraith, "Bury the Indian and get this damned thing over."

The undertaker, looking at Red as though he was suddenly afraid of him, sprang to his work, and he and his assistant prepared to lower the coffin into the grave.

But Jim Black was not yet done.

The big man's coat had been folded neatly and placed on the ground, his holstered Colt laid on top. The gun would help him save face, otherwise he knew he was finished in El Paso and probably in every other town. The cut above his eye dripping blood, Black crawled on all fours for his revolver. His battered face took on a demonic expression as he drew the Colt from the leather. Ryan had his back turned to him. No, a shot in the back would not look good to the crowd. Better to give it to him in the belly.

"Ryan!" Black yelled.

Red turned, and an instant later a single gunshot hammered apart the morning.

CHAPTER THIRTY-THREE

Big Jim Black rode a .45 bullet into hell. It was a beautiful shot, right in the middle of the forehead, and the man who pulled the trigger . . . was Seth Roper.

Red Ryan took in the situation at a glance, as did the gawking, unbelieving crowd.

Roper holstered his gun and said, "I won't see any man shot in the back."

It was bald-faced lie.

Killing Black had been on Roper's mind for a while, his ace in the hole. If things didn't work out as planned with the widow Morgan, he'd take Black's place as the premier gunman in El Paso with all the financial and social gains that implied. As an alternative scheme, it was strictly second best, but Roper had figured all the angles and it would do for now.

Red Ryan was stunned and puzzled. He buckled on his gun and then stepped to Roper. "Why?" he asked.

"You heard what I said, Ryan."

"Not allowing a man to be shot in the back wasn't the reason," Red said.

Roper shrugged. "Believe what you want."

"You saved my life," Red said.

"Yeah, I did, didn't I?"

"I'm beholden to you."

"Don't let it prey on your mind, Ryan. I would've done it for anybody."

"But not for me, unless you thought you had something to gain."

Roper smiled. "Like I said, believe whatever the hell you want. Now bury your Indian. Killing a man before breakfast makes me hungry, and steak and eggs are calling me."

Roper turned away and flung over his shoulder, "I did you a favor, Ryan."

"I know you did," Red said.

"I'll call it in one day," Roper said.

He walked away, and the crowd, abuzz with excitement, followed him, eager for breakfast in the same restaurant as the town's new premier gunslinger. The Apache was forgotten.

"In the end, they didn't care where the hell we buried the Indian," Buttons said.

"Seems like," Red said.

Buttons shook his head. "There's just no telling about folks."

"They have a new hero. Now Seth Roper is the biggest, baddest man in El Paso."

"You spoke to him, why did he save your life?"

"You heard him, he didn't want to see me shot in the back."

"Hell, Red, he hates your guts. You tried to get him hung, remember."

"I know. The whole sorry business has me buffaloed," Red said.

Thaddeus Wraith called out, "Mr. Ryan, Mr. Muldoon, you wish to say a word before we place earth on the dear departed?"

Red, light-headed and hurting all over, and Buttons stepped to the graveside, and Red said, "Anybody know an Apache prayer?"

"Do Apaches pray?" Wraith said.

"I don't know," Red said.

"We really should say something," Wraith said. "I mean, it's the Christian thing to do."

"He's not a Christian," Red said. "But you're right. We should say something." He took off his derby and said, "Well, by all accounts this Apache was a brave man, and he's got a medal on his chest to prove it. May he ride forever in the happy hunting grounds. Amen."

"Amen," Buttons said.

"Very nice," Wraith said. "Amen."

CHAPTER THIRTY-FOUR

"I'm so sorry, Mrs. Morgan," the Southern Pacific ticket agent said, "but the Younger Creek trestle bridge was long overdue for repair."

"Then how much longer must I wait?" Stella Morgan said. She wore widow's weeds and a vexed expression. "You do know that I buried my dear husband in the fort cemetery this morning, and I am anxious to visit his grieving loved ones in Washington."

"Another three days, dear lady," the clerk said. He looked harried, his pince-nez glasses askew on his nose. "And possibly a day longer."

"This is intolerable," Stella said, her anger rising. "Do you know what it's like to be stuck in this hellhole of a town?"

"Indeed, I do," the clerk said. "Man and boy, I've always lived in El Paso." He smiled, revealing yellow teeth. "It's not so bad when you get used to it."

"I'd never get used to it," Stella said. "Never in a hundred years."

She turned her back on the clerk and stormed out

of the ticket office onto the platform, Lucian Carter trailing behind her.

"We can wait it out, Stella," Carter said. "Now that the Indian is dead and buried, no one can pin your husband's murder on us."

"On you, Lucian. You mean on you, not me."

"Yes, I killed him, but I was following your orders," Carter said.

Stella's smile was vicious. "And who is going to believe that? I play the grieving widow very well, remember?" She saw Carter's hostile reaction and said, "Lucian, I'm only teasing you. Of course, we're in the clear, and I mean both of us. It's only . . . well, it's this awful town that's getting on my nerves, making me say things I don't mean."

"I would never betray you, Stella," Carter said. "Never."

"No, I don't believe you ever would." The woman took Carter's hand and placed it on her left breast. "I will always keep you here, Lucian, in my heart."

The platform was deserted, and Carter was in no hurry to remove his hand. Finally, Stella took his wrist and pushed it away. She smiled, "Later, Lucian, when we're alone, maybe tomorrow or the next day."

Carter looked as though he'd tasted something bitter. "We're never alone. It seems that Seth Roper is always lurking around."

Stella smiled. "Jealous, Lucian?"

"You bet I'm jealous."

"Don't be. Roper means nothing to me. I wouldn't let him touch me."

"Then why is he still around?"

"Because I am beset by enemies, that redheaded

stagecoach shotgun guard for one, and I might need Roper's gun."

"You don't need Roper, Stella. I can take care of Red Ryan."

"No, Lucian. We've got to arrive in Washington clean, as though we'd just stepped away from John's muddy grave and washed our feet in our tears. Let Roper handle Ryan." She lowered a black veil over her face, took Carter's arm, and said, "Now shall we promenade back to the hotel and let El Paso see the grieving widow dressed all in black . . . with a bright red corset underneath?"

As they walked down the paved incline that lead from the station, Stella turned her beautiful face to Carter and said, "There is one thing I forgot to mention, Lucian."

"And what is that?"

"Please return the carpetbag to my room."

Carter stopped mid-stride. "You don't trust me?"

"Of course, I trust you, silly," Stella said, smiling. "But there are many outlaws and crooks in El Paso, and the bag will be safer with me. I mean, who would dare try to steal from the room of a dead army hero's widow?"

"Any man tries to take the carpetbag, I'll kill him," Carter said.

"No, I told you, I don't want shootings before we leave for Washington," Stella said. "You will return the bag, and I'll keep it safe, Lucian, and there's an end to it."

"What the hell . . ." Carter said. His eyes were fixed ahead of him.

Then Stella Morgan saw what he saw . . . Seth

Roper marching at the head of a hundred-strong crowd of noisy people.

She and Carter stopped to let the crowd pass, and Stella was relieved when Roper politely touched his hat brim to her as he passed, as though they were not close acquaintances . . . or lovers.

Carter stopped a man as he passed and asked what the hell was going on. The man grinned and said, "Didn't you hear? Seth Roper killed Big Jim Black." He pulled free of Carter's restraining hand and said, "There's a hell of an excitement in this town."

After the crowd passed, Carter said, "Well, Stella, no killing, huh?"

"I'm sure it was justified," Stella said. "Seth Roper knows how high the stakes are in this game."

"Game? It's no game," Carter said. "The sooner we get out of El Paso the better, or the whole plan could come tumbling down around our ears."

"You're being alarmist, Lucian," Stella said. "You heard the ticket agent. Three more days and we can leave."

"What about Roper?"

"What about him?"

"He's attracting too much attention, and that attention could be bad news for you and me. Hell, Stella, Roper knows too much."

"The only law in El Paso is that idiot, the marshal. He blamed my husband's killing on the Apache, didn't he? He's hardly going to pin it on you now."

"If Roper finds himself in a corner, he could blab."

"Blab about what? He's in too deep himself for that. He helped plan John's death, didn't he?"

"Still, I wish you would let me gun him," Carter said.

"No, Lucian. I want Seth Roper in Washington with

us. He's a killer, and I may have need of his future services."

Stella Morgan lay naked in bed and stared at the plastered ceiling. Without turning her head, she said, "Lucian wants to kill you. Did you know that?"

Seth Roper grinned. "A lot of men want to kill me."

"We need him for a while longer," Stella said. She sounded drowsy.

Roper kissed the woman's sweat-damp shoulder. "Why?"

"I don't know. We might need him to take care of Red Ryan."

"This morning I saw Ryan beat Jim Black to a pulp with his fists. He's dangerous, more dangerous than I thought."

Stella turned and leaned on her elbow. "Why should Ryan concern himself with what we do? I mean, it's no business of his."

"Hanging the Indian troubled him. He knew the man was innocent. And on top of that, he's a do-gooder who wants to keep his halo polished, all nice and shiny."

"Do you think he knows that it was Lucian who killed my husband?"

"I doubt it."

"Could he find out?"

"Only if Carter tells him."

"Seth, Carter is a weak link. He's jealous of you, and jealous men do foolish things. Push him hard enough and he could spill the beans."

"I'll get rid of Carter," Roper said. "Don't worry about it."

"What about Ryan?"

"Him too."

"It's got to look good. When we arrive in Washington I don't want any lawmen on our trail."

"There won't be. You can trust me on that."

"Did you look in the carpetbag?"

"I know what's in it."

"We'll live well, Seth, you and I."

"Maybe we'll get hitched, huh?" Roper said, pulling Stella closer to him.

"Marriage is in the cards, yes, but not to you, Seth. I have other plans."

"Then you plan to marry well," Roper said, his throat tight

"Marry into more money, you mean. I disposed of one husband, I can dispose of others. No one plays the grieving widow better than me."

"You mean, I'll dispose of others," Roper said.

"Yes, you will, and you'll continue to share my bed. We'll have to be discreet, that's all."

Roper grinned. "Well, we don't need to be discreet tonight."

"No, we don't." Stella pushed herself against Roper. "So let's be indiscreet again," she said.

CHAPTER THIRTY-FIVE

"Oh, Mr. Ryan, we came as soon as we heard," Edna Powell said. She and Rhoda Carr had barged into Red Ryan's small hotel room like a couple of forty-gun frigates under full sail.

"Heard what, Mrs. Powell?" Red said.

"That you'd been in a fistfight with a dreadful man and that there had been a shooting," Edna said. "Corporal Powell is most distressed."

"And so is Corporal Carr, and so am I," Rhoda said. She threw up her hands in horror. "Lordy, look at your face and your poor head! Bring the medical supplies, Edna."

"How did you hear about the fight?" Red said.

"Hear about it! It's all anyone's talking about!" Rhoda said. "Corporal Carr said that he heard from a sergeant who heard it from an eyewitness. They say you were at the cemetery and took on a giant of a man and gave him a good thrashing."

"And then the giant of a man got himself shot," Red said.

"We heard that too," Edna said. "One ruffian shooting

another over where to bury the savage that murdered poor Major Morgan. Hold on, Mr. Ryan, this will sting."

And it did.

"Here's more stinging stuff," Edna said, applying liberal doses of brown liquid to his cut and bruised face. "Did you know that dear Mrs. Morgan fainted at the major's funeral this morning and had to be revived with Rhoda's smelling salts, poor thing? She didn't like the salts very much, and who can blame her? Now let us take a look at your head, Mr. Ryan. My, my, but you're a brave little soldier. When I tell Corporal Powell, he'll be very proud of you."

Red suffered the further ministrations of the two women in silence. The proceedings were closely watched by Buttons Muldoon, who visited his room smelling of rye whiskey and faintly of cheap perfume.

Red refused a bandage for his head, but Edna insisted that he take a spoonful of Dr. Lawson's Tonic and Vitality Restorer. "It will make you feel better in no time, Mr. Ryan," she said. "Corporal Powell swears by it."

Since the tonic was about ninety-nine percent alcohol, Red had no difficulty in swallowing the concoction, and Edna and Rhoda left, happy in the knowledge that they'd restored him to, as Rhoda said, "rude, good health."

After the door closed on the two women, Buttons said, "I got news."

"Have you been drinking?" Red said.

"Yes, I have, and you'll want a drink too when I tell you what I'm gonna tell you."

Red smiled. "Then tell me. And you smell like perfume."

"That's another story," Buttons said.

"All right, then tell me your good news first, the story later," Red said.

"I didn't say it was good news, Red. It's bad news."

"Then I don't want to hear it."

"Well, it's only kinda bad."

"All right, so I'll only half listen," Red said.

"The Indian is gone," Buttons said.

"What?"

"Somebody took him. Left the pine box and stole the Indian."

"How do you know?" Red said, horrified.

"Sheriff Lyons told me."

"How did he find out?"

"The feller who helped the undertaker lost a fob from his watch and he went back up to the cemetery to look for it. He didn't find the watch fob and then he couldn't find the Indian. Poof! Gone!"

Someone pounded on the door, and Buttons said, "I bet that's Lyons. He said he was coming to see you."

"Open the door, Buttons," Red said, sitting on the bed. "Let's hear what he has to say."

Marshal T. C. Lyons's opening remarks were short, sweet, and to the point. "Ryan, you look like hell. Are you ever going to leave El Paso?"

"Soon, after I get a few things sorted out," Red said.

"How soon is soon?" Lyons said. "No, don't answer that. Soon is when six men carry you by the handles to Concordia Cemetery. You make a habit of sticking your nose into other people's business, Ryan, and in this town, that's not healthy. Hell, are you going to offer me a drink or not?"

"Buttons, over there on the table. Pour the sheriff a drink and one for me."

"And one for yourself," Buttons said. "Thanks for asking."

Lyons sat in the only chair in the room and when he was settled, Red said, "You came to tell me about the Apache."

"Later. First, let's talk about the prank you played at the cemetery with the dead Indian and then the fistfight with Big Jim Black—"

"I won that fight, but barely," Red said.

"Yeah, looking at your face I can believe it. And then Seth Roper plugs Black to save your life, and him a man that's got no love for you, Ryan. How do you explain that?"

"I can't," Red said.

"Me neither. But from what I hear, Roper is on the brag at the Platte River saloon, and suddenly he's the biggest man in El Paso. Maybe that's why he shot Black, to clear the way for himself."

"Could be, Sheriff. Now what about the Indian?"

"Somebody dug him up," Lyons said.

"Who?"

"Ryan, stick a pin anywhere in a list of the names of every gent in this town and you've got your man."

"Will you go looking for the body, Sheriff?" Red said.

"Look? Where?"

"I don't know. Around."

"If the Apache's body is within the city limits, I'll find it. If it's outside the city limits I'll leave it to—"

"I know, the county sheriff," Red said.

"You finally got your saddle on the right hoss, Ryan. You're a slow learner, but once you learn a thing, you don't forget it." Lyons drained his glass and stood. He eyed Red with little affection and said, "Here's how it's coming down. You got three days to leave El Paso, and I'm being generous because I'm too kindhearted for my own good. Maybe you and your driver can pick up some passengers in that time, or maybe not. But starting tomorrow you're on notice."

"And suppose I don't want to leave, what then?" Red said. His quick temper simmered.

"Then, I'll toss you in the lockup and throw away the key."

Buttons became suddenly belligerent. "On what charge?" he said.

Lyons's smile was as thin as a fiddle string. "Gee, I'm glad you asked that, stagecoach man, because I've got a crackerjack charge just for Ryan . . . *incitement to riot,* in accordance with the Texas Penal Code of 1850. I read all about it in a lawbook just this morning." Lyons slapped his hands together and did a little jig. "Hell, boy, I could keep you behind bars for years."

"What riot did I . . . say that word again," Red said.

"Incite. Incite is a ten-dollar law word," Lyons said.

"I didn't incite a riot," Red said.

"Yes, you did. By burying an Indian in Concordia, you incited the assemblage of seven or more persons and created an immediate danger of damage to property or injury to persons. Well, property was damaged by a drunken mob breaking a mirror in the Platte River saloon, and Big Jim Black was injured by you in a brawl and was then shot and killed." Lyons shook his head. "If that sorry business over the Indian wasn't inciting a riot, I don't know what was." He glared at Buttons. "And, Muldoon, knowingly participating in a riot is a serious offense, so you're not off the hook."

Red smiled. "Lyons, you'll never make all that stick in court."

"And that's where you're wrong," Lyons said. "Earlier today I talked with Judge Azariah J. Thorndike the Third and he said that in fifty years of presiding over courts he's never tried an incitement-to-riot case before, but he reckons he might well deliver a fifteen-year sentence, and possibly a hanging, as a warning to others. He's very keen to get started."

Lyons stepped to the door.

"Ryan, you and Muldoon study on that for a spell and let me know what to tell Judge Thorndike. Bless him, he's eighty-three years old, and his heart is set on a trial. He'll be very disappointed if you don't decide to stay in town."

CHAPTER THIRTY-SIX

Red Ryan was tired out from the events of the day and he didn't let the dire warning from T. C. Lyons stop him from falling asleep as soon as his battered head hit the pillow.

Awakened with a start a couple of hours later by a shuffling noise in his room, he sat up and reached for the Colt on the bed stand—but never made it. Rough hands dragged him from the bed, and a callused, horny palm covered his mouth as the muzzle of a gun was shoved into his belly.

"Make no sound, white man," a voice whispered in his ear.

Red's sleepy grogginess vanished as his eyes grew accustomed to the gloom, and he saw two Apaches in the room with him. Both wore blue cavalry shell jackets, one with shoulder boards, and Red wondered if they'd once belonged to soldiers of C Company's lost patrol. He had no time to ponder that question before he was dragged to his feet and one of the

Indians, a Winchester in his hands, said, "Get dressed. Quickly."

"You boys are making a big mistake," Red said. "I'm not army."

"Be silent, get dressed," the Apache with the rifle said.

Red did as he was told and then he was pushed toward the open window.

"Out," the Apache said.

"Hell, I'm on the second floor. You mean jump?" Red said.

"Out," the Indian said.

The young warrior looked as though he'd use the Winchester without hesitation, and Red stepped to the window and looked down into the darkness. An Apache sat a gray horse in the alley, holding the reins of three other mounts, and Red reckoned one of the ponies was for him. An irritated rifle prod in the ribs pushed him to climb out the window and drop to the ground. He landed hard on both feet and then fell forward on all fours, his head pounding from the effort. Immediately Red was joined by the two Apaches from his room, who landed soundlessly beside him, graceful as leaping panthers. Red's hands were tied behind his back and then he was hustled onto a horse. The other Indians mounted, one of them taking the reins of Red's pony, and they left the hotel at a walk, keeping to the shadows like gray ghosts.

Despite the closeness of blaring saloons and busy streets, the Apaches led Red Ryan out of El Paso unseen, and only when the lights of the town lay behind them did they push their horses into a canter, riding into the vast blackness of the night.

After an hour, hurting on a pony with a rough gait and bony back, Red saw a speck of red light in the distance, like a cinder glowing in the darkness. The light was a small fire, and around it sat three Apaches. One of them, who had thin gray braids, stood at his approach. Red was dragged from his horse and pushed toward the old man, his face a network of deep wrinkles, a sign of his age and a legacy of a lifetime spent under the merciless desert sun. At a short distance from the fire was a fresh grave the Apaches had covered in rocks, something they always did to protect a body from scavenging coyotes.

Now Red was surrounded by six Apaches, and the expressions on their faces revealed one thing in common . . . an implacable hatred for the white man and all he stood for. In later years, Red Ryan would say that he knew he was a dead man that night and his only hope was that he would not scream too much when the torture started. He'd no doubt that these Apaches had taken part in the attack on the Patterson stage and they blamed him for the death of Ilesh, their promising young war chief, and now he must pay the penalty.

Red felt fear ice his belly. *My God, how many days of torture must I endure?*

But this proved not to be the case, and his fears were unfounded.

The old Apache ordered the bonds removed from Red's wrists, and then he pointed to the grave and spoke. "My son Nascha lies in yonder grave. He was a great warrior." The old man turned his head and spat.

"You have my deepest sympathy," Red said, since he could think of nothing better.

"Red Ryan, you wished to bury my son with honor and fought the man who tried to stop you," the old man said. "We are in your debt." He spat again.

"But . . . but how do you know all this?" Red said.

The old warrior managed a thin smile. "The little people the white men don't notice, the ones that build your iron roads across the land. Like the Apache they are hated and not seen, and they come and go, and the Apache welcome them to our lodges for the news they bring." He spat.

"You mean the Chinese? They talk with you?" Red said.

"Does that surprise you so much? Have the little people not suffered much at your hands?" the old man said. He spat.

Now that torture seemed less likely, Red found his voice. "I don't think any Chinese have suffered at my hands," he said. "I assure you, if a Chinese or any other Oriental person wishes to be a passenger on a Patterson and Son Stage and Express coach, I will assure him that his safety and comfort would be the company's only concern."

The old Apache stared hard at Red and then said, "I no longer wish to talk with you, Red Ryan. The white man's language tastes as bitter as wormwood on my tongue." He spat and then walked away.

A moment later a young warrior emerged from the gloom leading a grulla mare wearing a cavalry saddle and bridle. "For you," he said. "Go now, and never come near the Apache again."

Red said, "Well, good luck to all of you."

But the fire was already extinguished and the Apaches were gone and he spoke only to the hollow darkness.

CHAPTER THIRTY-SEVEN

After the trials of the night, Red Ryan was still asleep in bed when Stella Morgan decided to take a morning promenade around El Paso on the arm of Lucian Carter. That decision, made on the spur of the moment, would set in motion events that would result in the deaths of two people and put Red on a collision course with destiny.

Stella was dressed in rustling black silk. Her bustle was even larger than those worn by the fashionable El Paso belles, her veiled hat smaller, and her milk-white décolletage more spectacular, a state of affairs that drew frowns from the respectable matrons of the town and furtive, appreciative looks from their husbands.

The West was then very much a Victorian society, and it was not proper for a recently widowed woman to flaunt herself in that way, but Stella, counting the hours until she could leave the godforsaken burg, didn't give a damn.

Then fate, in the form of an unloading brewer's dray that blocked the boardwalk, forced Stella and

Carter to cross the street. They passed an alley where a sign hung above a narrow, wooden store that proclaimed:

ISAK RABINOVICH
JEWELER TO THE GENTRY

~

☞ Masonic Watch Fobs
Always in Stock

Stella stopped, read the sign and said, "Oh, Lucian, let's go in."

Carter shrugged. "Sure, but don't expect too much. This is El Paso, remember, not New York."

"I know that, silly, but it could be amusing, and I might pick up something nice."

"Whatever you say." Carter smiled and bowed. "After you."

Isak Rabinovich's store was small, dingy, and dusty and that description also fit its owner, who was saved from being completely nondescript by a pair of bright blue eyes that were large and prominent, as though everything he saw startled him. His wife Raisa, at least twenty years younger than her husband, was small and plump with a mane of beautiful black hair that she piled on top of her head and held in place with pins.

Both had fled the Russian pogroms, settled for a while in Austin, and then moved to newly booming El Paso. Together they scratched out a living from the store because, childless, their needs were few. Raisa's feet had been frostbitten when, as a child, she'd hid under a farm wagon in the dead of winter as Cossacks pillaged her village. Never strong, she and Isak agreed that moving farther west had greatly improved her health. The couple was well liked in the town, and Raisa had a growing reputation as a cook, her *bubliki*, delicious little round breads, the stuff of legend.

When Stella Morgan and Lucian Carter stepped inside, Isak smiled and said, "And what can I do for such a beautiful lady?"

"And you are in mourning," Raisa said. Then, putting two and two together, "Why, you must be the lady wife of the officer who was murdered at the fort."

"Yes, I am," Stella said.

"Major Morgan was a fine man," Isak said. "I repaired a watch for him once, and he was a perfect gentleman."

"Yes, he was," Stella said. Then, with a straight face, "A perfect gentleman and a fine officer."

"We have a large selection of mourning jewelry," Isak said. "In the glass case here." Stella briefly glanced at some black-enameled rings, bracelets, and necklaces, and Isak said, "All are suitable for the first two to three years of the deep mourning period, Mrs. Morgan. I can change the black stones in the rings to jade, pearl, and then ruby over the course of the next ten years of half-mourning."

Stella felt a laugh bubbling to the surface and coughed it away before she looked over the shelves and said, "You have a great many clocks, Mr. ah . . ."

"Rabinovich. Yes, clock repair is a specialty of mine, and I get broken watches up and running in no time at all. Can I interest you in the rings in this case, Mrs. Morgan?" Isak said, moving to his left. "Perhaps one that can hold a lock of the deceased loved one's hair? These are German made and of high quality." He smiled. "I stock them mainly because Germany is so much kinder to Jews than my native Russia."

Stella wasn't listening, her eyes fixed on an oval cameo brooch of a goddess with a bow in her hand and stags at her feet. "Let me see that," she said, pointing at the glass dome that covered the piece. "Oh, I must have it."

"Ah, that is Diana, the Roman goddess of the hunt," Isak said. "It's made of onyx and gold, and it belonged to my wife's grandmother. It's the only thing of value we managed to smuggle out of Russia."

"Let me see," Stella said.

Isak brought the dome to the counter and removed the brooch. He didn't pass it to Stella but held it up where she could see it, and Raisa explained, "My grandmother was a midwife, and she delivered the baby of a Russian noblewoman whose name was Countess Isolda Mamatova. The delivery was a difficult one, and afterward the countess was so grateful that she'd given birth to a healthy son, she presented my grandmother with the brooch. It is beautiful, isn't it?"

"Yes, it is," Stella said. "It's exquisite, and I must have it. Name your price."

Raisa smiled. "I'm afraid it's not for sale. It's the only connection that Isak and I have with our family and our former lives. To us it's priceless."

Stella's face flashed annoyance. "Five hundred for the brooch, and that's more than you'll earn from this place in years."

Isak shook his head. "As my wife says, the goddess brooch is not for sale." He brightened. "But I do have another cameo, Italian made, that might interest you."

Stella glared at the little man and then turned on her heel and barged through the door. Carter lingered a moment and said, ice in his eyes, "Better for you two if you'd sold her the brooch."

"Since when did killing become such an easy thing, Lucian?" Stella Morgan said, smiling. "I mean when you want a thing, say, like the death of a husband, you just make it happen and in an instant all your problems are solved."

"Not getting caught is the hard part," Carter said.

"Only the stupid are caught, Lucian."

The man smiled, "Then it's just as well that we're smart."

Stella held the Diana cameo up to the hotel room's gas lamp. "This is beautiful. I can wear it for afternoon tea in Washington. It will set off a white blouse very nicely."

"They didn't want to part with it," Carter.

"But you convinced them otherwise."

"I stabbed the old man and then the woman. They didn't put up much of a fight."

"So, as I said, the killing was easy," Stella said.

"You could say that."

"Thank you for getting the cameo for me, Lucian. You're such a dear."

"It's easy to kill and get away with it in El Paso," Carter said. "Washington will be different."

"In what way?"

"It has an efficient police force and a detective

division. Murders still happen quite frequently, but usually among the lower classes."

"We'll become selective, Lucian, specialists if you will. Rich husbands who meet unfortunate accidents or fatal illnesses . . . you and Seth Roper must make it look good."

"Convincing, you mean?"

"Well, enough to convince the police," Stella said.

"My father trained me well in the ways of murder," Carter said. "Poison, carefully applied, is the weapon of the gentlewoman or gentleman. Seth Roper is a blunt instrument, a violent man who knows the gun and the garrote and little else. He will be of limited use in Washington."

Stella's laugh rang like a silver bell. "A blunt instrument, says the man who just used a knife to kill a couple of doddering old Jews."

"Two gunshots would have alerted everyone in the street. The job had to be done silently," Carter said. "The blade considerably lowers the risk of being caught in the act." He was silent for a while, and then said, "Stella, when we live in Washington the stakes must be higher, a lot higher. We don't murder someone for a five-hundred-dollar cameo."

"Leave that to me, Lucian," Stella said. "I'll raise the stakes high enough that we'll both be rich. As for Roper, he's a bodyguard, nothing more." She studied Carter and said, "Your jacket is torn and your pants are bloodstained. Get rid of them."

"Yes, I'll dump them somewhere," Carter said. "The old fool's struggles ruined my new tweed suit."

Stella smiled. "Who would have thought the old man to have had so much blood in him. *Macbeth*, act five, scene one."

"You know your Shakespeare, Stella. I'm surprised."

"Thanks to the stupidity of men, an education in art and literature is all a woman is allowed these days." She rose from her chair. "Ah, well . . ."

Stella crossed the floor and lay on her back in the bed. "Come, Lucian, you did something nice for me, now let me do something nice for you."

"I love you, Stella," Carter said. "At first, I didn't think I did, but I do now."

"How sweet," Stella said. She opened her arms. "Come get your reward, my dearest boy."

CHAPTER THIRTY-EIGHT

"Why are you telling me all this, Sheriff?" Red Ryan said, his fork poised over his plate in the steamy interior of Ma's Kitchen. "You said yourself that I'm not a lawman."

T. C. Lyons took time to order coffee before he answered with a question of his own. "Ryan, you know how many cuttings there's been in this town since I took over as Marshal?"

Chewing on bacon, Red shook his head.

"None," Lyons said. "El Paso is not a cutting town. Hell, even the whores use guns. Now, in the space of . . . what? . . . three days, three people have been stabbed to death. Don't you think that's a little unusual?"

"You don't think Major Morgan was killed by the Apache?" Red said.

"No, I don't, not any longer. And I think the same person that murdered Isak and Raisa Rabinovich did for the major."

Not that he was finished with his steak and eggs,

Buttons Muldoon spoke up for the first time. "Stretching it, ain't you, Lyons?"

"Maybe. But I have a feeling in my gut that I'm right."

"Tell me again what happened," Red said. "Just bear in mind that the murdered people were never passengers on a Patterson and Son stage and therefore not really my concern."

"All right, shotgun guard, then I'll talk to you only in your capacity as an unconcerned citizen," Lyons said.

"Then let's hear it," Buttons said.

"I never met them, but I'm told the Rabinovich couple were well liked in this town," Lyons said.

"No enemies of any kind?" Red said.

"None that I know of, but I'll get to a possible motive later. As far as I can tell from the bodies, they were killed sometime last night. Mr. Rabinovich always closed his shop at seven every evening, but last night it seems he opened the door to someone, their killer, after business hours."

"They live on the premises?" Red said.

"Yes, they have a small apartment in the back of the store."

"Who found the bodies?"

"A man named Harry Mandelbaum. Mrs. Rabinovich baked some kind of bread rolls for him that he picked up every morning when the store opened at eight."

"Does he have a good alibi?" Red said.

"The best. He's ninety years old and in poor health."

Lyons set down his coffee when a man threaded his way through the crowded restaurant then bent over and whispered something in the sheriff's ear. Lyons nodded and the man left.

"Harry Mandelbaum is dead," he said. "He was frail and I guess the shock of seeing his friends murdered was too much for his old ticker. Fifteen minutes ago, he keeled over and died in the Addams Apothecary store, where he was buying something for the ague. The undertaker is on the way." Lyons looked at Red. "As far as I'm concerned, Harry is the killer's third murder victim."

"Why would someone murder a harmless old couple?" Red said. "I mean, it doesn't make any sense, unless robbery was the motive."

"And robbery was the motive, Ryan. After Harry found the bodies he noticed something was missing, a cameo brooch, the kind women wear, that the Rabinovich couple kept under a glass dome."

"They were killed for a brooch?" Red said.

"Apparently," Lyons said. "The brooch was quite valuable, and it was Raisa Rabinovich's treasured possession. She said it once belonged to a Russian empress or some such." He drained his coffee cup. "Ryan, I want this killer found, and I want to see him hang."

"And for some reason I can't figure, you want my help," Red said.

"Then figure this . . . I trust you, and I believe you stand for law and order. Those are reasons enough, and here's another, I think you want to see this killer caught as badly as I do."

"Sheriff, just so you know, I stand for the Patterson and Son Stage and Express Company," Red said. "Buttons and me will be moving on in a few days."

Buttons said, "I'm right glad to hear that, Red. For a spell there, I thought you were thinking of settling down in El Paso, working in a mercantile maybe."

Lyons said, "I can't see you working in a mercantile, Ryan, or doing any kind of honest work. Listen up, the man who killed the old couple had some knife training. Isak Rabinovich was a tough old coot, and he fought for his life. It took five stab wounds to bring him down, all in the chest and belly. The man who killed him had used a knife before, and he took time to wash his hands at the pump, I noticed that from the blood splashes in the sink. He was a cool customer."

"And you think this same cool customer stabbed Major Morgan?" Red said.

"I think it's possible, and that's all I'm saying," Lyons said. "It's possible, no more than that."

Now Red Ryan did some thinking of his own. The death of Major Morgan benefited his wife enormously and Stella was a suspect in his mind . . . but would she have an old couple murdered for a trinket? No, it was unthinkable. Cold and calculating she may be, but Stella Morgan knew where to draw the line.

"Of course, could be I'm barking up the wrong tree," Lyons said. "Maybe the killer saw the brooch and figured it would make a nice present for a lady friend."

"There you go, Sheriff," Buttons said. "Find the lady, or maybe a whore, wearing the brooch and she'll lead you right to the killer." He smiled. "Case closed . . . and now it's high time me and Red lit a shuck out of this burg."

T. C. Lyons, an isolated man marooned in a sea of lawlessness, made one last plea for Red's help. "Ryan, give me a week. Your accommodation and grub will be provided at city expense. Help me find the killer of Isak and Raisa Rabinovich."

"Hell, Sheriff, what can I do that you can't do your

ownself?" Red said, frowning as a portly gent bumped into the back of his chair and made him spill coffee on his shirt. He wiped the coffee away with his napkin and said, "Besides, I've never been too keen on helping the law."

"Ryan, maybe you can do nothing, maybe everything. I'm the law in this town and a marked man, but you can go where I can't, talk to people, make inquiries. Also, if you get into a tight corner, you're handy with your dukes and a gun and I am not."

It came as a surprise to Lyons that Buttons Muldoon favored the idea.

"Free hotel and free grub right here at Ma's Kitchen for seven days," he said. "And a hundred dollars in gold when the murderer is caught. Those are Mr. Ryan's terms."

"Done and done," Lyons said.

Red said, "I don't think—"

"Red, we got to fatten up before we head back east," Buttons said. "A week will pass in no time. And besides, we can't leave a mad killer running loose in the streets. It just wouldn't be decent."

"Buttons, I hope you know what you're doing," Red said.

Buttons grinned. "You would have agreed to help anyway. I just negotiated better terms."

"Ryan, just to make things legal, I hereby deputize you as deputy sheriff," Lyons said. "I won't give you a star since you'll be working in secret as a detective."

"Thank God for that," Red said.

Buttons grinned and said, "Now that's all settled . . . Waiter! Burn me another steak . . . and send the bill to Sheriff Lyons!"

CHAPTER THIRTY-NINE

Rachel Tyler fixed her cameo brooch to the high collar of her white shirtwaist and studied herself in the mirror. Yes, along with a long red skirt, wide black belt, and high-heeled ankle boots she looked very ladylike, as befitted an aspiring physician.

"I won't be gone long, Papa," she said, walking into the dining room as she adjusted her hat. "I just want to buy a few things in El Paso."

Holt Tyler, dressed in dusty range clothes, looked up from his breakfast, smiled, and said, "You look just as pretty as your Ma did when she went to town."

Rachel gave a little curtsey. "Why, thank you. Is Manuel ready?"

"He's outside with the buggy. Be careful, Rachel, and don't talk to any strangers."

"Father, I think Manuel Cantero would shoot anybody who got within talking distance."

Tyler grinned. "I reckon he would do just that. You're still a little girl in pigtails as far as Manuel is concerned."

When Rachel stepped out to the buggy, Cantero

grinned. "You look real pretty today, Miss Rachel. I'll think I'll have to fight off the young El Paso bucks."

Rachel's smile acknowledged the vaquero's compliment. "Not the handsome ones, I hope," she said.

"Ah, those most of all," Cantero said. He was short, stocky, and had an ivory-handled Colt stuck into the waistband of his pants. The vaquero had killed five outlaws during his time on the ranch, and Holt Tyler trusted him implicitly.

"The New York Hat Shop first," Rachel said, as Cantero assisted her into the buggy. "And then the shoe store and then Madame Blanche's Gowns & Dainties and then . . . well, we'll see how our time goes."

If Manuel Cantero's heart sank, he was gentleman enough to not let it show.

At the same time Rachel Tyler left the Rafter-T, a man stepped off a C. Bain and Company stage in El Paso. He was short, only five-foot-six, and slight with careful brown eyes above a great beak of a nose and under that a trimmed, military mustache. He wore a brown ankle-length tweed overcoat, a ditto suit of the same color, a bowler hat, and elastic-sided boots. In the right-hand pocket of his coat he carried a .41 caliber self-cocking Colt that he'd used several times, twice resulting in a fatality for the other party. Phillip "Pip" Ogden was a forty-three-year-old San Antonio Police detective and by all appearances he was a mild-mannered man, but in the opinion of his contemporaries, crooks and police officers alike, "no meaner *hombre* ever drew breath." A human bloodhound, so far in his twenty-year career he'd sniffed out hundreds of lawbreakers and sent fifty-six of them to the gallows without a single moment of regret. As fate would have it, Pip Ogden was soon to cross paths with Rachel Tyler and Red Ryan, Rachel for the better, but Red for the worse . . . much, much worse.

Rachel Tyler found nothing that suited her in the New York Hat Shop, but Madam Blanche's was a different matter. After two hours of shopping, Manuel Cantero struggled out of the store to the buggy under a mountain of boxes and sundry packages tied with pink ribbon. Thus, fully occupied, the vaquero didn't notice the two men who stopped on the boardwalk and took up position on either side of Rachel, who was uncomfortably aware of their presence but as yet unaware of their intentions.

Cal Lawler and Kit Maxwell were a couple of troublemakers and small-time criminals with no obvious means of support, two of the hundreds of drifters who came and went in El Paso and were always a headache to the town's law enforcement and respectable citizens. Petty theft and burglary provided Lawler and Maxwell with enough ill-gotten gains to keep them in whiskey and whores, but they were attracted to Rachel's fresh-faced beauty and looking for some fun.

"Buy you a drink, little lady?" said Lawler, an illiterate, unshaven, brute who smelled worse than he looked.

Maxwell, tall and skinny with badly decayed teeth, grinned, put his arm around the girl's waist, and said, "We got us a nice, cozy cabin nearby. You'll like it, girly."

The two thugs should have been aware of two men who looked on that scene with disfavor. One of them was Manual Cantero, a skilled gun handler who, with a few notable exceptions, had no qualms about shooting gringos. The other was a small man wearing a bowler hat and troubled expression who had no qualms about shooting gringos either.

Both men now went to Rachel's rescue.

Cantero pulled his Colt but then hesitated, afraid of hitting Rachel. Pip Ogden walked between Rachel Tyler and her pair of assailants and said, "You men, be off with you now. Leave the young lady alone."

Lawler, a braggart and a bully, grinned, threw a curse at Ogden, grabbed him by the front of his coat, and pushed him away. "In El Paso, I'm the cock o' the walk, and I do as I damn well please," he said.

"And we do who we please," Maxwell said, baring his rotten teeth.

Three events followed very quickly.

Rachel wrenched away from Maxwell's arm, Cantero moved a step to his right, seeking a clear shot, and Ogden, as he was pushed away, dropped his hand to his coat pocket, came up with his Colt, and slammed it into the left side of Lawler's head. The man groaned and dropped to his knees, and Ogden swung the heavy revolver again, this time into the back of Lawler's bent head and then, mean as hell, kicked him in the teeth before the man bellied onto the boardwalk.

Cantero, a gunfighter, reacted the way he knew best.

He triggered his Colt, and Maxwell shrieked as he took the hit in his chest and staggered back against the front door of Madam Blanche's store. An old Texas lawman had once told Cantero, "Keep shooting 'em till they fall." Now he heeded that advice and pumped two fast shots into Maxwell's belly. The man's rotten mouth opened in a soundless scream, and he dropped into a sitting position, his back to the door, and died within moments.

Gunsmoke drifted in the street as onlookers gathered, and there were calls to send for the sheriff. Madam Blanche, tall and slender, dressed in severe black, opened her door and Maxwell's body fell inside and she stared at the bloodied corpse for a moment and then fainted. Seeing her employer faint, her teenaged assistant, newly arrived from France, promptly followed suit, and suddenly the doorway was blocked with bodies, two living, one dead.

Rachel Tyler, a rancher's daughter, was made of sterner stuff. She quickly went to the aid of the two women while Ogden and Cantero stood together on the boardwalk and silently awaited the arrival of the law.

Attracted by the gunfire, Red Ryan and Buttons Muldoon were already on the scene when T. C. Lyons arrived. The body of Kit Maxwell was still in Madam Blanche's doorway, but she and her assistant were inside, Rachel Tyler busy administering smelling salts and medicinal brandy. Cal Lawler was on his hands and knees spitting blood and teeth, and Pip Ogden was seriously thinking about kicking him in the face again.

Lyons carried a shotgun in the crook of his arm as he surveyed the melancholy scene and said, "What the hell happened here? Ryan, did you have a hand in this?"

Red shook his head. "No, I didn't, Sheriff. Me and Buttons just got here."

Ogden stepped forward. "Sheriff, two men were troubling a respectable young lady," he said. "One got shot and I buffaloed the other one."

"Oh, you did, did you? Well, we'll just have to see about that, won't we?" Lyons said. "Who did the shooting?"

"That would be me, señor," Cantero said.

"And who are you?"

"My name is Manuel Cantero and I ride for the Rafter-T."

"Holt Tyler's outfit?"

"*Sí, señor.* Mr. Tyler is my boss."

Lyons felt the ground shift under him. Tyler was one of the most powerful ranchers in Texas and a man to be reckoned with. He'd have to tread carefully.

"You in the bowler, who the hell are you?" Lyons said.

"My name is Phillip Ogden, but most people call me Pip if they call me anything at all. I'm a detective with the San Antonio Police Department."

"Then what the hell are you doing in El Paso?" Lyons said

"I'm conducting what could be a murder investigation," Ogden said.

"You have no jurisdiction in El Paso . . . Pip," Lyons said.

"Right, none at all, other than that Governor John Ireland is a personal friend of mine who takes a close interest in my work."

Lyons felt the earth move under his feet again.

"We will talk about this later," Lyons said.

"Yes, we will," Ogden said. He put his ankle boot on Cal Lawler's shoulder and pushed hard so that the man tumbled heavily on his side. "It's too late for the other one, but this animal needs a doctor."

Lyons stepped onto the boardwalk and glanced at the groaning Lawler. "I don't know this man, but I think the dead one's name is Maxwell. I arrested him for public drunkenness a while back." He pointed out a couple of men. "You and you, take this fellow to Dr. Williams and get him patched up."

"Then what do we do with him?" one of the men said.

"Take him to the jail and throw him inside. The door is open." Then to Ogden, "Where is the young lady?"

"I'm right here." Rachel stepped from the dress shop door. "What can I do for you, Sheriff?"

"And your name is?"

"Rachel Tyler."

"Ah yes, Holt Tyler's daughter," Lyons said, smiling. "Red Ryan and Buttons Muldoon recently rescued you from road agents. They told me all about it."

"They were both very brave," Rachel said, smiling at Red, who stood in the crowd.

"It seems that gentlemen are always saving you from brigands, Miss Tyler," Lyons said.

"Let's hope that it doesn't become a habit," Rachel said.

Lyons pointed at Manuel Cantero. "This man works for your father?"

"Yes, Manuel is one of our vaqueros. I've known him since I was a child."

"Why did he kill Maxwell?"

"Why don't you ask Manuel, Sheriff?"

"I'm asking you, Miss Tyler."

"He thought the man was about to harm me," Rachel said.

"Did you think that?"

"Yes, I did." Rachel reached into her purse and produced her derringer. "I would have shot him myself, had not Manuel fired first." She frowned. "I hope you're not thinking of arresting him, Sheriff. My father sets great store by Manuel."

Lyons had his back to the wall. The last thing he needed right now was an angry rancher showing up on his doorstep with fifty equally irate waddies demanding their vaquero back.

"The way I see it, is that you, Miss Tyler, were in fear for your life and the Mexican came to your defense, as did Mr. Ogden," Lyons said. "Now, others may not see it that way, but since you and Cantero are not residents of El Paso, addressing the community's concerns will be a job for the country sheriff."

"I'd like to speak with him on other matters," Ogden said.

"And you will, as soon as a county sheriff is appointed," Lyons said.

"When will that be?" Ogden said.

Lyons blinked and said, "Soon."

CHAPTER FORTY

T. C. Lyons decided that a show of cooperation with the little San Antonio detective might not go amiss, and could even help him in his bid to become the first chief of police in El Paso's history. To that end, he palmed off Red Ryan on Pip Ogden, introducing Red, with considerable exaggeration, as "a detective in training."

"Detective Ogden, you and Ryan must have many matters to discuss," Lyons said. "So I'll leave you to it."

But Red would have none of it. After he and Ogden left Lyons's office, he said, "To set things straight with you, Ogden, I'm a representative of the Patterson and Son Stage and Express Company and it is with them that my loyalties lie."

Ogden stopped on the boardwalk to light a cigar, and then said, "In what capacity are you a representative?"

"Shotgun guard," Red said.

Ogden ran his eyes over Red's beaded, buckskin shirt, his derby hat with the bullet holes, the cavalry blue bandana loosely tied around his neck, and the holstered Colt on his hip. "As a detective in training you were a considerable disappointment to me, Ryan, but as a shotgun guard, well, I guess you pass muster."

Red bristled, not liking the sound of that, and said, "Shotgun guard is a fine profession."

Ogden smiled. "Ah yes, the dignity of the job. Honor lies in honest toil, *n'est-ce pas?*"

"Damn right," Red said. "And whatever the hell else you said is right as well."

Ogden nodded. "Keep telling me I'm right, and you and I will get along just fine, Ryan. Now tell me about the double murder this morning."

"An old couple was killed by a robber," Red said. "It's nothing that would interest you."

"Violent crime is always of interest to me," Ogden said. "How were they killed?"

"They were stabbed to death," Red said. "After a struggle, I'm told."

"Ah, yes, like the feather pillow, the blade is silent. Take me to the crime scene."

"The bodies are gone, and there's nothing to see except blood," Red said.

"I'll be the judge of what there is to be seen or not seen. Lead the way."

"It's a small space, isn't it?" Pip Ogden said. "Very confined. And the old man put up quite a struggle, you say?"

"He fought hard for his life and got stabbed five times," Red said.

"I see," Ogden said. He looked around the tiny store and then his gaze fixed on a small display table that had been overturned in the struggle. "Hello, what have we here?"

A tiny scrap of fabric clung to a nail that stuck out from a corner of the rickety table. Ogden pulled the cloth free and held it up to Red. "What do you think of this, Ryan?"

Red shrugged away the question. "All I see is a few threads."

"That's all you see?"

"Yeah, that's all."

"Hmm . . . interesting. There are none so blind as those who will not see."

Ogden reached into a pocket, produced a chrome magnifying glass with an ebony handle, and used it to study the cloth scrap. "Tweed," he said. "Light brown in color, possibly woven here in the United States, but more likely it's British, Scottish to be exact, Harris tweed it's called. Yes . . . hand-spun, hand-woven and dyed by peasant craftspeople in the Outer Hebrides, northern islands at the edge of nowhere."

Red was puzzled. "So, what does that tell you, Ogden?"

"Let me ask a question first . . . the old couple, Izak and Raisa Rabinovich, were poor people, were they not?"

"Look around you, Ogden. What do you think?"

"Tiny living quarters, selling bric-a-brac to scrape a meager living, yes, they were poor." Ogden stared into Red's eyes. "The man who wore the tweed was not. Since British nobility began wearing tweed, it's become very fashionable in our country. Tweed jackets, tweed coats, tweed suits . . . the young San Antonio bucks are wearing it everywhere, even to the opera house."

"Maybe the Rabinovich couple had a rich customer who tore his pants," Red said.

"Why would a rich customer frequent a store like this? If he wanted a watch repaired, he could go to one of the big jewelers in El Paso. I'm sure there are a few?"

"I understand that there are several used by high rollers with expensive mistresses," Red said.

"An expensive mistress would not like to be taken to this store," Ogden said. "No, the table was over-turned in the struggle, and the killer snagged his pants on a nail. You told me this was a robbery. What was stolen?"

"A cameo brooch," Red said.

"A what?"

"A Russian cameo brooch," Red said.

"Valuable?"

"It seems that Raisa Rabinovich thought so. She and her husband were Russian, and it was her link to the old country."

Ogden said, "Why would a man of apparently ample means murder two people for a cameo?"

"Sheriff Lyons thinks maybe the killer wanted the brooch to give to a lady friend," Red said.

Again, Stella Morgan came unbidden into Red's mind, but he dismissed the notion immediately. She would not condone a double murder for a bauble when she could easily buy better. It was preposterous to think otherwise.

But the thought led to another, and he said, "There was another murder a few days ago. An army officer was stabbed at the fort."

"Stabbed, you say?" Ogden said. "Who was this officer?"

"Major John Morgan. An Apache army scout was blamed for the killing and then lynched by a mob."

"Was he guilty?"

"I don't think so."

"Then who did it?"

"I don't know," Red said. "My driver and me brought Morgan's wife, as she was then, from Fort Concho. She's still in town. You could talk with her." And then, a fact worth adding, "Major Morgan was about to retire. His mother died and made him a wealthy man."

"The widow's name is Stella Morgan," Ogden said. "She lived with Martha Grace Morgan before the old lady's death at the age of eighty-two. There were rumors that Stella was having an affair with a man named Lucian Carter. But I have no proof of that. Stella Morgan insisted that they were just friends."

"How do you know all this?" Red said.

"Because I investigated Martha Morgan's death. I suspected murder, but my superiors told me her death was due to natural causes, and I was ordered to drop the case."

"Then why are you here in El Paso?"

"I took a leave of absence. I still think Martha was murdered."

"Ogden, have you ever heard of Elijah Carter, worked out of New Orleans?" Red said.

"Yes, he was a paid assassin and well known to law enforcement in Louisiana and Texas. He was hung for a murderer."

"Lucian Carter is his son," Red said.

Ogden was silent for a while, then shook his head

and said, "Damn me for a shortsighted fool, I never made the connection."

"Well, here's the nub of it, Ogden . . . a few years back I was told by a truth-telling feller that Lucian Carter learned the murder-for-hire trade at his daddy's knee, and when he grew old enough to use a gun, he did some killing for profit his ownself."

"Stella Morgan and Lucian Carter are the reason I'm here in El Paso," Ogden said. "The police doctor said Martha Morgan died of natural causes. I didn't believe it then, and I don't believe it now. She was a suspicious, distrustful old biddy who was said to be very rich, but she didn't trust banks. The thing was, when I searched the house I found no money, not a red cent, no jewelry, nothing of value. The place had been picked clean. I believe Lucian Carter smothered Martha with one of her own feather pillows, and he and Stella Morgan then stole everything they could lay their hands on. Then they sold the old lady's house for a tidy sum and lit a shuck for El Paso."

"And on my stage," Red said.

"Did Stella ever mention—"

"That she carried a large sum of money? No, she didn't, and neither did Carter, though he held onto a carpetbag that seemed important to him. But Stella did take up with an outlaw and gunman by the name of Seth Roper and on the trail here they became real cozy, if you get my meaning."

"What about Carter?" Ogden said.

"I don't know what Carter thinks about Roper, but I do know that he's still with Stella."

Ogden looked at his watch, snapped the case shut, and said, "It's about time for lunch." And then, "Ryan, a shotgun guard is paid to keep his eyes open, now think about this . . . did you ever see inside the carpetbag that Lucian Carter kept close to him on the journey here from Fort Concho?"

Red smiled. "Ogden, most of the time I was too busy fighting off Apaches, but I did notice that Lucian Carter didn't let much space get between him and the bag."

"A large carpetbag?"

"Large enough."

"Then I must see what's inside that bag, and you're going to help me."

"Help you, how?" Red said.

Ogden told him . . . and Red Ryan's hair stood on end.

CHAPTER FORTY-ONE

Red Ryan and Pip Ogden's conversation over lunch centered on the murder of Major Morgan and the subsequent lynching of the innocent Apache. They were drinking coffee when Buttons Muldoon walked into Ma's Kitchen with Rachel Tyler in tow. "I thought I might find you here," Buttons said. "Miss Tyler has something to say to you, Mr. Ogden."

Red and Ogden had both stood, and now Red directed the girl to a chair. "Please sit. Rachel."

"No, thank you, I must be getting back to the ranch." Rachel said. "I'd just like to thank you again for what you did for me this morning. Mr. Ogden, you must come out to the Rafter-T one day and meet my father."

Ogden bowed and smiled. "It will be a great pleasure, Miss Tyler. And there's no need to thank me. I was merely doing my duty as a concerned citizen."

Red smiled and said, "It was nice seeing you again, Rachel. But next time I hope we meet in happier circumstances."

"Me too, Red," the girl said. "I think I've had enough excitement to last me a while."

"Miss Tyler, just before you go, may I compliment you on the cameo you're wearing," Ogden said.

Rachel touched the brooch. "It was my deceased mother's. She wore it on her wedding day."

"I see," Ogden said. "Then she had exquisite taste."

"Thank you," Rachel said. "Now I really must go, and do take me up on my invitation to the ranch, Mr. Ogden."

"You can depend on it," the little detective said.

After the girl left, Red said, "Damn it, Ogden, do you have to suspect everybody?"

"Yes, I had to ask," Ogden said. "It's a detective's duty to ask questions. Ninety-nine percent of the answers lead nowhere, but there's always that one percent that does. You'll learn that as a detective, Ryan."

"I'm not a detective," Red said. "I'm a shotgun guard."

"And speaking of that, I have news," Muldoon said. He sat, called over a waiter, ordered the beef stew, bread rolls, and a wedge of apple pie and said, "Send the bill to Sheriff Lyons."

"Buttons, I swear, you're going to weigh five hundred pounds before we leave here," Red said.

"Don't worry, we're leaving soon," Muldoon said. He reached under his sailor's coat and with a flourish produced a telegram that he slapped on the table in front of Red so hard that it made the cutlery lying on his empty plate rattle. "I picked this up at the depot. It's from Patterson and Son," he said. "A passenger to be picked up at Fort Concho."

"Fort Concho again?" Red said. "Another army wife?"

"Wrong sex. Wrong army. Read the wire."

Red picked up the telegram and read:

PASSENGER PICKUP FORT CONCHO
SOONEST. BRITISH ARMY DESERTER AND
COWARD. TRANSPORT THIS OFFICER TO
GALVESTON FOR ARREST BY ROYAL NAVY
FRIGATE HMS HEPHAESTUS.
ABE PATTERSON

Red passed the wire to Ogden without comment. The little detective scanned the paper, his eyebrows crawling up his forehead like hairy caterpillars. After a while he said, "Ryan, you've already made a commitment to me and to Sheriff Lyons."

"Hardly a commitment," Red said. "More like following an order."

Ogden opened his mouth to speak, but Red headed him off when he said, "When do you want to leave, Buttons?"

"Tomorrow morning, I guess."

Now Red turned to Ogden and said, "You heard the man."

"Leave tomorrow and some guilty parties could escape justice," the little detective said.

"I know that," Red said. "Buttons, what do you think?"

"According to what I hear at the stage depot, no trains will leave El Paso for points north until a bridge is repaired," Muldoon said. "They say it will be another couple of days."

"Can we delay picking up the Limey officer that long?" Red said.

"He's in Fort Concho, so he's not going anywhere,"

Buttons said. "But I don't know how long the navy ship intends to stay in port at Galveston."

"Until they get their prisoner, I guess," Red said. "Remaining in Galveston with its saloons and brothels is no hardship for sailors."

"They must want the coward real bad to send a warship after him," Buttons said.

"Seems like," Red said. "But maybe it's a small warship." Then to Ogden, "All right, I can give you two more days."

"Two days is enough if we make the most of them," Ogden said.

"Since time is short, lay it out for me, Ogden," Red said. "You came all the way from San Antonio through some rough country that could still have hostile Apaches roaming around. You must have had good reason to believe that Stella Morgan and Lucian Carter really are murderers."

Pip Ogden nodded. "Here's the bottom line, Ryan . . . yes, I firmly believe Stella Morgan and Lucian Carter killed Martha Morgan for her money and jewelry. I talked with the lawyer who drew up Martha's will, and he said she left all her considerable fortune to her soldier son, Major Morgan. I believe Stella knew she'd be a rich widow one day, but she decided to hasten the process and have her husband murdered. In my opinion, the killer was Lucian Carter. Are the murders of Isak and Raisa Rabinovich somehow connected to Carter? I don't know."

Buttons said, "Hell, Ogden, haul T. C. Lyons out of his office and go arrest Stella Morgan and Carter. Seems simple enough to me."

"Everything I've said is suspicion and conjecture, and it won't stand up in a court of law. What I need is proof," Ogden said. "Examining the contents of Stella Morgan's carpetbag would be a good start."

"And that's not going to be easy," Red said. "Lucian Carter never allows the damned thing out of his sight."

"Nothing in a murder investigation is ever easy," Ogden said. "Ryan, recovering the bag is of the utmost importance, so we have it to do. We're lucky we already have a plan, aren't we?"

CHAPTER FORTY-TWO

"It's him, I tell you. That little San Antonio detective with the big nose."

"Lucian, we're above suspicion," Stella Morgan said. "The old girl's death certificate said she died of natural causes, and as far as the law is concerned it ends right there."

"I know, Stella, but he worries me. He's only just arrived in town and already he was involved in a shooting scrape."

"Was that the shooting we heard?" Stella said.

"Yeah. But the detective didn't do the shooting. He buffaloed a man with his revolver, and another was shot by a cowboy. Apparently, the dead man and his friend were trying to spark a woman who objected to their advances."

"And the detective and the cowboy rode to her rescue like good little knights in shining armor," Stella said, smiling.

"Something like that," Carter said. "I spoke to a man who saw the whole thing, and he said the little fellow in the bowler hat was real mean, laid into the man he'd downed with his gun and the boot."

Stella shook her head. "Lucian, you get too worked up about things. If the detective gets to be too much of a nuisance, I'll have Seth Roper take care of him."

"I can take care of him myself, Stella," Carter said. "You don't need Roper."

"No, I don't want you involved in another killing, at least not until we're in Washington." Stella said. "Besides, Roper wouldn't do it himself. Now he's the big auger in El Paso he can hire a man to do his dirty work for fifty dollars."

"Stella, you simplify things so well," Carter said, his eyes shining.

"Life is simple because it's so short, Lucian. You have to grab everything you can, while you can, and consider no one else but yourself."

"You consider me, though, don't you, Stella?"

"Yes, Lucian, I consider you. You're my good right arm, and another hand to grab with. Together, we'll take anything and everything we want, and we won't spare a backward glance at the human wreckage we leave behind us. I want to die rich, and I want to die young. Can you think of a fate worse than growing old?"

"But not too young, huh?" Carter said, smiling.

"Come here, Lucian," Stella said. She rose from her chair, took Carter's hands, and placed them on her breasts. "Squeeze. Now do you like that?" she said.

"Of course, I do," Carter said.

"When the time comes that a man no longer wants to squeeze my tits, I'll have grown old enough and I'll shoot myself," Stella said. "It will be time for Miss Stella to leave the ball."

Carter shook his head. "That will never happen."

"Oh, yes it will. And when the time comes, I'll be ready."

Knuckles tapped on the hotel room door and Stella said, "I'll answer it."

A young man wearing a deputy's badge on his vest and a Colt on his hip stared openmouthed at Stella in her sheer dressing grown and stammered, "Sh . . . Sheriff Lyons wishes to see you in his office at your earliest convenience, ma'am."

Stella smiled. "Today?"

"Now, ma'am. And . . . he wants to see Mr. Carter as well."

"Tell him we'll be right over," Stella said.

"Yes, ma'am." After one last, lingering look at Stella's breasts, the deputy turned on his heel and left.

As Stella closed the door, Carter said, "This doesn't bode well, Stella. I told you the detective was a troublemaker."

"We were invited . . . invited, mark you . . . to attend by Sheriff Lyons," Stella said. "This may have nothing to do with the San Antonio detective. And if it does, I'll handle it, Lucian. Let me do the talking."

"I say we kill the detective tonight," Carter said.

"It may come to that," Stella said. "I really don't think it will, but we'll keep our options open."

T. C. Lyons's office smelled of the coffee simmering in the pot on the stove and the usual tang of gun oil, ancient vomit, and man sweat. He'd surrendered the chair behind his desk to Pip Ogden and had arranged three more, confiscated from a saloon, around the available floor space.

Ogden didn't rise when Stella entered, his face unreadable, but Lyons ushered her into a chair with a considerable show of good manners, impressed by the black severity of the widow's mourning dress with its tantalizing hint of cleavage.

After Stella and Carter were settled and had refused coffee, jailhouse brews justifiably reviled throughout the West, Ogden said, without much ceremony, "My name is Pip Ogden, and you're both here today to discuss the manner of Martha Morgan's death. Does that surprise you?"

Stella seemed to take what the detective said in stride. "Not really," she said. "I thought the matter closed, but you obviously have questions about dear Martha's passing."

"Questions?" Ogden said. "No, I only have one . . . which of you murdered the old lady?"

That last hit Stella like a blow to the belly, and silenced her. But Carter stepped into the silence and said, "That is a very serious allegation and one I will not answer without the presence of my lawyer."

Ogden grinned like a Louisiana alligator. "Ah yes, Lucian Carter, good of you to speak up. Martha's coroner's report failed to mention the bruises I found on both her upper arms. Old people are easily bruised, and I believe the bruising occurred when you kneeled on Martha's arms while you smothered her with a pillow. Or did you hold her down, Mrs. Morgan? After all, she was a frail old lady, and you are a strong, healthy young woman."

Lyons said, "Ogden, don't go too far, old fellow."

"He's gone too far already," Stella said. She jumped to her feet. "I will not listen to your vile, baseless accusations a moment longer. Good day to you, sir."

Stella strode for the door, her high-heeled boots clacking on the wood floor.

"One thing, Mrs. Morgan, before you go," Ogden said.

Stella stopped, her back stiff.

"I'm a good detective, Mrs. Morgan, and do you know what makes me good? I'll tell you. I'm like a terrier with a rat, or in this case two rats, and once I sink my teeth in, I never let go, be it in El Paso . . . or Washington town."

Without a word, Stella opened the door and stepped outside. Carter followed, but he stopped at the desk and said, "You've made enemies today, Ogden."

"Is that so, Carter?" the detective said. "I make enemies very easily, and I see most of them hanged. Good day."

"Ogden, that was mighty strong," T. C. Lyons said.

"It may be a fault of mine, but I can't be civil to murderers," Ogden said.

"You're convinced they murdered the old lady in San Antonio?"

"Yes, I am. Aren't you?"

"I don't know," Lyons said. "Maybe."

"What about Mrs. Morgan's husband? Do you think the Apache killed him?"

"No, I don't."

"Do you think Stella Morgan killed him?"

"Had him killed . . . maybe. I don't know."

"Or you don't want to know, Sheriff."

"Ogden, you come to me with evidence that will stand up in court, and I'll do my duty," Lyons said.

"I will, and I'll see Stella Morgan and Lucian Carter hang, and I'll piss on their graves," Ogden said.

Lyons shook his head. "Detective Ogden, you're one mean son of a gun."

"Damn right, I am," Ogden said. He smiled as he said that, but he was worried. He should have kept Carter and the woman longer, much longer. How the hell was Red Ryan doing? Did he have the carpetbag yet?

CHAPTER FORTY-THREE

"I'm here to see Mrs. Stella Morgan," Red Ryan said to the hotel desk clerk. "Is she to home?"

"Who wants to know?" the clerk said.

"I'm her brother."

The clerk sneered. "Mrs. Morgan is the widow of an army officer. I doubt she could be sister to a man wearing a shirt made by a savage." And then to drive home his distrust, "And a hat with bullet holes in it and a face that's recently felt the knuckle side of a fist."

The clerk was a medium-size man, possessed of a medium-size intellect, and he should have known better than antagonize a ranny with red hair and a Colt on his hip that had seen a considerable amount of wear. But he didn't.

"I'll ask you again," Red said, holding on to his patience with both hands, "is Mrs. Morgan in her room?"

"And I'll tell you again, Mrs. Morgan is not here, so she's not receiving visitors," the man said. "Now be off with you."

Red held back his growing irritation and said, "I'd

like to surprise Stella, so if you'll just give me the key to her room, I'll wait for her."

"Mister, I told you to git. Go buy yourself a new shirt and a new hat, and come back when Mrs. Morgan is in residence. For your information, she's in room twenty, but that won't do you any good until you show up properly dressed. Oh, and bring flowers."

"My name is Red Ryan, and I'm a representative of the Patterson and Son Stage and Express Company. Does that make a difference?"

To Red's shock, the man said, "No, it doesn't, mainly because I don't give a damn." He reached under his desk and Red tensed, but instead of a gun the clerk came up with a greasy bacon sandwich in a paper sack. "Now beat it, and let me finish my lunch in peace."

Time was a-wasting, and Red was very conscious of the foyer clock striking noon. To the clerk he said, "What's your name?"

"What's it to you?"

"I just want to know. When I walked in here I took you for an Archibald."

"It ain't Archibald. They call me Bill, and you call me Mr. Fowler."

"Well, Bill, I'm in a hurry and I'm really sorry to do this, but—"

Red drew and clattered his Colt against the side of Fowler's head. The men's eyes got big, then small, and he spat out a mix of bread, bacon, and saliva and tumbled backward in his chair, sprawling with his legs tangled, out like a dead man.

Red sighed and said, "See, Bill, that's what refusing to be sociable gets a man."

He ducked behind the counter, retrieved the key for room 20, one of a pair on the hook, and then took the stairs two at a time. Now time was of the essence.

Room 20 was the middle door on the left. Red used the key and stepped inside. He saw no sign of the carpetbag. A quick look under the bed. It was not there. Unless Stella Morgan had taken the bag with her, the only other possible hiding place was in the armoire. To Red's relief, that's where it was, covered only by the hems of Stella's long dresses. Because of the summons from T. C. Lyons, she'd had no time to find a better hiding place, or, more likely, her arrogance was such that she believed no one would have the audacity to search her room.

Well, she was wrong about that.

Red hauled out the bag and then cussed under his breath. It was padlocked. From downstairs in the foyer she heard a woman's voice yelling, cussing out the clerk, who must have regained consciousness. It was a heart-stopping moment, and Red didn't hesitate. He flung open the window and dropped the bag outside. It was a long drop from the second floor, but he followed it. He landed hard on the boardwalk and then fell on his back, his breath gushing out of him. Groggy, his left knee and broken toe paining him, Red staggered to his feet. The carpetbag was a few feet away . . . in the hands of a drunk who looked skyward and yelled, "Thank'ee God!"

"Not this time, pardner," Red said. He limped to the drunk and said, "Give me that. It's mine."

The drunk, his whiskey-hazed brain trying to focus

on what was happening, held the bag tight to his belly and turned away. "No, it's mine," he said.

Red didn't have time to argue. He dropped the drunk with a chopping right to the chin, grabbed the bag, and hobbled into a nearby alley. He stood in shadow, his back to the wall of a hardware store, and listened for sounds of pursuit, but none came.

After a few minutes, Red shouldered himself off the wall and then froze. The drunk man stood silhouetted against the bright rectangle of the street and then lurched toward him. Red held the bag's handle in his left hand, drew with his right. "Stop right there or I'll drill you," he said.

The slurred voice of the drunk answered. "I want my bag back. It fell from heaven right at my feet."

"It fell from a hotel room window," Red said.

"You're lying, mister," the drunk said.

"And you're drunk."

Red holstered his gun, reached into his pocket, and came up with two silver dollars. He held them out for the drunk to take. "Here, go buy yourself a drink."

The man grabbed the money, hugged it close to his chest, raised his eyes skyward and said. "You're an angel, sent from heaven."

"No, I'm a shotgun guard sent by the Patterson and Son Stage and Express Company. Time you left or you could get yourself shot."

"I'm leaving, I'm leaving," the drunk said as he made his uncertain way back along the alley. Then, thrown over his shoulder, "You're an angel from heaven, shotgun guard."

"Right about now I reckon there are some who'd say different," Red said.

* * *

"Were you seen?" Pip Ogden said.

"By Stella Morgan? No," Red Ryan said. "By a drunk member of the citizenry, yes."

"He won't remember," Ogden said.

He and Red stood at a table in Ogden's hotel room, the carpetbag between them.

"How do we open the padlock? Do you have a pick you can use?" Red said.

"No."

"No? You're a big-city detective, for God's sake."

Ogden almost smiled. "Don't believe all you read in the dime novels and the *Police Gazette*. This is a cast heart padlock, made of bronze, and it's very strong. I've never known one to have been opened without a key."

"Maybe I can shoot it off," Red said.

"And your bullet will bounce off and ricochet around this room and kill us both," Ogden said. "No, there's a simpler way."

The little detective reached into his pocket and produced a pocketknife. He opened the blade, tested the edge with his thumb, then began to saw on the wide leather strap that covered the hasp and padlock. It was the work of a few minutes to cut the strap and open the bag.

"I wouldn't have thought of that," Red said.

"I'm sure you would have . . . eventually," Ogden said. "Now, what have we here?"

Red looked in the bag and whistled between his teeth. "Hell, no wonder it was padlocked."

"An astute observation, Ryan," Ogden said. "Shall we inspect the Morgan loot?"

It took a while to count the money, mostly in banknotes but also in gold double eagles, and then Ogden called on his police experience to put a value on the jewelry.

Finally, Ogden said, "I put a value on the contents of this bag, money and the diamond jewelry, at a hundred thousand dollars. Martha Morgan was a rich old lady, and that is why Stella Morgan and Lucian Carter murdered her." He stared hard at Red. "Ryan, as I expected, we have the motive for murder, but not the proof."

"We have the bag," Red said. "Surely that proves something."

"It proves nothing. As any competent lawyer will point out, although she left everything to her son in her will, Martha could have given the money and jewelry as a gift to Stella."

Red thought that through and then said, "So, stealing the bag was a waste of time. I twisted my damned knee and hurt my sore toe for nothing."

"Not quite. We have the bag and its contents, so Stella Morgan will not profit from her crime. There is satisfaction in that. But wait . . . I just had a thought."

Ogden took time to light a cigar and Red followed suit by building a cigarette. The detective thumbed a match, lit Red's smoke and then his cigar. "How discreet were you at the hotel, Ryan? Come now, be frank."

"I told you, nobody saw me."

"How about the desk clerk?"

"Well, I . . . I mean . . ." Red's face fell. "Oh, my God . . ."

"You had a confrontation with the clerk?"

Red nodded. "Yeah, over the room key." He hesitated, then said, "I hit him over the head with my gun."

Ogden beamed. "Excellent, Ryan, well done." A serious look crossed his face. "He can describe you?"

"Yeah, he can, and more than that, I told him my name and that I was a representative of the Patterson and Son Stage and Express Company." Red shook his head. "How could I have been so stupid?"

"It's my opinion that you're a man of action, Ryan, not much suited for cloak-and-dagger work, but your stupidity . . . if you want to call it that . . . will very much work in our favor."

"I'm not catching your drift, Ogden," Red said.

"Don't you see? Stella Morgan can hardly go to Sheriff Lyons and report her carpetbag stolen. That could lead to some awkward questions that I'm sure she'd rather avoid."

"So, what does she do?"

"Do? Why, she'll come after you, or her henchmen will. I imagine the lady will be driven by desperation and will soon overplay her hand. The crux of the matter is to keep her here in El Paso until I gather the evidence I need to charge her with murder."

"And I could end up dead," Red said, not liking a word Ogden had said.

"Ryan, that is a risk we have to take."

"We? There's no we, there's only me," Red said. "She knows I took the bag, so I'm a walking target."

Ogden slapped his hands together. "Excellent,

Ryan! You catch on fast," he said. "This is our best hope of catching a cold-blooded killer and her cohorts."

"Over my dead body," Red said, meaning every word.

CHAPTER FORTY-FOUR

"According to the stationmaster, we can get out of here by the morning train, seven o'clock sharp the day after tomorrow," Lucian Carter said. "That's how long we have to get the bag back from Red Ryan."

Stella Morgan nodded. "All right, get Seth Roper."

"You're going to kill Ryan?"

"Yes, and Ogden."

"Ogden?" Carter said. "Since we're headed out of town soon, maybe we should leave him alone."

"No, we must kill him, Lucian. You heard what he said. He's a bulldog. A man of his kind will follow us all the way to Washington."

"I can kill him in Washington, Stella. Hell, in the big city, it would be just another unsolved murder."

"No, I don't want to take that chance. What if Ogden spoke to the Washington police before we could strike? Lawmen stick together, and his death would not go unnoticed." She shook her head. "We'll let Roper take care of this."

Carter's face flushed with anger. "Damn Ryan, he's always been a troublemaker."

"He's a nobody, a stagecoach guard, but he has our bag. Roper can get rid of him first and get the bag back. When we step on the train I want to leave nothing behind us, except the good wishes of the Fort Bliss army officers bidding the heartbroken widow a fond farewell." Stella smiled. "Boo-hoo."

"Let me do it, Stella," Carter said. "I can eliminate Ogden and force Ryan to return the bag. A bullet to the kneecap is a powerful convincer."

"The answer is still no, Lucian. It's a job for Roper. I don't want any blunders. There's too much at stake . . . at least half of our fortune."

Stella sat in a chair and looked out the hotel window at the street below. Carter rose, placed his hands on her shoulders, and began a gentle massage.

"Get your hands off me, Lucian," she said. "I'll tell you when you can touch me, and now is not that time." Stella rose to her feet and turned on Carter, frowning. "Now go and do what I told you. Bring me Seth Roper."

Seth Roper listened as Lucian Carter bent over and whispered in his ear. Roper nodded and pushed his chips to the faro banker. "Cash me out, I have to go," he said.

Roper tossed the banker a ten, then stuffed his winnings into his pocket. "Step to the bar with me, Carter," he said. "I'll buy you a drink."

"But Stella says for you to come right away," Carter said.

"She can wait," Roper said.

As usual, the Platte River saloon was busy with the early crowd, and deferential men made way on the floor when Roper waded through them to the bar. He ordered whiskey for himself and Carter and then said, "What does she want?"

"Best you hear that from Stella," Carter said.

Roper smiled. "Then it's a killing."

"I don't know," Carter said.

"You do know, you just don't want to tell me."

"Stella's mighty nervous."

"She's a woman. Women are always nervous." Roper drained his glass.

"There's a lot of money at stake, Roper. I mean a lot of money."

"I'm aware of that, and I want my share," Roper said.

"And you'll have it. You'll get everything that's coming to you," Carter said.

"That's good enough for me," Roper said. "All right, let's go."

Stella Morgan touched the back of Seth Roper's hand with her fingertips. "You'll do it for me, won't you, Seth? I'll be so grateful."

"Me, do it? No, I won't." Roper saw the disappointment on the woman's face, smiled and said, "But I'll have it done. Ogden is easy, but Ryan is a tougher proposition. It won't be cheap."

"Seth, all my money is in the bag, and Ryan has it," Stella said.

"All *our* money," Roper said.

"Of course, that's what I meant," Stella said.

Roper stared across the hotel room and said, "What about you, Carter? You got a problem with that? Our money, I mean."

Carter shrugged off the question. Now wasn't the time or the place for a confrontation. "I have no problem. We're all in this together, the three of us."

"So, Seth, how do we pay to have the killings done?" Stella said. "Ryan has my money, remember?"

"I'll fund the killings and get paid back later," Roper said. "I have a couple of good men in mind who'll cut Ryan's suspenders for two hundred dollars."

"Make sure they get the bag back from him," Carter said. "Then they can shoot him in the belly."

"You want him gut-shot, Carter?" Roper said. "Holding a grudge, huh?"

"Yeah, I am," Carter said.

"And so am I," Stella Morgan said. "Shoot the redheaded rogue in the guts. He's plagued us for too long."

Henry "Skull" Jackson's face had been burned away by a forest fire as he lay wounded between the lines during the Battle of the Wilderness in 1864. The scarred skin of his features lay tight to the bone, and this coupled with lidless eyes had given Jackson his dreadful nickname.

Seth Roper could hardly bear to look at him.

Along with Jackson at a table in the Platte River saloon was Danny Kline, a tall, loose-limbed man with a long, soulful face made remarkable by eyes the color of a blue sky in winter. Kline was a sharp dresser who had a growing reputation as a draw fighter, and like Jackson he was a killer for hire who wasn't fussy about who he gunned so long as the money was right.

Between them, Jackson and Kline had killed eighteen men, and all that Red Ryan represented was the two hundred dollars they'd earn to make him number nineteen.

Jackson, who'd once been the possessor of a strong, baritone voice, had breathed in flames in the Wilderness that had scorched his vocal cords, and now he talked in a high screech, like an angry parrot.

"Three hundred, Roper," he squawked, struggling to form the words. "This ain't just a killing, we got to take this Ryan feller alive and make him show us to the carpetbag."

"Yeah, I understand, Skull—"

"Don't call me that name, Roper. I don't like it," Jackson said.

"Hank is sensitive about his face," Kline said. "Hell, he carries a mask with him to the cathouse so he don't upset the whores."

"Shut your trap, Danny," Jackson said. Then, "Three hundred, Roper, and that's my rock-bottom price."

Roper forced himself to look at the man. It was like coming face-to-face with death. "I'm agreeable," he said. "Three hundred it is. Once you get the bag, gut-shoot Ryan. My clients want him to suffer a spell."

Jackson shook his nightmare head. "That ain't happening, Roper. Gut-shot men can still talk, and I'm real easy to describe. Ryan gets it between the eyes like everybody else."

Roper shrugged off that last. "Fine by me, Jackson. The main thing is to recover the bag, *compre*?"

"Yeah, I *compre*," Jackson said. "What makes a damned carpetbag so important?"

"That's none of your business," Roper said. "Just do the job you're being paid to do."

"Your best chance of catching Ryan alone is at his

hotel, The Inglenook," Roper said. "He might have a scattergun, watch for that, and he has a sidekick goes by the name of Buttons Muldoon who's handy enough with a pistol."

"I'll bear all that in mind," Jackson said. "I'll have another whiskey. Roper, you're buying."

CHAPTER FORTY-FIVE

"Buttons, you're buying," Red Ryan said. "My throat's dry after all the talking I've done."

Buttons ordered two more beers and said, "So now that detective feller has the bag with all the loot, what's he gonna do with it?"

"Right now, he's hoping that Stella will come after me and make a mistake."

"What kind of mistake?"

"The kind that gets her hung."

"Big mistake," Buttons said.

"She'll come after me to recover the carpetbag," Red said. "Maybe Ogden hopes he can pin her with an attempted-murder charge."

"It's only attempted murder if you survive, Red," Buttons said. "If she kills you, it's just plain murder." He shook his head. "Damn, it all seems mighty thin to me."

"Ogden figures Stella and Lucian Carter killed the old rich lady in San Antonio. And he believes the murder of Major Morgan and the Rabinovich couple are connected, but he doesn't have a shred of proof."

"He has the bag, though," Buttons said.

Red smiled. "Yeah, he has the bag. You don't trust him?"

"I don't trust anybody, including the mean-looking ranny who just came in. He's sitting over there on a high lonesome."

Red looked in the mirror behind the bar and saw what Buttons saw, a tall, lanky man dressed like a gambler sitting at a table, his long slender fingers manipulating the deck of cards that were lying on the table.

"Gambler," Buttons said, dismissing the man.

"Maybe he's a gambling man, but most of all he's a gun," Red said. "I reckon he followed us here from The Inglenook."

"That how you read him, a pistol fighter?" Buttons said.

"That's how he reads himself," Red said.

The Silver Slipper saloon was off the beaten track, known more for its quiet, its excellent selection of brandies and cigars and available out-of-town newspapers than its gambling, and mostly the sporting crowd avoided it. To see a gambler in the place was rare, like spotting a unicorn in church . . . a gambler who had the casual arrogance and careful eyes of a shootist was rarer still.

"He's taking a good look at you, Red, summing you up," Buttons said. "You gun any of his kinfolk?"

"Not recently that I recollect," Red said.

"Then maybe he just don't like the way you look, huh?" Buttons said.

"Could be, but since he followed us from the hotel, that's a heap of not liking a man's appearance," Red said.

"Ah, maybe he's just be bored and looking around, huh?" Buttons said.

That question was answered when the man rose from his chair, slowly, elegantly, unwinding one piece of himself at a time. He stepped across the floor, his spurs chiming, and stood at the bar. Without turning his head, as though he talked directly to the mirror, he said, "Going by the color of your hair, I'd say your name was Red Ryan."

"You got my name, mister, so what's yours?" Red said.

"Name's Danny Kline. Mean anything to you?"

"Not a thing," Red said. "Are you somebody I should know?"

Kline ignored that and said, "I'm only going to say this once and I won't repeat it . . . I'll stay for the next thirty minutes. Bring back the carpetbag before I leave or you're a dead man."

"What carpetbag?" Red said.

"You got thirty minutes and time is a-wasting. You get back here a minute late, I'll kill you. Don't come back at all and I'll kill you. Mister, you got a decision to make."

Danny Kline had scored too many easy kills, gunned too many scared or unskilled men, and his overconfidence was his undoing. He'd measured Red Ryan all wrong. Red would not be pushed, browbeaten, or threatened, and above all he was good with a gun and had sand.

"I've made my decision, Kline," he said. "And now it's time for you to make yours . . . walk out of here while you still can or draw your pistol and get to your work."

The bartender leaned across the bar and said, "Here, that won't do. I run a respectable place here."

An elderly man with a fashionable imperial beard and mustache sat in an easy chair by the far wall. He looked over his newspaper, said loudly, "Tut-tut-tut," and went back to reading again.

"You heard the bartender, Kline, this is a respectable place. Now get the hell out of here and tell Stella Morgan to come for the bag herself." Red stood loose, ready, his hand by his holstered Colt. "Otherwise, I can accommodate you at your earliest convenience," he said.

Kline didn't like the taste of his own medicine, he didn't like it one bit. But he'd been fairly called and his pride would not let an uppity stagecoach messenger put the crawl on him.

"Well, mister, it seems like I got to kill you," he said. "Pity, because that's not how I planned it."

Kline went for his gun and cleared leather faster than Red. A gunfight is measured in fractions of a second, and Kline drew with blinding speed and fired first. It is said that in later years Bat Masterson penned a newspaper account of the Silver Slipper draw-fight and wrote that the noted shootist Danny Kline should have taken an extra half-second to place his shot against such an inferior opponent. And he was right. Kline's bullet went wide to the left by a couple of inches and splintered into the bar. But Red's first shot, slower but accurate, was on target and hit the gunman's right bicep, tearing through muscle and shattering bone. Again, referring to Masterson's account, Danny may have been attempting a border shift, tossing his Colt into his left hand, when Red steadied, placed his second shot on the money, and hit Kline's breastbone dead center. The gunman staggered back, stared at his bloody chest in horror for long seconds, and then collapsed onto the wood floor and died.

Masterson wrote, *"Danny Kline passed away secure in the knowledge that he'd been bested by a less-speedy opponent. And so it was with many fast-draw gunfighters who fell to lesser, but coolheaded men who took their time and placed their shots where they would do the most damage."*

His ears ringing, Red Ryan stared at Kline's body as he reloaded his revolver, and he was vaguely aware of Buttons Muldoon saying, "Hell, Red, you cut that too close."

It took a while before Red answered, and when he did he said, "He was good, fast on the draw and shoot, and I reckon there will be more where he came from."

"Then it's high time we quit this burg," Buttons said. "What do you say we hitch up the team right now and head for Fort Concho and pick up that Limey coward feller?"

"No, I've been wronged, and I'll see this through to the end, no matter what that end may be," Red said. He glanced at the dead man again. "Danny Kline, you tried to scare me, and all you did was make me angry. The mistake was yours, not mine."

The old man with the imperial stepped to Red's side, bringing along his newspaper. "Suh, my name is Major Augustus Bennett, late of the 8th Virginia Infantry, and I saw this whole sorry affair as it happened. You defended your honor as a true Southern gentleman should and you were not to blame, suh, not to blame."

"Thank you, Major," Red said.

"Hey, Major, tell that to the sheriff," Buttons said.

Ten minutes later T. C. Lyons stalked through the open door, a Colt at his waist and a scowl on his face. "What's all the shooting about?" he said. His eyes went to the dead man on the floor and then to Red. "I might have known. Ryan, did you have a hand in this?"

"He drew on me, and I killed him," Red said. Then, with a mind to Major Bennett, "I was defending my honor."

"And I can attest to that, Sheriff," the major said. "Fair fight, suh, fair fight."

"Hell, that's Danny Kline, runs with Skull Jackson and them," Lyons said. He looked at Red. "It's a miracle you're still alive."

Red nodded. "He was good, real good."

The bartender said, "Sheriff, I run a respectable place here. There hasn't been a gunfight in the Silver Slipper in three-month."

"Seems to me there was a shooting not so long ago," Lyons said.

"A dispute between Southern gentlemen over a game of cards," Bennett said. "I saw that too, Sheriff."

Lyons nodded. "Major, one of those Southern gentlemen died of a bullet in the heart and I hung the other one."

The bartender turned surly. "When it's only one man doing the shooting, it don't count as a gunfight," he said. "Everybody knows that."

Lyons ignored the man and turned his attention to Red. "Ryan, what happened here?"

Red decided not to mention the carpetbag, and implied that Kline picked a fight because he was in the mood to kill a man. The major, well gone in brandy, didn't contradict that account, nor did the bartender, who wanted the whole matter forgotten as quickly as possible, and for once Buttons kept his mouth shut.

"All right, so it was self-defense," Lyons said. "But you're in a heap of trouble, Ryan. You said Danny Kline was fast, and he was, but Skull Jackson is a sight faster. He set store by Kline. They drank together, whored together, and killed together, and he won't let this stand." The sheriff shook his head. "I thought Pip Ogden would keep you out of trouble, but obviously that hasn't happened."

"We're still investigating Stella Morgan," Red said.

"Forget it, Ryan. Do as I do and leave it for the county sheriff when we get one. Climb on your stage and head west, east, north, south, anywhere but El Paso. Ogden is a trained police detective. Let him investigate Stella Morgan."

"I'll see it through, Lyons," Red said. "There's a train headed north the day after tomorrow, and Stella Morgan will be on it unless I stop her."

"I told you, let Ogden stop her." Lyons studied Red's face. "I can see you won't take my advice, so on your head be it. In the meantime, steer clear of Skull Jackson. I won't describe him for you, Ryan, because you'll know him when you see him . . . and he may be the last thing you'll ever see." He turned to the bartender. "I'll send the undertaker to clean up this mess."

CHAPTER FORTY-SIX

"Danny Kline dead. It's hard to believe," Seth Roper said.

"The word I hear is that Ryan shot him in the back," Skull Jackson said. "He couldn't shade Danny in a fair fight, and he knew it."

Roper smiled. "I never thought Danny Kline was much of a one for a fair fight either."

"Danny was my friend, Roper. With a face like mine, he was my only friend. Don't talk bad about him. I don't like it." He tossed his fork on the plate and said, "I can't eat this garbage."

"I can tell the bartender to scramble you some eggs, Henry," Roper said. "Or maybe some cheese. You like cheese?"

"I won't have any appetite until I kill Ryan," Jackson said. He looked around at the expectant faces in the Platte River saloon and said, "Yeah, you all heard me right. Go spread that word that I aim to shoot Red Ryan on sight."

Roper shook his head. "Henry, listen, that won't do. We need to get the carpetbag. It's likely Ryan has stashed it someplace, and he has to tell us where it is before you gun him."

"Probably in his hotel room," Jackson said. "Damn it, Roper, I told Danny not to go it alone."

"Don't underestimate Ryan. He's a hard man to kill," Roper said.

"I can kill him," Jackson said. "I'll kill him tonight."

"We must get the bag first, Henry. Please, understand that. Killing Ryan is way less important than the carpetbag."

"Killing Ryan is important to me," Jackson said. He and Roper locked eyes, a pair of pitiless, vicious predators with very different priorities. Finally, Skull looked away. "All right, Roper, here's how it will go down, and I don't want to hear any objections." He reached into the inside pocket of his frock coat and produced a straight razor with a yellowed, ivory handle. "Roper, you ever worked over a man with one of these?"

"No, I never have," Roper said. "I save razors for my chin."

Jackson opened the blade and it glinted in the saloon's gaslight. "The razor is so sharp, so keen, the cut is subtle. At first there is no feeling, but after a few heartbeats the pain hits and burns like fire. A strong man, Red Ryan for instance, will take many, many cuts before he screams in his torment and begs for the final slash . . . the merciful one across the throat." The man's face was a grinning skull. "Set your mind at rest, Roper. I'll find out where the bag is hidden." He closed the razor. "Ryan will tell me."

Roper, a hard-edged man not lacking in a self-serving brand of courage, swallowed with difficulty and then because he could think of nothing else, he said, "There will be blood."

Jackson nodded. "Much blood, rivers of blood. When I am done with my butchering, Ryan's hotel room will look like a slaughterhouse."

Roper drained his whiskey and then said, "Henry, tonight I wouldn't want to be in Ryan's shoes."

Jackson's smile was grotesque. "Tell me, who in his right mind would?"

"Red Ryan will breathe his last tonight, Stella," Seth Roper said. "Skull Jackson has it all planned."

"The carpetbag, Seth," Stella Morgan said. "We must get the bag."

"Jackson will get it." Roper smiled. "Ryan has had close shaves before, but the one he'll get tonight with Jackson's razor will be his last."

"Seth, who is this Skull Jackson?" Stella said. "Can we trust him?"

"As to who he is, or what he is, you don't want to know. And yeah, we can trust him. Skull always earns his wages."

"Lucian told me that Ryan killed a man last night," Stella said. "Is it true?"

"Yeah, in the Silver Slipper saloon, a draw fighter by the name of Danny Kline," Roper said. "Kline worked with Skull Jackson and he was warned not to go after Ryan by himself, but he did, and got himself shot."

"I hope Jackson is faster on the draw than Kline was," Stella said.

"He is, don't worry about that. Kline was told that Ryan is no bargain, but he went ahead and braced him anyway. The word coming down was that Ryan shot Danny in the back, but I talked to the Silver Slipper bartender, and he said it was a fair fight. Ryan didn't shoot first. But he shot straighter."

"Well, hopefully after tonight Red Ryan won't be around to trouble us," Stella said.

Seth shook his head. "There's no hopefully, Stella. When Jackson puts his mind to killing a man, he sees it through."

Stella rose from her chair by the hotel-room window and sat on the bed. She picked up a hairbrush from the table and then said, pointing it at Roper for emphasis, "Seth, what about Lucian?"

"Carter? What do you want to know?"

"Do we take him with us to Washington?"

"I guess he has the manners of a gentleman, when he wants to."

"And so?"

"He could come in handy as a front when you meet your future rich husbands. Introduce him as your brother and let him help you talk your way into high society." Roper saw the question on Stella's face and grinned. "I can't play that role, Stella. I'm too rough around the edges. Let me stay in the background, like we planned."

Stella began to brush her luxuriant hair. "Just so you know, Lucian will want to be rewarded, and I don't mean with money."

Roper laughed. "Hell, woman, you're a whore, a beautiful, desirable whore, but a whore nonetheless. In Washington, you'll use your body to lure rich men to your bed, so giving Carter a taste now and then won't hurt a bit." Roper shrugged. "If that arrangement becomes distasteful, I'll kill him for you." He rose to his feet and sat beside Stella on the bed. He took the brush from her hand and said, "Here, let me do that for you."

As Roper brushed, Stella said, "Am I that, Seth? Am I really a whore?"

"You plan on selling your body to the highest bidders," Roper said.

"So that makes me a whore," Stella said.

Roper kissed Stella's naked shoulder. "Yes, but you're more than that, Stella. You're a beautiful spider . . . a black widow spider that kills with a bite a dozen times deadlier than any rattlesnake."

Stella smiled. "I like being a black widow better than a whore."

"You're both, my love," Roper said. "You're both."

CHAPTER FORTY-SEVEN

"I'm a whore, Mr. Ryan," the girl said.

Red Ryan was puzzled. "Then, I think you have the wrong room, lady."

"No, number fourteen. It says so right here on the door."

Red shook his head. "I don't understand. Why are you here?"

The girl smiled. She was small, brunette, and pretty.

"I'm a present, a present for you." She held up a bottle. "And look, I brought some wine."

"Who sent you?" Red said.

"All I can say is that he's a gentleman admirer. Now, can I come in?"

Red looked out in the hallway. It was deserted, shadowed by the pale blue light of the gas lamps. "I'd guess you'd better," he said.

The girl's silk dress rustled as she stepped into the room. She smelled of lavender water. "My name is Trudy," she said. "Trudy True, and I'm all yours for the night."

The girl sat on the bed and bounced. "Comfy mattress," she said.

"Who is this gentlemen admirer?" Red said.

"I can't tell you. But I know he's rich." She smiled. "I don't come cheap, and neither does this wine." Trudy patted the bed. "Come sit beside me, Mr. Ryan."

There was nothing about this girl that Red didn't like. She had the kind of pert, poised prettiness that would make any man cut a dash in her presence, and Red was no exception.

"Well," Trudy said, "how do you want me? Do you want to undress me or should I do it myself?"

Red opened his mouth to speak, but the girl said, "No, not yet. We've got the whole night to get better acquainted. Let's have a glass of wine first."

Trudy rose and stepped to a side table where there was a carafe of water and two glasses. She took a small corkscrew from her purse, opened the wine bottle with practiced ease, and poured. She returned to the bed and handed a glass to Red. "I declare," the girl said, "it's a trifle warm in here." She turned her back and said, "Please unbutton me, Mr. Ryan. I'll be much cooler without my dress."

Red grinned, downed his wine in a gulp, let his glass drop to the floor, and began to fumble with tiny buttons and eyelets. "Damn, you're right, it is hot in here," he said. He fumbled . . . blinked . . . fumbled . . . blinked again . . . he couldn't feel his fingertips . . . fumbled . . . the girl giggled . . .

"Damn it's . . . hot . . ." Red said. He couldn't speak properly, as though his tongue was too large for his mouth.

The girl rose, laid her untouched wineglass on the table, and collected her purse from the bed. She smiled sympathetically at Red and said, "Poor boy, you just can't handle your liquor, can you?"

"Wha . . ." Red said. The room grew darker and his head spun. He tried to get to his feet, failed, tried again and finally stood upright . . . but not for long. He was vaguely aware of Trudy True stepping back from him, smiling, and he tried to reach her, but he staggered and then fell on his hands and knees. The walls of the room closed in on him, and he found himself crawling across the floor in darkness . . . and then he fell heavily on his side. He tried to rise, but could not move his arms or legs. He was fully conscious now . . . but paralyzed.

Red Ryan woke to dim gaslight. He opened his eyes and tried to focus his hazy brain. At some point he'd fallen asleep, but slowly the events of the evening returned to him . . . the girl . . . the wine . . . his paralysis . . .

Damn, the wine had been drugged! He'd been taken in by a whore's false smile like a teenage rube just off the farm.

Red attempted to move his arms and realized he was no longer immobile, but his wrists were tightly bound to the brass bed as were his ankles. Then it dawned on him, he was stark naked, spread-eagled on the bed like a human sacrifice in some lurid dime novel.

He raised his head . . . and saw death.

Then from the lipless skull, a thin whisper. "Ah, the sleeper awakes. The potion from my little Celestial friends did everything they said it would. Oh, I see you frown, Mr. Ryan. Did you hope you were dead? How unlucky for you that you are not."

"What the hell are you?" Red said. "What are you doing in my room?"

The skull grew closer, grotesque in the eerie glow of the gaslight.

"What am I? I am the razor man. I am the bringer of pain. I am the herald of your screams, of your shrieks, of your squeals . . . of your death. Woe to you, Mr. Ryan, your dying will not be quick and it will not be pleasant, but your screeching for mercy will be like sweet music to my ears."

"Damn you, you're Skull Jackson," Red said. "I was warned about you, and you sound like Edgar Allan Poe in them stories of his."

"You were warned, and it was a warning you should have heeded." Jackson shook his horrific head. "Undone by a paid whore. How easy it all was." A razor appeared in Jackson's hand. "When it comes to horrors, Edgar Allan Poe is an amateur compared to me. See the blade, see how it shines . . . how keen it is . . . and very soon now soon you will feel its bite. Holla! Here is a splendid idea! A taste of the steel as an appetizer."

Jackson moved to the bed, stared down at Red, and smiled. The razor flashed . . . and laid open the top of Red Ryan's chest from armpit to armpit. Red raised his head and saw a thin ribbon of seeping scarlet that caused little pain . . . at first. Then the fire began.

"You wince, Mr. Ryan, but that is just a little taste," Skull Jackson said. "There's much, much more to come, oh, a thousand cuts more."

"You go to hell," Red said.

"Ah, bravado. I like that in a man. An obstinate

man does not die too quickly." Jackson rubbed his deeply scarred chin. "Now we'll play a little game. It's called question and answer. I will ask the question and you give the answer. Comfy? Good, then we'll begin. Where is the carpetbag?"

"Go to hell," Red said.

The razor slashed again, from the middle of the cut across Red's chest to his navel, forming a bloody T. Again, the cut was not too deep, but it hurt like a hundred beestings.

"Don't worry, Mr. Ryan, the cuts will get deeper as our little game goes along," Jackson said. "An hour or so before the end you'll watch your guts spill out onto the bed. Not an agreeable sight, I grant you. Now, back to our game . . . Where is the carpetbag?"

Red felt blood trickle down the sides of his chest and enter the conduits between the ribs. He felt that his upper body was on fire, and for the first time he felt real fear. "I don't have the bag," he said.

"I know you don't," Jackson said. "Where is the carpetbag?"

"Go to hell."

The razor was poised. "Where is the carpetbag?"

"I don't know."

Another slash, this time a little deeper, to the left side of the bloody T, a six-inch-long vertical cut that readily spurted blood. This one made Red gasp in pain.

"Where is the carpetbag?"

"Go to hell. I don't know."

The razor poised again, the blade gleaming pale blue in the gaslight.

"Where is the carpetbag?"

Red bit back a groan. "Go to hell."

The razor did its work. A gash similar to the last, this time on the other side of the T. And it was deeper.

"Where is the carpetbag?"

"I don't know."

The bloody steel blade hovered over Red's face.

"Where is the carpetbag?"

Red opened his mouth to spit out his defiance, but the words were never uttered.

The hotel room door crashed inward with tremendous force, and a man's voice yelled, "Drop it!"

Skull Jackson roared in surprise and anger. He let the razor fall from his hand and went for his holstered gun. A gunshot racketed like thunder in the confines of the small room, and Jackson shrieked as he took a hit. Red turned his head and saw the small figure of T. C. Lyons standing wide-legged just inside the room, the shattered door at his back. He held his Colt in both hands at eye level, his arms extended straight out in front of him. Jackson, unsteady on his feet from a chest wound, thumbed off a shot that missed, and Lyons fired again. For a man who'd never been in a gunfight, he acquitted himself well. His second bullet hit Jackson's gun hand, caromed off the cylinder of his revolver, took a path upward and crashed into the bottom of his chin. Jackson, choking on lead and his own blood, staggered back, tossed his mangled Colt aside, and bent and grabbed his razor. When he straightened up he went for Red, his nightmare face contorted with hate. He raised the razor for a killing throat slash, but Lyons advanced on him, shooting. Three .45s slammed into Jackson's body, punching great holes in his chest, and the man let out one last shriek of rage and frustration and dropped to the floor.

Lyons emerged from the gunsmoke, stepped to the bottom of the bed and said, "Ryan, are you still alive?"

"Yeah, more or less," Red said.

"Damn, that's discouraging. I was sure Skull Jackson had done for you."

"He tried, Lyons. He tried."

"You're all bloody, Ryan. Stay right there, I'm sending for a doctor."

"I'm not going anywhere. I'm roped to this damned bed."

"I wish I could keep you there," Lyons said.

He walked through the doorway and into the hall, and Red was left to gaslight and pain.

CHAPTER FORTY-EIGHT

The elderly doctor, a tall, thin white-haired man by the name of Tom Malone, declared Red Ryan's wounds to be superficial except for the last cut that was deep enough to cause him concern but was not life-threatening, and he discounted any danger from tetanus.

Directing his pedantic words at T. C. Lyons and Buttons Muldoon, not his patient, he said, "Bleeding wounds are always alarming to the nonprofessional bystander, but—"

"Doc, they're alarming to me," Red said.

Malone ignored that and continued, "In this case a bandage may be conveniently employed, once the wounds have been thoroughly cleaned with alcohol. Later, if the patient expresses discomfort from pain, laudanum may be administered at the caregiver's discretion."

Hope fled Lyons's face. "So, Ryan is going to pull through?"

"I appreciate your concern, Sheriff, but I see no reason why he should not," the doctor said.

Lyon's nodded, disappointment writ large on his face.

After Red was freed from the ropes that bound him to the bed, Dr. Malone bandaged his chest, left a bottle of laudanum and then stepped aside as Thaddeus Wraith and an assistant carried out Skull Jackson's body, the death mask of the gunman's face made even more grotesque by the manner of his dying.

After the doctor and the undertakers were gone, Red got up from his bloodstained bed and with difficulty dressed.

"How are you feeling, Ryan?" Lyons said.

Red managed a smile. "Sorry to dash your hopes again, Lyons, but I'll survive." He stuck out his hand. "Thank you for saving my life. You played a man's part tonight."

Lyons thought it over and finally shook Red's hand. "I've never killed anyone before," he said.

"You didn't kill a man, you killed a monster," Red said. "Skull Jackson intended to slice me up piece by piece."

"Maybe you should thank Trudy True," Lyons said.

"You mean the treacherous little whore that got me into this mess?" Red's shirt bulged over his bulky bandage, and he felt light-headed.

"She thought Seth Roper was playing a practical joke on you," Lyons said.

"Roper hired her?"

"That's what she told everyone in Joe Dolan's saloon. One of my sometime deputies heard her." Lyons smiled. "Whores don't keep secrets."

"And Skull Jackson was the practical joke?" Red said.

"The girl didn't know that. But her loose talk in the

saloon led me here, so if I were you, I wouldn't be too hard on her."

"All right, what did the girl know?"

"Roper told her it was all a big joke, that's all. The girl didn't know he planned on Jackson killing you one cut at a time."

"He wanted Stella Morgan's carpetbag."

"And you didn't tell him?"

"No. I told him nothing."

"You're a tough man, Ryan."

"I don't know how tough I'd have been after a few more cuts. I think I would've told Jackson what he wanted to know."

"Maybe, maybe not," Lyons said. His watch chimed, and he snapped it open and looked at it. "One o'clock."

"Then Stella doesn't have much time," Red said. "She sent two killers after me, Danny Kline and Jackson, and she'll send more. The first train out of El Paso leaves this morning at seven, six hours from now, but without the carpetbag she won't be on it."

"I still don't have the proof I need to arrest her," Lyons said.

"You can arrest Roper."

"He wanted to play a practical joke on you, Ryan. He didn't know that Jackson would show up to avenge his friend. He's horrified about what happened, just horrified. That will be his defense, and there's no way around it."

Buttons Muldoon said, "On the bright side, so long as she doesn't have the carpetbag we can keep Stella Morgan in town until Pip Ogden can pin a murder charge on her." Buttons gave Red a sidelong look and said, "Though me and Red won't be in El Paso much longer."

"I'm not leaving until I see this through," Red said. "Now it's become a personal thing with me."

"Just to remind you, Red, we got a date with a yellowbelly in Fort Concho," Buttons said.

"He can wait. I have a feeling that one way or another, this whole business will be settled real soon."

"Ryan, watch your step," Lyons said. "I don't want you breaking the law."

"Whatever it takes," Red said.

"Ryan . . . I don't like where you're headed," Lyons said.

Red looked the sheriff in the eye. "Neither do I," he said.

Lyons left, to be replaced by the hotel owner and a couple of maids who had been roused from sleep and looked irritable.

"I'm here to assess the damage," said the manager, a bearded man named Pollock who looked a heap more irritable than the maids. "Door wrecked, bedsheets destroyed," he said. "Mr. Ryan, you've brought ruination to my house."

"Send the bill to Sheriff Lyons," Buttons said. "He busted down the door and did the shooting. And as it's still early yet, Mr. Ryan will need another room."

"Then he can move in with you," Pollock said. "I won't trust him with another of my rooms. Not after what he's done to this one."

One of the maids looked at the bloody bed, shrieked, and scampered out of the room, adding to Pollock's annoyance. "That's it!" he yelled. "Ryan, get the hell out of here, or do I have to throw you out?"

A split second later he found himself looking into

the muzzle of Buttons Muldoon's Remington, the hammer back and ready. "I don't advise that," Buttons said. "But you suit yourself, mister, state your intentions."

Pollock's gaze went from the Remington to Buttons's bleak eyes, and he decided he wanted no part of either. "At your convenience, of course, Mr. Ryan," he said.

"Now is convenient," Buttons said. "Gather up your stuff, Red."

Red Ryan sat on the corner of Buttons's bed and said, "Well, where do we go from here?"

"I don't know," Buttons said. "Do you?"

"Wait for Stella Morgan to make the next move, I guess," Red said.

Buttons nodded. "I thought that might be your way of thinking." He stepped to the corner of the room and grabbed Red's shotgun. "Keep this close. You do a sight better with the Greener than you do a Colt's gun."

"Danny Kline is the one that's dead," Red said, slightly miffed.

"Yeah, he is," Buttons said. "And you're the one that was almighty lucky."

CHAPTER FORTY-NINE

It was well after midnight, and Stella Morgan was still awake. And Lucian Carter and Seth Roper were also sleepless. Roper had just brought news of the death of Skull Jackson at the hand of T. C. Lyons, and Stella had summoned Carter to join in what was an emergency meeting.

"I'm not leaving El Paso without my money and jewels," Stella said. "It's out of the question."

"Red Ryan is badly cut up and is at death's door," Roper said. "That's what I heard in the Platte, and that's why I'm here."

"We can delay our departure for a few days if need be," Lucian Carter said.

"We may have to," Stella said. "Does Ryan even have the bag?"

"Him and that fat driver of his?" Carter said, "I'm sure they do."

"Seth, saloons are full of gossips. Did anyone in the Platte mention a carpetbag?" Stella said.

Roper shook his head. "No, but it's possible Lyons has it, especially if Ryan is about to turn up his toes."

"Lyons or the driver, what's his name? Muldoon," Carter said.

"There still might be time," Stella said. "The train doesn't leave until seven."

Roper shook his head. "That's pushing it, Stella. T. C. Lyons killed Skull Jackson, not an easy thing to do, and if Lyons doesn't have the bag we go after Muldoon, and he's no pushover either."

"Damn it, Seth, don't tell me what we can't do," Stella said. "Tell me what we can do."

"We need time, that's all," Roper said.

"How much time?" Stella said.

"Two more days. I can arrange things in that time," Roper said.

Carter said, "Roper, you arranged the Ryan business, and look where that's gotten us . . . nowhere."

"Well, hell, Carter, can you do better?" Ryan said.

"It wouldn't be hard," Carter said.

"Stop it, you two," Stella said. "There's no use quarreling among ourselves. Seth, we know what has to be done, so you and Lucian put your heads together and come up with a solution."

"It's easy," Carter said. "Roper spelled it out . . . first Lyons, and if he doesn't have the bag, then Muldoon. But as Roper said, we need some time."

"Well, it's not all bad news," Stella said "It seems pretty obvious that Ryan will die, so that only leaves Lyons and Muldoon. Get the bag and use two bullets and we can leave for Washington free and clear." Stella's smile was as beautiful as ever. "Seth, Lucian, why don't you draw straws for who kills who?"

"I'll take Muldoon," Carter said. "I never liked that man from the git-go."

"I can kill Lyons," Roper said. "But he's a lawman and it has to look good."

Stella said, "That leaves Pip Ogden. Do we have to worry about him?"

"I'll take care of him too," Carter said. "I don't like him worth two bits either."

"Then it's settled," Stella said. "Lucian, pour us a drink. I think we all need one."

Seth Roper grinned. "Hey, maybe Ogden has the carpetbag."

"Stranger things have happened," Stella said. "But I don't think Ryan would trust him. I mean, he hardly knows the man."

Carter raised his glass. "Well here's to Red Ryan," he said. "May he rest in peace."

"Amen to that," Stella said. "One down, three to go."

Stella Morgan lay in bed sleepless, her mind racing. Once the present difficulties were resolved and the carpetbag safely returned to her, she would have a decision to make . . . Roper or Carter . . . which one should accompany her to Washington? Though wouldn't there be plenty of tough men in the big city willing to do her bidding, at least as long as she remained desirable and had something to offer in bed? Carter was jealous of every man she met, and he might become a burden after a while. Roper was a western man and as rough as a cob. He had muscle and a gun and was willing to kill for her, but she could not see him at home in Washington society. Now if Carter and Roper killed each other, it would solve her problem. Stella smiled into the darkness at the thought. How could she make it work? There had to be a way. Well, she'd think about it once her money and jewels were returned. Plenty of time then to . . . arrange things.

Stella closed her eyes, and whispered in her mind, "John, thank you for dying so conveniently and leaving me a rich woman with so many things to think about."

Someone knocked on the door, a soft, discreet rapping. Who could it be at this time of the night? Had Roper or Carter come back hoping for some mattress time?

The soft, tap-tap-tap again.

Stella rose, hurriedly put on her dressing gown and picked up her Colt, keeping it behind her back. She stepped to the door and said, "Who is it?"

No answer.

Well, she never could resist a mysterious caller.

Stella opened the door a crack, saw who stood in the hallway, and opened it wider.

"Oh, it's you," she said, smiling. "Do come in."

CHAPTER FIFTY

Buttons Muldoon stood in the recessed entrance of Mark Kidd's Rod & Gun Store and watched into the night, his gaze moving from the street to the entrance of the hotel and back again. He'd had a hard time convincing Red Ryan to lie in bed and get some rest. Although his wounds were mostly superficial, Red had lost blood, and it had weakened him. Buttons didn't really expect that there would be another attempt on Red's life . . . yet something nagged at him, a feeling that all was not well, that there was danger in the darkness, unseen, unheard . . . but out there, waiting to strike.

Buttons had the Irish gift. As his sainted mother had once told him, "Patrick, hindsight is to be admired and so is foresight, but second sight is the most admirable of all. You have the gift, so be sure that you use it well."

He was using it well that night.

A careful man, Buttons had propped Red's scatter-gun in the corner of the doorway. He was a fair hand with a revolver, but knew he'd be no match for the kind of gunman Stella Morgan would send to make sure Red was well and truly dead. A 12-gauge Greener loaded with double-aught buck was a great equalizer.

It was two in the morning, a Tuesday night, and El Paso was winding down early, the sporting crowd saving themselves for Friday. A strangely solemn quiet had descended on the town, and a waxing moon rode high in the heavens. Across the street from the hotel, behind a row of stores, a scattering of outbuildings and cabins were bathed in moonlight, like so many old men in white nightgowns who'd wandered off and lost their way. A tiny calico cat strolled past Buttons, hunting for rodents of the smallest kind, ignoring the human who was much too big to eat. Buttons glanced at his watch. Ten after two. Would this night ever end?

Room 14.

Lucian Carter looked up at Red Ryan's hotel and the windows stared back at him with dark, blank eyes. Behind one of those windows in room 14, Ryan lay at death's door, and if he wasn't dead yet he would be soon. Carter adjusted the lie of his guns, but he had no intention of using them. Way too much noise. The knife was better, and Ryan was already cut up, so who would notice yet another wound? What was it the French called it? Ah yes, the coup de grace . . . hilt deep into the heart. Hilt deep . . . that reminded him of Stella Morgan, and Carter smiled. She would be proud of him. Ryan, Lyons, and Ogden the nosy detective, all killed on the same night. And the bag? One of them would have it, and he'd return to Stella with it in triumph, just in time for the morning train.

Carter consulted his watch. Ten after two. Time was

short. He had to make his move. He was supremely confident. His father had taught him the assassin's profession well, and he'd always said that Lucian was the most gifted of his students, and now the prodigy would prove it.

Buttons Muldoon saw the man emerge from the shadows and stand on the edge of the boardwalk, his eyes fixed on the hotel. A few moments later, as though he'd just made his mind up about something, the man stepped into the street, and it was then, in full moonlight, that Buttons recognized the slim figure of Lucian Carter. He didn't try to outguess himself. Carter was there for one reason and one reason only . . . he planned to kill Red.

Buttons grabbed the Greener and moved quickly to cut Carter off before he reached the hotel. "Hold up there," Buttons said.

Carter turned and his face registered shock. He hadn't even seen that fat fool lurking in a doorway. Now he'd have to go to the gun, kill Muldoon, and beat a hasty retreat before a crowd gathered. Carter didn't think about it any further. The situation was clear cut, and he knew what had to be done and he did it.

He went for his guns.

Then a spiking instant of alarm . . . in the uncertain light he hadn't seen the scattergun!

Carter cleared leather with dazzling speed, but he couldn't outdraw Muldoon's trigger finger. Even as his brought his Colts level, Carter was hit by both barrels of the Greener. Buckshot tore into the left side of his pelvis, and he staggered back. He'd been hit hard, and he knew it. Like a wounded animal, Carter fought back, but he was unsteady on his feet, and his fusillade of shots missed Muldoon, who had his own revolver in his hand and was getting his work in. None of Buttons's bullets took effect, but it didn't matter, because all Carter wanted was to get out of there. He staggered away, Buttons, not the most forgiving of men when he'd been wronged, taking pots at him until Carter merged with the gloom, leaving behind him a trail of blood.

Then Red was on the hotel porch, along with a half-dozen other guests in night attire led by Pollock the manager, looking stunned. "Ryan, you again," Pollock said.

Red nodded in the direction of Buttons to the street. "Not me, him." Then, "Who was he?"

"Lucian Carter. I reckon he was here to make sure you was dead."

"Are you hit?" Red said.

"No, but he is, took two barrels of buck."

Red stepped into the street and looked at the blood pooling in the street where Carter had taken the hit. "He's badly wounded, Buttons," he said.

"Man who takes both barrels from a scattergun usually is," Buttons said.

Pollock stepped beside Red and said, "My God, man, are you two trying to ruin my business?" He waved a hand in the direction of his guests. "Look at them. These people are terrified."

"A man named Lucian Carter came here tonight with the idea of killing me," Red said. "Me and Buttons can hardly be blamed for that."

"Well, I am blaming you, Ryan," Pollock said. "I want both of you out of my hotel—now!"

Buttons was outraged. "Mr. Ryan is sore wounded. You'd throw a sick man into the street?"

"Yes, I would," Pollock said. "Out now, before I send for the law!"

"You wouldn't dare," Buttons said.

"Try me," Pollock said.

Red Ryan and Buttons Muldoon sat on the step of the hotel porch, their meager belongings around them.

"Well, I guess he meant it," Buttons said.

"Seems like," Red said.

"I should've plugged him," Buttons said.

"Maybe you should, but it's too late for that now," Red said. "He locked the door behind him. What time is it?"

"Gone four," Buttons said. "I wonder if Ma's Kitchen is open?"

"That's just what I was thinking," Red said.

"It's a walk, can you make it?" Buttons said.

Red rose to his feet. "Just watch me," he said, wincing.

CHAPTER FIFTY-ONE

Lucian Carter knew he was hit bad. Gore stained the front of his pants, and as he staggered through the empty, shadowed streets of El Paso he left a scarlet snail trail of blood behind him. Like a wounded animal seeking its lair, he had but one thought . . . he must get to Stella Morgan. His face twisted in pain, he knew everything would be fine once he reached Stella. She'd take care of him and send for a doctor. Yes, the wound was serious, he was aware of that, but with proper treatment and care he'd recover.

Carter stumbled on. Stella, bright, luminous, was his light at the end of this tunnel. Stella, his angel of mercy . . . the woman who loved him.

A gusting wind picked up and tugged at Carter, teasing him unmercifully as he tottered forward through the deserted streets on leaden feet. The pain in his lower belly was now a living thing that gnawed at him with fangs of fire. His head reeled, the world spun around him, and he stumbled and fell . . .

Then, glory be, salvation!

Carter looked up and realized he was outside Stella's hotel.

Slowly, painfully, Carter climbed to his feet. He staggered toward the entrance and lurched inside. There was no clerk on duty, but a single gas lamp glowed behind the desk. He stood and waited until the pain subsided a little, and he shuffled to the stairs. Outside, the spiteful wind howled in frustration as Carter regarded the mountain he had to climb . . . the staircase that soared before him, the last few carpeted steps before the landing deep in shadow. He thought about crying out for help, but immediately dismissed the idea. A shout would draw too much attention, and questions would be asked. Once he was safe in Stella's arms, she would make the decisions from there.

Lucian Carter had it to do.

One cruel step at a time, in agony and bleeding like a stuck pig, he began to climb the stairs. It took Carter an eternity of pain to reach the landing . . . then the gaslit hallway . . . stumbling, groaning . . . then Stella's door.

Safe at last. Stella would cry over him, care for him, make him well again.

Carter pounded on the door and, his voice weak, he said, "Stella, let me in . . ."

He'd thought Stella would be asleep in bed, but to his surprise the door swung open almost immediately. Carter staggered inside. "Stella, for God's sake help me," he said.

Then he saw the man sitting at the table with the carpetbag in front of him, and painful as a blow to the gut, Lucian Carter knew he'd been betrayed.

* * *

Stella gave Carter no time to react. The man looked dead on his feet, and the push she gave him had the desired effect. Carter cried out in pain as his back slammed against the wall, and as he fell Stella reached inside his coat and relieved him of his Colts.

She turned her head and said, "He's been shot."

"Is it bad?" Pip Ogden said.

Stella nodded. "Yes, it's bad."

"Then we have to get rid of him."

"How, Pip? He's here."

Carter tugged on the hem of Stella's nightgown. "Help me, Stella," he whispered. "I need a doctor."

Stella pulled away from Carter's clutching hand and said, "We can keep him here. He'll die soon, and by the time his body is found we'll be on our way to Washington."

Ogden shook his head. "I don't want to take that risk. It's just possible that the body could be found early. I don't want T. C. Lyons showing up at the station asking why there's a dead man in your hotel room and why I'm with you on the train."

"Then what do we do with him?" Stella said.

"Before he bleeds all over the floor, out a back window with him," Ogden said. He saw the puzzlement on Stella's face and said, "It will look like he'd been shot and crawled into an alley to die."

"There's a linen closet with a window, but we'll need to cross the hallway," Stella said.

"Then let's get it done."

Ogden rose, took his revolver from his coat pocket, and stepped to Stella's side.

Carter looked up and said, "Help me. I'm hurt, and I need a doctor real bad."

Ogden smiled. "Sure, I'll help you." He raised his Colt and slammed the barrel into Carter's head. The man groaned and fell on his side. "Stella . . ." he whispered. "Stella . . ."

"He won't give us any trouble now," Ogden said. "Look in the hallway and make sure it's clear. If it is, open the closet door and then the window. I'll drag him over there."

"Stella . . ." Carter said, his eyes pleading.

"Lucian, shut the hell up," Stella said. "You'll be out of your misery very soon."

She opened the door, saw that the hallway was clear, then crossed to the linen closet. The window was a large casement, and Stella opened it wide. She looked down and saw to her joy that Lucian, wounded as he was, would land on a jumbled pile of bricks that pretty much guaranteed a fatal fall.

"Is the coast clear?" Ogden's hoarse whisper from the doorway.

"Yes. Hurry."

Ogden dragged the semiconscious Carter into the hallway and then through the open door of the linen closet. He lifted the upper half of the man's body into the window frame but got stuck. "Stella, you've got to help me," he said.

Stella made a face. "Ooh . . . he's covered in blood."

"I know, but I can't get him through this damned window by myself, so help me lift him," Ogden said.

Stella and Ogden got ahold of Carter's legs and pushed him through the window.

"He hit the ground hard," Ogden said. "He's done for."

"Lucian still had enough life in him to squeal though, didn't he?" Stella said.

"Yes, he did," Ogden said. "Quick, close the window and let's get back to your room. We've got some planning to do."

"Why did you bring back my carpetbag, Pip?" Stella Morgan said. "You could've kept it and made your escape. Why are you here?"

"You want the main reason?" Ogden said.

"I'm all ears," Stella said. She smiled. "Now that I'm over my surprise."

"Because I want you, Stella."

"You want to be my lover?"

"More than anything else in the world. I thought that from the first moment I set eyes on you, and then I told myself that I was being a fool. How could a man on a policeman's salary ever possess a woman like you? But when Red Ryan brought me the bag and I saw what it contained, I knew I'd found a way."

"That's the main reason," Stella said. "What are the others?"

"Others? There is only one other. After twenty years of servitude as a police officer, of harsh discipline, being overworked, badly treated, made to know my place and that place no better than a common laborer, when I retired I'd receive a pension of two-thirds my annual salary, enough to die a slow death in genteel poverty. When I came here to El Paso I saw a way out, and I took it." Ogden took Stella's hand. "So, dear lady, that's why I'm here. In the carpetbag alone, there's money enough for both of us."

Stella thought that through. A trained detective

would be a great help in the kind of criminal enterprises she planned once she reached Washington. But how far would Ogden be willing to go? She could control him with her body, but could she trust him? Once a lawman, always a lawman, isn't that how the saying went? No, the risk was too great. She had what she wanted, the carpetbag and Seth Roper to supply muscle when needed, and that last was just a half-formed idea. The truth was, she didn't really need anybody. After all, it was cheaper to have a killing done than share her fortune with a thug like Roper. She summed it up in her mind: Ogden would have to go, but not here in El Paso. The runt's death would be her first order of business after her arrival in the capital.

"I'd love for you to be in Washington with me, Pip," she said. "But there are many beautiful women in Washington, and I fear you would soon tire of me."

"Never, Stella," Ogden said. "I'll devote the rest of my life to making you happy."

And the rest of your life will be very short, Pip, you ugly little pip-squeak.

"Then I'm very content," Stella said. "All this is very sudden, but I know we can have a wonderful life together, you and I."

Ogden rose from the chair, took Stella by the hands, and raised her to her feet. He pulled apart the top of her nightgown and let it slip from her shoulders and cling to her hips. "I love you, Stella. Do we have time?" he said, his voice hoarse.

"Of course, we do, dear Pip," Stella said, dropping her gown to her ankles. "All the time in the world."

CHAPTER FIFTY-TWO

Seth Roper made up his mind as he tossed some clothing into a bag and checked his watch for the sixth time within the past fifteen minutes. Leaving with Stella Morgan was not an easy decision to make. Remaining in El Paso where he was the premier gunman had its attractions, as there were opportunities to make money, especially a protection racket that had been perfected up Fort Worth way by his sometime acquaintance Jim Courtright. But there was a downside to that plan. When a man sat himself up on a pedestal as top gun there were any number of wannabes who wanted to knock him off it. One day, someone would come along who was faster or just luckier and leave him with his beard in the sawdust.

Roper was a realist, and Stella was obviously a better bet. She would hustle her bustle and make him rich without the need to put his life on the line every time a wild kid with a quick gun and a chip on his shoulder rode into town.

Three hours until train time.

Roper closed the bag and pondered how to kill

time. Visit Stella? No, she'd be packing, and he'd only
be in the way. Kill Lucian Carter? Nah, that too could
wait. Breakfast? Sure, why not? Ma's Kitchen opened
early and steak and eggs would sustain him until he
and Stella had a romantic supper in the dining car.

Roper buckled on his gun, left the hotel, and
walked into the dark, windy morning.

"Red, do you see who just came in?" Buttons Muldoon said.

"I see him," Red said. "What's he doing up so early?
No, no need to answer that. My guess is he's leaving
on the seven o'clock train."

"Him and Stella Morgan," Buttons said, an odd
tone of defeat in his voice.

Roper looked across the restaurant. A few work-
men sat at tables eating breakfast along with several
bleary-eyed representatives of the sporting crowd
suffering from the whiskey hunger. Roper met Red's
gaze and stepped to his table.

"You gents mind if I join you?" he said.

"If we said no, you'd do it anyway," Buttons said.
"Pull up a chair."

A waitress filled a coffee cup for Roper and took his
order. When she left, he said, "Heard you had some
trouble earlier, Ryan."

"You heard right, Roper," Red said. "But I doubt it
came as a surprise to you, since you hired it done."

"Yet another of your false accusations, Ryan, though
I was sorry to hear about Skull Jackson," Roper said.
"Sheriff Lyons done for him, huh?"

"Yeah, he did," Red said.

"Who would've thunk it?" Roper said, shaking his head.

"I think Lyons surprised himself," Red said. "He was no match for Jackson."

"Did he cut you up bad?"

"Some. Before Lyons stopped him."

"I'm sorry to hear that."

"No, you're not."

"I mean sorry that Lyons stopped him."

"Why are you up so early, Roper?" Buttons said. "It ain't like you to be an early bird."

"Leaving town on the seven o'clock train. Me and the widow Morgan."

"I thought she wouldn't leave without the carpet-bag," Red said.

"Maybe she has it," Roper said.

"She doesn't," Red said.

Roper shrugged. "Well, I'll be at the station anyway. There could be something in it for you, Ryan, if you tell me where the bag is located."

"I don't know where it is."

"I'd say Stella would go as high as five thousand, cash."

"She won't go without the carpetbag, Roper," Red said. "You'll be at the station alone."

"We'll see. Ah, and here's breakfast." Roper smiled at the waitress and then picked up his knife and fork. "I can talk while I eat."

"We've got nothing to talk about," Red said.

Roper chewed on steak and then said, "You don't look too good, Ryan. Lost a lot of blood, huh?"

"I'm just fine."

"You don't look it. Shedding blood is bad for a

man, makes him weak and slows him up real bad, if you get my meaning."

Seth Roper looked big and muscular that morning, a strong man in his prime ready to take on any challenge thrown at him. On the other hand, Red did feel used up, the knife cuts working on him.

Roper dipped a chunk of steak in egg yolk, pushed the dripping forkful into his mouth, chewed, his eyes reading Red's face. "Either of you boys seen Lucian Carter recently?"

Buttons face didn't change. The less he told Roper the better. He said, "Can't say as I have."

"I haven't seen him," Red said.

"I guess he'll be at the station," Roper said.

He finished his breakfast in silence, paid his bill and then rose to his feet.

"A word of advice, Ryan," he said. "Don't be at the station. I'll take it hard if you are."

"I've got no reason to be there, Roper," Red said. "I can't stop you leaving. I'm not the law. But Detective Ogden might have a different way of seeing things."

Roper nodded. "Better for him if he's not at the station either." He moved away from the table, turned, and said, "Well, so long, Ryan. Come visit me in Washington sometime. I'll buy you a stogie."

CHAPTER FIFTY-THREE

A pounding on his hotel room door woke Sheriff T. C. Lyons from a sound sleep. He jolted upright in bed and yelled, "Who the hell is it."

"It's me, Sheriff, John Bryce. I'm the owner of the Parker Hotel." A pause, then, "There's been a murder."

"Damn it all, man, who was murdered?" Lyons said

"I don't know, Sheriff."

"How do you know he was murdered?"

"Looks like he was gut shot."

Lyons swung his legs off the bed. "Sounds like murder, all right."

"Then he fell over a pile of bricks," Bryce said.

"Fell over a pile of bricks?"

"Yeah, Sheriff, in the dark."

"I'll be right over," Lyons said. "Wait a minute, Stella Morgan has a room in your hotel, doesn't she?"

"Yes, the widow Morgan is an honored guest."

"I'll be there in ten minutes," Lyons said.

The sheriff took time to rouse Lou Hunt, one of his more competent deputies, and the two men made their way to the Parker, walking through a blustery wind that pulled at their clothing and lifted mustard-colored veils of dust from the streets.

John Bryce, looking worried, wringing his hands, met Lyons on the hotel porch. "He's round back, Sheriff." Then, "Isn't this a terrible thing?"

"Let's take a look at the body, and I'll tell you if it's terrible," Lyons said.

"It's terrible, all right," Lyons said. "Looks like he was hit with a scattergun."

"And then he tripped over the bricks," Parker said.

"That would explain the bruises on his head, huh?" Deputy Hunt said.

"Maybe," Lyons said. And then to Bryce. "The dead man's name is Lucian Carter. He was a close friend of Mrs. Morgan."

"Oh, she'll be so upset when she hears about this," Bryce said, wringing his hands again.

Lyons said nothing. He examined the body again, closer this time. When Carter tripped and fell he'd hit hard, and there was a deep, almost triangular indentation in his skull above his left eye, that could have been caused by the corner of a brick. Lyons examined the ground, deep in thought. A shotgun blast to the belly causes massive bleeding, but there was no blood trail leading to the brick pile. Then it dawned on him. Carter didn't trip over the bricks . . . he fell on them from a height. The sheriff's eyes scanned the hotel wall. There was a second-story window almost directly above where the body lay, and Lyons said, "Bryce, what window is that?"

The man glanced upward and said, "Ah, that's the window of the linen closet." He puffed up a little. "The Parker prides itself on its clean linens."

"Let's take a look up there," Lyons said.

"Sheriff is . . . is that the deceased's blood on my closet floor?" John Bryce said. His face was ashen, and he looked as though he was washing his hands without soap or water.

"That would be my guess," Lyons said. He examined the windowsill and pointed out some dried, rust-colored stains. "Blood," he said.

"Oh, dear," Bryce said. "My poor sheets."

"Lucian Carter was tossed through this window," Lyons said. "And that was sometime after he was shot. There's a blood trail across the floor and into the hallway." He stepped out of the closet and examined the carpet. "Bloodstains lead to this room," Lyons said.

"Ah, that is Mrs. Morgan's room, but I doubt—"

"Open the door, Bryce," Lyons said.

"I have a master key, Sheriff, but I don't think I wish to disturb—"

"Open the damned door," Lyons said. "He pulled his Colt from his waistband and let Bryce smell the muzzle. "Am I going to have trouble with you?" he said.

"No, not at all, Sheriff," Bryce said, flustered. "Now just let me knock first to be polite."

"Lou," Lyons said.

Without a word, Hunt raised his boot and crashed the door in. The deputy grinned, bowed, and said, "After you, Sheriff."

Gun in hand, Lyons stepped into the room and looked around. "She's flown the coop," he said. His eyes went to the blood on the floor and wall. "And that's Lucian Carter's blood for sure."

Hunt said, "Looks like she dragged him from here to the linen closet window and tossed him outside,"

"Not she, they," Lyons said. "Stella Morgan couldn't manhandle Carter across the hall and into the closet by herself. And she sure as hell needed help throwing him out the window."

"Sheriff, what about my broken door?" Bryce said, wringing his hands at a rapid rate.

"Send your bill to the county sheriff as soon as one is appointed," Lyons said. He smiled at Hunt. "The shotgun wound didn't kill Lucian Carter, the fall from the window did. I finally have enough to charge Stella Morgan with murder." He thought about that for a few moments.

Bryce said, "Detective Pip Ogden has a room in my hotel. I'll go talk with him first and see what he thinks."

Lyons consulted his watch. "It's almost six. I don't have much time."

CHAPTER FIFTY-FOUR

"We'll go talk with Pip Ogden and ask him if we've any legal way of stopping Stella Morgan from taking the train," Red Ryan said. "If Roper is right, it seems she's willing to leave without the carpetbag and settle for what she can get in Washington."

"That just don't seem logical, Red," Buttons Muldoon said. "Stella was willing to kill to get her hands on the bag. She wouldn't leave without it."

"Maybe she feels the law closing in on her and decided now was the time to light a shuck," Red said. "Well, let's go hear what Ogden has to say."

He and Buttons stepped off the boardwalk in front of Ma's Kitchen and headed in the direction of Ogden's hotel. As far as Red was concerned, the little detective was probably a forlorn hope. Ogden had no more evidence to arrest Stella Morgan than he did himself, but it was only an hour before the train pulled out of El Paso and anything was worth a try. There was one consolation though . . . Ogden had the carpetbag.

* * *

"Well, fancy meeting you here," T. C. Lyons said, eyeing Red Ryan with considerable disfavor. He stood on the porch of the Parker Hotel.

"We came to talk with Ogden," Red said.

"Everybody wants to talk with Ogden, only he isn't here," Lyons said. "He checked out late last night."

"Did he say where he was going?" Red said.

"Nope, he didn't. Paid his bill, turned in his key, and left." Lyons's eyes glowed. "Ain't that strange, though?"

"Maybe Ogden thought Stella Morgan was getting too close to the carpetbag and went into hiding," Red said.

"And maybe pigs will fly," Lyons said.

"I'm not catching your drift, Lyons," Red said.

"All right, let's start with this—Lucian Carter is dead."

Button Muldoon spoke up. "We know. I killed him."

Lyons let his surprise show. "It was you that gut-shot him with a scattergun?"

"I shot him," Buttons said. "As I recollect, I wasn't aiming for his belly."

"Why did you plug him, Muldoon?" Lyons said.

"He was trying to sneak into the hotel to kill Red and recover the carpetbag."

"He didn't know that Ogden had it?"

"I'd say that's pretty obvious," Buttons said.

"Well, you shot him, but you didn't kill him," Lyons said.

Red said, "Then who did?"

"Stella Morgan for one. And she had an accomplice."

"For God's sake lay it out for me, Lyons," Red said. "I've lost blood, and I'm not thinking real clear."

"As far as I can figure it, after Muldoon shot him,

Carter made it to Stella's hotel looking for help." Lyons bladed his hand and made a downward motion. "The only help he got was to be thrown out of a linen-closet window. He landed on a pile of bricks, and that's what killed him. The corner of a brick bashed his brains out." The sheriff sighed. "Ah well, may he rest in peace."

"Stella didn't do all that by herself," Red said. "Carter wasn't a big man, but he was heavy enough."

"Roper?"

"We spoke to Roper this morning at Ma's Kitchen," Red said. "The impression I got was that he hadn't spoken with Stella in a while."

"So, if Roper wasn't involved, who was the other party?"

Red thought about that and a light went on behind his eyes. "You don't think it was Ogden?"

"Do you?"

"Hell, I don't know."

"It could be that Stella now has the carpetbag and Ogden has Stella, or at least he thinks he does," Lyons said. "I'm sure she's made promises and maybe given him a taste to whet his appetite."

"Can you pin the death of Lucian Carter on Stella and make it stick?" Red said.

"I came here to ask Ogden that very question," Lyons said. "But he wasn't here to answer it."

"What time is it?" Red said.

"Almost six-thirty and the sun is coming up," Lyons said.

"Then we don't have much time," Red said.

Lyons's smile was thin. "Ryan, if Seth Roper takes a hand in this game, time could be running out for all of us."

CHAPTER FIFTY-FIVE

When Stella Morgan and Pip Ogden arrived at the station, the locomotive that would take them north stood impatiently at the platform and belched steam like an angry dragon.

Stella was on edge, worried that it had all been too easy. But there was no sign of the law, and Ogden seemed relaxed, the precious carpetbag hanging by his side.

"Twenty-five minutes until we leave, Stella," Ogden said. "Do you wish to board?"

"No, not yet," Stella said. "Let's see if Seth Roper shows up."

"I don't want any trouble with Roper," Ogden said.

Stella smiled. "There won't be, silly. Seth is on our side, remember?" Then, as an afterthought, "No one will get past his gun. What time is it now?"

"Now it's twenty-four minutes until we leave, Stella," Ogden said. "Are you getting anxious?"

"Extremely. I'll be so glad when we're finally out of El Paso."

"You don't have a thing to worry about," Ogden said. "Nothing can stop us now."

"I so hope you're right, Pip," Stella said. "Keep an eye on the time. We'll board in ten minutes."

A dozen other passengers waited on the platform, a young couple who stood very close to one another and smiled constantly, the rest businessmen in suits and a lone cattleman, a portmanteau and a saddle at his feet. Last night's wind had blown itself out and the day dawned clear, and a few white clouds floated in the blue sky like lilies on a pond.

Stella Morgan's eyes constantly scanned the platform, looking for Seth Roper. Would he ever come? Behind her the stationmaster, the conductor, and the locomotive engineer had their heads together in a conference. Finally, the conductor walked down the platform and said, "Time to board, folks, and get settled. We leave in fifteen minutes."

"Where is Roper?" Ogden said, echoing Stella's own thought.

"He'll be here," Stella said.

"He's cutting it fine, isn't he?" Ogden said.

Stella said, "There's still plenty of time, Pip. Oh, look, I see him now in the ticket office."

Ogden began to look worried, his eyes cagey on each side of the bridge of his unlovely nose. His hand dropped to the pocket of his coat where he kept the Colt self-cocker and he seemed to take confidence in the feel of blue steel and walnut. "He's all packed, carrying his bag." He'd uncoupled that vapid statement from his train of thought because the mere act of talking helped restore his confidence. Roper was an unforeseen complication, and Ogden was worried.

Roper left the ticket office, stepped onto the

platform, and grinned when he saw Stella. "All ready to leave?" he said.

"More than ready," Stella said.

"So am I," Roper said.

Stella grabbed Ogden by the bottom of his sleeve and urged him forward. "Seth, this is Pip Ogden. He brought me the carpetbag."

Roper nodded, but didn't extend his hand. "Heard about you, Ogden. Heard you were a lawman of some kind."

"I was a lawman, but I'm not now," Ogden said.

Roper gave Stella a quizzical glance, and she said, "Pip will help us in Washington, Seth. He's a former detective and knows how the law operates."

"Do you know how outlaws operate, Ogden?" Roper said.

"Yes, I do," Ogden said. "I've had many years of study."

"Good, then you'll feel right at home with us. Is this the first time you've changed sides, or have you done it before?"

"I changed sides because I don't want to be a policeman any longer. And no, I've never done it before."

"Then don't ever think about doing it a second time," Roper said.

"I won't," Ogden said. "And you don't scare me, Roper."

"I should," Roper said.

"I don't like where this conversation is headed," Stella said. "Let's board the train, and I want you two to be friends. After all, you'll be working together."

Ogden missed the sly look Stella exchanged with

Roper, his eyes widening until the white showed around the iris. "Oh my God," he said.

Stella looked down the platform, where Red Ryan, Buttons Muldoon, T. C. Lyons, and deputy Lou Hunt walked toward them. "Seth, stop them," she said.

Roper turned and swept his frock coat away from his gun. "Damn you, Ryan. I warned you not to come here," he said.

Red ignored that as T. C. Lyons said, "Lou, go tell the engineer to keep his engine where it's at. We got legal business to conduct here."

"Lou, you stay right there," Roper said.

"The hell with you," Hunt said. He walked in the direction of the huffing locomotive and then dropped as Roper drew and shot him.

"Damn you, Roper!" Lyons said. He ran to his downed deputy and took a knee beside him.

"Stella, get on the train!" Roper yelled.

"No, you don't, Stella!" Red said.

His hand went for his Colt. Beside him Muldoon reacted and reached for his Remington.

"Ryan!" Roper yelled.

He fired the instant before Red's bullet hit him in the chest.

Roper's shot was high and to the left, and the thick padded bandage on Red's shoulder absorbed some of the .45 impact to Red's right shoulder, and he backed up a step, firing, two misses and another hit that tore into Roper's heavy trapezius muscle where it joined his neck. The big man was hit hard and he knew it, but he stayed on his feet, getting his work in. Red took a second bullet, low on the right side of his waist, just above his gunbelt. He swayed on his feet, thumbed his

Colt dry, a miss, and in that moment, he knew he'd lost the gunfight.

But Buttons Muldoon didn't see it that way.

He fired at Roper, a hit, shot again, missed . . .

But Seth Roper had absorbed all the lead he could handle. His legs gave out, and he dropped to his knees, his face gray as death. Red, unsteady on his feet, advanced on him, reloading his revolver from the cartridge belt. But Seth Roper was done. He looked up at Red and said, "How the hell did you best me, Ryan? I don't understand it."

"I gritted my teeth and took my hits, Roper."

"Why, for God's sake?"

"Why, because your friend Skull Jackson made me good and mad, that's why."

Blood all over the front of his shirt, Roper grinned. "You done good, shotgun guard." Then he fell forward on his face, and all the life that had been in him fled.

"Lou is dead," T. C. Lyons said. He shucked his Colt and yelled, "Ogden!"

The little detective dropped the carpetbag as though it was red hot. "Sheriff, it's all a mistake," he said. "I was working undercover. Stella Morgan confessed to everything, the murder of her husband . . . the old lady in San Antonio . . . everything." Pip Ogden walked toward Lyons. "Don't you see, thanks to my investigation we now have enough to hang her."

Somewhere close by a band struck up with "Goodbye," then a popular parlor song by the composer Paulo Tosti, and for a moment time seemed to stop, Red, Buttons, Lyons, Ogden, and Stella frozen in place.

The spell was broken when a ten-piece military

band, led by Colonel David Anderson, marched onto the platform, several more army officers trailing behind. Stella Morgan's farewell had arrived at the worst and best of times.

"Ogden, you damned traitor!" Stella screamed.

She pulled her Hopkins & Allen revolver from the pocket of her gray traveling dress, extended her right arm straight out in front of her, sighted, and fired.

The bullet hit Pip Ogden in his left temple. The man didn't even have time to cry out as death took him, and he fell to the platform, a trickle of blood seeping from his terrible wound.

Then horror piled on horror . . .

As the music wailed to a discordant stop, Stella smiled and yelled, "Thank you, Colonel Anderson, for the grand adieu." She shoved the muzzle of her revolver between her breasts and pulled the trigger.

CHAPTER FIFTY-SIX

"She said, 'I'll never grow old,' and then she died," T. C. Lyons said. He sighed. "Well, Stella Morgan was right about that."

"There was nothing I could do for her," Dr. Tom Malone said. "The bullet burst her heart asunder." He looked at Red Ryan with less than affection and said, "As for you, young man, you've been shot up and cut up, and it seems that patching you up has become my full-time job."

"How is he, Doc?" T. C. Lyons said.

"He'll live."

"Maybe you could tell me how I am," Red said, irritated and in some pain now as the ether the doctor had administered was wearing off.

"The shoulder wound was not as serious as it could have been because the bullet hit the bandage over one of your knife wounds," Dr. Malone said. "Nevertheless, I had to extract the ball. It was in quite deep. As for the wound on your waist, well, you were shot through and through, but no vital organs were damaged. You were very fortunate, Mr. Ryan.

However, you're a strong young man, and you'll soon recover, that is, if infection can be avoided. That's why you'll remain in my surgery for a week or so." The doctor picked up Red's bloodstained buckskin shirt and his plug hat with its bullet holes and said, "I suggest you buy yourself a new wardrobe as soon as you leave."

"When will he be on his feet, Doc?" Buttons Muldoon asked.

"Hard to tell," Dr. Malone said. "A few weeks, a month, maybe." He saw the disappointment on Buttons's face and said, "Why do you ask?"

"We got a coward to pick up in Fort Concho, Doc," Buttons said.

"A coward?"

"Yeah, a Limey coward. We'll carry him to New Orleans, where he'll be taken into custody by a British ship."

"Then he'll just have to wait, won't he?"

After Dr. Malone left to visit patients, Red raised himself in the cot and said, "What happened to the carpetbag, Lyons?"

"I gave it to the army," the sheriff said. "Maybe Major Morgan has next of kin." He smiled and said, "Ryan, that damned bag has caused enough death and suffering. I wanted to get rid of it as quickly as possible."

Buttons whistled and said, "That was a lot of money to give away."

"Yes, a small fortune," Lyons said. "Was I tempted? The answer is, yes, I was, but only for the best part of a day. I was glad to hand it over to Colonel Anderson."

"Now he'll be the one tempted," Buttons said.

"Well, that's up to him," Lyons said. "What do you think, Ryan? Did I do the right thing?"

"I'd have left it up to the county sheriff to make that decision," Red said.

Lyons smiled. "I thought about that. But I'm glad I decided to let the army deal with it."

"Where's Stella Morgan being buried?" Red said, the thought coming to him.

"In Concordia, later today. And so will Carter and Roper and Deputy Hall. I'll be in attendance in an official capacity," Lyons said.

"What about Pip Ogden?" Red said.

"I wired San Antonio and asked what they wanted done with the body. I haven't had an answer yet."

"Will you tell them how he betrayed his badge?"

"I don't think that will serve any useful purpose. As far as San Antonio is concerned Detective Ogden died in the line of duty."

"I suppose that's all for the best," Red said.

"I think so. By the way, when I searched Stella's trunk I discovered the cameo brooch taken from the old Rabinovich couple," Lyons said. "I'd already found letters in their store between Raisa and a cousin in Boston. Since it's a family heirloom, I'll send the cameo to her."

Red said, "Two people murdered for a bauble. It seems that Stella was born without a conscience."

"I'd say that's pretty common among the criminal class," Lyons said. "Now, I got to leave for the cemetery." He smiled. "I hope you recover real soon, Ryan, and then leave El Paso forever."

"And ever," Buttons said.

* * *

"Buttons, I want you to do a couple of things for me," Red Ryan said after Lyons left.

"Name it," Buttons said.

"Bring me a bacon sandwich from Ma's Kitchen. No, make it two."

"The doc not feeding you?"

"He fed me oatmeal for breakfast. Does that answer your question?"

"And what else?"

"Do we have money?"

"Some."

"Buy me a shirt and new hat."

"I can do that. But the shirt won't be buckskin."

"Maybe I can pick one up later from the tame Apaches at Fort Concho."

"Is that it?" Buttons said.

"No. Get the stage and the team ready. We're out of here tomorrow morning at first light."

Buttons was shocked. "But Red, you heard Doc Malone, you're all cut up and shot through and through. "

"And I'm much more likely to die of an infection in this place than I am on the stage," Red said.

"But Red—"

"I'll survive, Buttons. Just do as I say."

"I don't like this, Red. I don't like this one bit."

"Well, it has to be done, that's all. Now go, and don't forget . . . it's two bacon sandwiches, and the greasier the better."

EPILOGUE

The Franklin Mountains lay behind them, almost lost in the ribboning dust kicked up by the stage wheels. Before they reached Fort Bliss, Red Ryan and Buttons Muldoon had four hundred miles of prairie to cross, a vast wilderness of grass under the arching blue bowl of the Texas sky.

"How are you holding up, Red?" Buttons said, slowing the team to a distance-eating trot.

"I feel like hell," Red said.

"Where?"

"All over."

"I don't like this, Red. I don't like this one bit, you being cut up and shot through and through an' all," Buttons said.

"You already told me that back in El Paso."

"Doc Malone was real angry when you left, mad enough to chew a chunk out of the head of a double-bit axe, I'd say."

"Buttons, one of the times when I was snowed up I read *Doctor Darby's Maladies and Ailments of Women* from cover to cover. Now I know enough about doctoring to take care of myself."

"Red, I don't know if you've looked in a mirror recently, but you're a man," Buttons said.

"Man, woman, it doesn't make any difference," Red said. "A misery is a misery."

"Well, I hope you know what you're doing," Buttons said.

"If I'm still alive by the time we reach Fort Concho, I reckon you'll know I knew what I was doing," Red said.

Buttons drove in silence for a while, the team fresh and going well, and then he said, "Red, you ever met a real live coward afore?"

"Can't say as I have," Red said.

"What makes a man that way?" Buttons said. "Why does he become a yellowbelly?"

Red said, "Well, now I study on it, a coward gets scared and quits and a brave man gets scared and still does what has to be done. At least, that's how I see it."

"What are we?"

"I don't think we're cowards, Buttons."

"Me neither," Buttons said.

CUTTHROATS
A SLASH AND PECOS WESTERN

JOHNSTONE. KEEPING THE WEST WILD.
Not every Western hero wears a white hat or a tin star.
Most of them are just fighting to survive. Some of them can
be liars, cheaters, and thieves. And then there's a couple of
old-time robbers named Slash and Pecos . . .

Two wanted outlaws. One hell of a story.
After a lifetime of robbing banks and
holding up trains, Jimmy "Slash" Braddock and
Melvin "Pecos Kid" Baker are ready to call it quits—
though not completely by choice.
Sold out by their old gang, Slash and Pecos
have to bust out of jail and pull one last job to
finance their early retirement . . .

The target is a rancher's payroll train. Catch is: the
train is carrying a Gatling gun and twenty deputy
US marshals who know Slash and Pecos are coming.
Caught and quickly sentenced to hang,
their old enemy—the wheelchair-bound
bucket of mean, Marshal L. C. Bledsoe—shows up at
the last minute to spare their lives. For a price.
He'll let them live if they hunt down their old gang,
the Snake River Marauders.
And kill those prairie rats—with extreme prejudice . . .

Look for *Cutthroats*. Coming in July,
wherever books are sold.

CHAPTER ONE

In the early morning hours, the bounty hunters gathered around the remote mountain cabin, crouched in a shadowy clearing. They were thirteen in number—a dozen-plus wolves on the blood scent.

Ray Laskey walked up to where Jack Penny crouched in the pines roughly fifty yards from the cabin, running an oily rag down the barrel of his Henry repeating rifle.

"All the boys are in position, boss," Laskey said, slicing a hunk of wedding cake tobacco onto his tongue and chewing.

Penny turned to Laskey and winked in acknowledgment with the rheumy blue eye that always seemed to roll to the outside corner of its socket and that always made Laskey feel vaguely uneasy, for some reason. That wandering eye seemed like some separate living thing, rolling and bobbing around in Penny's ugly, bearded head . . . like some ghastly thing that lived inside a log at the bottom of a murky lake and only came out to rend and kill. . . .

Both men crouched lower behind their covering

pine when the cabin's front door latch clicked. Laskey drew a sharp breath as he turned to see the door open. He squeezed his Spencer tightly but then eased his grip when he saw that the person stepping out onto the cabin's small stoop was a woman with long, thick, copper-red hair.

The woman, nicely put together and clad in a man's wool shirt and tight denim trousers, turned toward the split firewood stacked against the cabin's front wall. When she had an armload, she straightened, turned back to the door, and stopped abruptly.

No, Laskey thought. *Don't do that. Keep goin'. Get back inside the cabin, dearie. . . .*

The woman turned ever so slowly to stand staring straight off into the trees, directly toward where Laskey and Penny crouched behind a stout ponderosa.

Laskey's gut tightened.

Had she heard or in some other way sensed the killers crouched in the forest around the cabin? Had she smelled their unwashed bodies made even whiffier from their long, hard ride over the course of the long night lit only by a small and fleeting powderhorn moon?

Penny glanced at Laskey. The bearded bounty hunter smiled darkly, then raised his Henry to his shoulder. He slid the barrel up over a feathery branch and leveled his sights on the woman. He crouched low over the long gun, resting his bearded cheek up snug against the stock.

Slowly, almost soundlessly, he ratcheted back the hammer with his thumb.

Laskey looked at the woman. His heart thudded. She appeared to be staring straight at him. Straight at Penny steadying his sights on her chest.

No, no, no, dearie. You didn't hear nothin'. You didn't smell nothin'. No one's out here. A coyote, maybe. A rabbit, maybe—up and out too early for its own damn good . . .

That's all.

Go on inside, stoke your stove, start cookin' breakfast for them two cutthroats in there. It's them we want. Not you, purty lady.

We got other plans for you . . . dearie. . . .

As though obeying Ray Laskey's silent plea, the woman turned slowly, stepped back toward the door, nudged it open, and stepped inside. She turned to look outside once more, then closed the door and latched it with a soft *click.*

Penny eased his Winchester's hammer down against the firing pin.

Laskey released a breath he hadn't realized he'd been holding.

Penny turned to him, spreading his ragged beard as he grinned. "She almost joined the angels."

"When, uh . . ." Laskey said, pressing the wedding cake up tautly against his gum, "when do you want to . . . ?"

"Start the dance?"

"Yeah, yeah. Start the dance."

"As soon as they show themselves. Best odds, that way. Won't be too long now, most like. We got time."

"What, uh . . . what about the woman?" Laskey said.

"What about her?" Penny asked him.

Laskey shrugged, toed a pinecone. "She's too purty to kill. Outright, I mean . . ."

Laskey grinned, juice from the wedding cake bleeding out from between his thin lips.

Penny scowled down at the shorter man. "We came here to kill, an' that's what we're gonna do, Ray, my boy. She's with them cutthroats, so she dies with them cutthroats. Hell, there's a reward on her head, too. Dead or alive. Same as them."

"Oh, boy," Laskey said. "The woman, too, huh? Seems a shame's all."

Penny placed a big, strong, gloved hand on Laskey's shoulder and squeezed. "The woman, too, Ray. We ain't here for none o' that nonsense you're thinkin' about, you randy scoundrel."

Penny brushed his gloved fist across Laskey's pointed chin.

He winked his weird fish eye again, and it rolled like that living thing in the dark lake, fleeing back to its log after feeding.

CHAPTER TWO

"What you two old cutthroats need is a job," said Jaycee Breckenridge.

James "Slash" Braddock lifted his head from his pillow, frowning at the pretty woman forking bacon around in the cast-iron skillet sputtering atop her coal-black range. "Jay, honey, please don't use such nasty language so early in the morning. Pecos an' me got *sensitive ears*!"

"What'd she say?" asked Melvin Baker, better known for the past thirty years of his outlaw career as the Pecos River Kid.

He lay belly down on the cot on the far side of the small cabin from Slash Braddock. His blue eyes were open, regarding his longtime outlaw partner in shock and disbelief. "I didn't just hear her use the bad word again—did I, Slash?" He closed his hands over his ears. "Oh, please, tell me I didn't!"

"Now, look what you done, Jay! Poor ole Pecos is beside himself over here! He's likely ruined for the whole dang day! I might have to hide his guns from him, so he don't blow his brains out!"

Pecos buried his face in his pillow and pretend bawled.

At the range, one hand on her hip as she continued to flip and shuttle the bacon around in the same pan in which potatoes and onions fried, Jay shook her long, copper-red hair back from her hazel-eyed face and laughed. "Look what time it is, you old mossyhorns!"

She glanced at the windows behind her through which slanted the crisp, high-altitude sunlight of the Juan Valley of southern Colorado Territory. "It's nigh on midmorning and you two are still lounging around like a pair of eastern railroad magnates on New Year's Day!"

"Lounging around—nothin'!" Pecos lifted his head from his pillow and looked over his shoulder at Jay. "I was dead asleep not more'n two minutes ago. You done woke me up with your foul language. You oughta be ashamed of yourself, woman. What would Pistol Pete think of such talk?"

"Ha!" Jay threw her head back, laughing. "Whenever I mentioned the word 'job' to that old rascal—as in he might want to quit ridin' the long coulees and try an honest job for a change—he'd howl like a gut-shot cur an' skin out of here like a preacher caught in a parlor house. He'd run clear across the yard and throw himself in the creek. Didn't matter what time of year it was. Spring, summer, winter, or fall—that's just what he'd do, Pete would."

Jay threw her head back again, laughing.

But then she turned a thoughtful look over her shoulder, gazing out the window toward the lone grave standing on a knoll about sixty yards out from the cabin, in a little pocket of ponderosas and cedars. Jay's shoulders, clad in a plaid work shirt tucked into tight denims, rose and fell slowly, heavily. Her lower lip trembled. She stifled a sob, clamping her hand over her mouth, then wheeled from the range and hurried to the cabin's front door.

"Excuse me, boys!" she said in an emotion-strangled voice as she opened the door and stepped out onto the small front stoop. She slammed the door behind her.

Through the door, Slash heard her sobbing.

He turned to his partner, scowling, and said, "Pecos, what'd you have to go and do that for?"

"Ah, hell!" Sitting up now, clad in his wash-worn longhandles that clung to his big, rawboned frame, Pecos slapped the cot beside him and hung his gray-blond, blue-eyed head like a young man fresh from the woodshed. "I reckon Pete's name just slipped out. I mean, hell, he *was* her man. And, hell, we rode with him for nigh on thirty years before he . . . well, you know . . . before he got himself planted over there in them trees."

Pecos turned a disgruntled look at Slash. He kept his voice down so he wouldn't be heard on the stoop from where Jay's sobs pushed softly through the door. "Come on, pardner, Pete's been dead almost five years now. We should be able to mention his name from time to time."

"Dammit, Pecos." Slash tossed his animal skin covers aside and dropped his bare feet to the timbered floor still owning the chill of the crisp mountain morning. "You an' I both know Pete didn't get himself planted in them trees over there. *I* did!" Slash jabbed his thumb against his chest that bore the hooked knife scar that gave him his nickname. "I'm the one that got him planted. My own damn carelessness did."

"It was a bullet from the gun of one of Luther Bledsoe's deputies that killed Pete, Slash, you stupid devil. Don't you start in with all this old Pete stuff now, too!"

"I didn't," Slash said, rising in disgust and grabbing his brown whipcord trousers off a chair. "You did!"

"Ah, hell!" Pecos twisted around and flopped belly down on his cot, burying his head in his pillow. His big Russian .44, snugged inside its brown, hand-tooled leather holster, hung by its shell belt hooked over elk horns mounted on the wall above his head, within an easy grab if needed. Such a move had been needed more than a few times in his and Slash's long careers as riders of the long coulees, or the owlhoot trail, as some called the life of a professional western outlaw.

Slash quickly stepped into his pants. Then his boots. He left his blue chambray shirt on the chair but he strapped his twin, stag-butted Colt .44s around his waist, which was solid as oak at his ripe age of fifty-seven, which he was not above crowing about to Pecos, who'd grown a little fleshy above the buckle of his own cartridge belt.

Slash rarely walked more than five steps without either the revolver or his Winchester Yellowboy repeater. As he grabbed his hat off the kitchen table his bone-handled bowie knife, also strapped to his shell belt, rode high on his left hip, behind the .44 positioned for the cross-draw on that side. He swept a hand through his dark-brown hair, still thick, he was proud to know, but well streaked with gray—especially up around the temples and in his long sideburns that

sandwiched a broad, strong-jawed, brown-eyed face—
the face of a handsome albeit middle-aged schoolboy.

One who'd spent the bulk of his life out in the
blazing western sun.

That he was no longer a schoolboy, however, made
itself obvious once again as it always tended to do
upon his first rising. As he tramped across the
kitchen, his hips and knees and ankles popped and
cracked, stiff from too long in the mattress sack after
too many years forking a saddle and sleeping on the
hard, cold ground of one remote outlaw camp or another. An old back injury, the result of being thrown
from a horse during a run from a catch party nearly
twenty years ago, made Slash curse under his breath
as he lifted the popping skillet off the range and slid
it onto the warming rack, so the vittles wouldn't burn.

He pulled a couple of heavy stone mugs down from
a shelf near the range and set them on the table. He
dumped two heaping helpings of sugar into one,
because he knew Jay liked her mud a little sweet—
"Just like her men," she often quipped—then used a
deer hide swatch to lift the hot black coffeepot from
the range, and filled both mugs to their brims.

"Is Jay gonna be all right?" Pecos asked, his cha-
grined voice muffled by his pillow.

"Of course, she's gonna be all right," Slash said,
heading for the door. "She's Jay, ain't she?"

He fumbled the door open and stepped out, draw-
ing the door closed behind him with a hooked boot.
Jay stood ahead and to his right, her back to him,
staring out over the porch rail toward the lone grave
on the knoll.

The sun glowed in her hair. Birds flitted about the

sunlit yard around the cabin ringed with pine forest. Tall stone escarpments flanked the place. The cabin, originally built by a hermetic, now-dead fur trapper, was situated here on this mountain shoulder in such a way that it couldn't be seen from any direction unless you rode right up on it. And the only way you were likely to ride up on it was either by accident or if you'd already known it was here and you were headed for it.

That's what had made the place such a prime hide-out over the years. After a bank or train job, the Snake River Marauders, as Slash and Pecos's old gang called themselves, often split up their booty and then separated themselves into small groups of twos, threes, and fours, scattering and holing up till their trail cooled. They'd meet up again later at some far-flung, prearranged place to plan their next job.

Sometimes Slash, Pecos, and Pistol Pete, the old outlaw from the far northern Dakota country, would meet Jay in Mexico, and they'd spend their winnings in Durango, Loreto, or Mazatlán. Sometimes they'd sun themselves on the beaches of the Sea of Cortez, drinking pulque and tequila and feasting on spicy Mexican dishes like *tortas ahogadas* and *chilorio*.

Sometimes they'd hole up here for weeks or months at a time, hunting in the San Juans and the Sawatch to the north, and fishing and swimming in the pure, cold mountain streams. It was the time between jobs spent either here or in Mexico that Slash had always preferred over the jobs themselves, but he could never deny his almost primal attraction to the danger and excitement, as well as the money, that had always lured him back to the outlaw trail.

Now he set the cup of sugary coffee on the rail in front of Jay and kissed her tear-damp cheek. "Cup o' mud for you, darlin'," he said. "Put hair on your chest."

Staring toward the grave atop the knoll, Jay laughed at the old joke she and her old friend Slash had shared all the years they'd known each other— going on fifteen now—and offered her usual retort, "I don't want hair on my chest, Slash. That doesn't sound appealing to me at all!"

Slash gave a wry snort and sipped his coffee. "How you doing?"

"Look at me," she said, still staring toward the grave. "It's been how long, now? Going on five years? And I'm still pining for that man turned to dust under those mounded rocks over there."

"That's all right. He was a good man. He deserves pining for."

"Yes, he does, at that." Jay hardened her voice as well as her jaws as she turned to her old friend. "But it's time for me to move on, dammit, Slash."

"You're right on that score, too, Jay." Again, Slash sipped the rich black coffee.

"I'm still young . . . sort of," she said with proud defiance. "I still have my looks. Or most of them, barring a few crows-feet around my eyes and a little roughness to my skin . . . as well as to my tongue," she added drolly.

Slash looked at her, which was one of his favorite things to do. She was a slight, petite woman but with all the right female curves in all the right female places. She wore each of her forty-plus years beautifully on a face richly tanned by the frontier sun.

The lines and furrows had seasoned her, refining her beauty and accentuating her raw, earthy character. Her hazel eyes were alive with a wry, frank humor.

She was the most sensuous and alluring woman Slash had ever laid eyes on, and he'd first laid eyes on her when she was well past thirty.

"Hellkatoot," he said. "You're still a raving beauty, Jay. There's not many women over forty who've kept their looks as well as you have. You'll find a man. You just gotta start lookin' for one, that's all."

Jaycee Breckenridge drew a deep, slow, fateful breath. "I'm not gonna find one out here, am I? The only men who come around here anymore are you and that lummox lounging around inside like Diamond Jim."

Slash smiled.

"And you two don't deserve me," Jay said with another laugh.

"We sure don't!" Slash chuckled and shook his head.

Besides, he knew, they shared too much history. Good history and bad history. He'd once gotten his hopes up about Jay, a long time ago. But then she'd tumbled for the older, wiser "Pistol" Pete Johnson, five years Slash's senior, old enough to have been Jay's father.

She'd preferred the astuteness and assuredness of the older man. She'd been taken by the burly Pete's rough-sweet ways and his bawdy humor. Mere days after she'd met the man at the country saloon she'd been singing in, she never looked back. At least, not as far as Slash knew, and he thought he knew her as well or better than anyone on earth, now that Pete was gone.

"I'm so sorry, Jay," he said, looking off in frustration. She frowned at him, puzzled. "For Pecos? Don't be silly. He only mentioned his old friend's name."

"No, not for Pecos." Slash turned to her. "For me."

Jay looked at him askance, with sharp admonishment. "Let's not go down that trail again, Slash."